MISTRESS TO A MONSTER

EVERNIGHT PUBLISHING ®

www.evernightpublishing.com

MISTRESS TO A MONSTER

MISTRESS TO A MONSTER

Sam Crescent

Copyright © 2022

Prologue

Milah Russo glanced around at the party her father had thrown to honor her eighteenth birthday. This wasn't really for her. He pretended it was because he liked to show off his wealth and power.

Staring at the people present who were not his friends, she felt a little sick to her stomach. These kinds of celebrations were never good. All they did was bring out the worst in people. None of them were interested in her.

They were all here to get in her father's good graces, but Antonio Russo was not interested in making friends. Ever since her mother's death at the hands of the De Luca family, their sworn enemies, he'd been on a warpath, determined to spill De Luca blood. This had been going on for the past five years.

She didn't understand why. It wasn't like there was any love between her parents. They had fought constantly. Her father was a brutal man, and he'd beaten her mother regularly.

As she watched him tonight, surrounded by many scantily clad women, he sickened her.

She hated being his daughter, but there was no way she'd ever let him see the truth. Hiding her feelings was what got her through.

Milah declined several opportunities to dance, and instead made her way out into the garden. Like so many other times before, there were plenty of guests. All of them pretty much tripping over themselves to greet her. She wasn't rude, so she smiled and nodded at them all, not caring one bit about doing her duty.

They would talk nicely to her face, but behind her back, it would be scathing. From the way she looked to how she dressed. Some felt she wasn't fit to be a Russo. Her mother had been a beauty. Considered to be the most beautiful woman in the whole country. Milah only possessed her raven hair. Where her mother had been slender, raven-haired, with brown eyes, Milah was curvy, with the same hair and blue eyes. She never bowed her head in the company of others and always listened to what surrounded her.

Rumor would have it that her mother turned a blind eye to everything. Ignoring all the warning signs.

Milah would do no such thing. In her world, she knew women were treated as objects to be bought and sold at the whim of men.

Everyone had thought her mother a fool, but Milah knew differently. Her mother had known the cost of bearing a daughter as opposed to sons. So while everyone treated her like an idiot, behind closed doors, her mother trained her well. She wanted a daughter who could fight back. Who wouldn't be afraid of the men her father brought, and also, who would be able to defend herself, unlike her mother.

She trained with the best guards. Learned from

the best the Russo had to offer, and now on her eighteenth birthday, she had never felt so alone.

Milah found a small maze at the bottom of the gardens and decided to have a few moments to herself before she needed to start worrying about faking it again. Being around these people for longer than a few hours was tiring.

She wanted to leave. To go back home where her father never visited and just live her life in peace.

The time would come when he'd use her, but until then, she hoped to find a means to support herself. To run from the Russo life. Even if it meant faking her own death and being reborn, she'd gladly do it.

Wrapping her arms around her body, she stared up at the night's sky. The moon glowed down, and it made her smile.

Closing her eyes, she stood perfectly still, and in a rare moment of her life, she felt a sense of peace. These times were always few and far between in her life. She had learned long ago to not always expect them, but to enjoy them while they happened.

After taking a deep breath, she released it slowly, counting the seconds.

"Well, well, well, if it isn't the rare beauty herself."

The dark voice sent a shiver down her spine, and not in a good way either. Opening her eyes, she stared straight ahead, feeling the man approach. He was the enemy. Her senses told her to be on high alert. She didn't have a single weapon on hand.

Gritting her teeth, she tried not to react.

"Are you not going to scream?" he asked.

His warmth seeped through her dress, and she tensed up as his hands suddenly appeared. The moon provided enough light for her to recognize the De Luca markings on his knuckles, but there was only one man in the entire family who would have that kind of ink.

Her mother had warned her about him.

Damon De Luca. The most feared and oldest son of the empire. Their sworn enemies.

What was he doing at her party?

No one was around. He'd be able to kill her easily.

She had done the unthinkable and let down her guard. She should have known there was nowhere in this world where she would be safe.

Her heart raced, but she didn't move. She didn't even flinch as those arms went to her waist, as if he had a right to touch her, which he did not.

No one was here to hear her pleas.

"You are making a big mistake," she said.

He chuckled. "Am I? Or is your father becoming too reckless with your safety?"

Her hands clenched into fists. No one insulted her father or her family.

The desire to hurt him was strong, but she kept herself in check, not wanting to give away too much.

Damon pressed his face against her neck. "You smell good."

What was his end game?

What did he want?

"You know, I could steal you away right now. None of your pictures do your beauty justice."

She had heard enough. Slamming her elbow into his ribs, she stomped her foot down on his and spun around to face him, landing a blow to his face.

Her attack caught him off guard, but as she went to slap him, he captured her wrist. His grip was firm, making her cry out from the sudden jolt of pain. "Let go of me!"

"You've got some fight in you. I like that. It will be so much more fun to watch you beneath me."

"You've got no chance in hell." She would fight him no matter what. "There is no way a Russo would ever be with a De Luca. You are filth and the worst plague to walk this fucking earth."

"Fighting words."

"I can do more than that." She was ready to kill him. He might not have been directly responsible for killing her mother, but he was a De Luca. They were all the same.

"Mark my words, Milah. You will be mine."

"I'd rather die."

"We will see."

Chapter One

Three years later

Milah spun around in a circle, taking in the grandeur of her surroundings. Her shirt was torn, exposing one shoulder along with her bra strap. Her hair had been pulled from the confines of her bun. Her jeans were still intact, but now there were tear marks where she'd been roughly kidnapped.

She wrapped her arms around herself, trying to ward off the sudden fear. There was no reason to be irrational. She didn't like the look of the house. It already screamed money. Being taken someplace that looked wealthy wasn't a good sign as far as she was concerned.

Gripping the back of her neck, she tried not to think too hard. This wasn't good. None of this was.

Her guards hadn't put up any fight either. She hadn't been able to find a means of escape from the Russo empire in the past three years. Every time she tried to find one possible avenue, her father thwarted it.

Either by stopping her from going away to college, or constantly having guards at her side. Her mother had warned her more than once that if her father saw her as a feasible income, or a means to get what he wanted, he'd use her.

Had that time come?

Had his enemies figured out who she was?

Her coming-of-age party had been a huge problem. Up until that point, no one knew who she was, or what she meant to Russo. It was like she didn't exist, but since then, all had known what she looked like and now there was no getting away from it.

There was a bed against the far wall, looking as imposing as ever. There was no way she was going to sit on it.

She stayed perfectly still and kept her gaze on the door, which was locked. That was the first thing she tried, to see if there was any chance of escape.

There wasn't.

Even trying to flee from the window was useless. It was far too high, and the windows were locked. The only way she'd be able to escape through them was if she had a rock or something to break the glass. That would only alert her captors to her intention of escaping.

No matter where she looked, there was nothing she could do.

Absolutely nothing.

The large, imposing bed was the only piece of furniture in the room. Only one door. There wasn't even a closet or any drawers. Nothing. She'd already tried to look under the bed, and nothing was there.

This was impossible.

She wasn't going to beg or cause a scene. A Russo never did any such thing. She was highly embarrassed that even after all of her training, she hadn't been able to stop the men from taking her.

Milah had to wonder if her mother would be ashamed if she could see her now. She shook her head, refusing to think of that. She couldn't.

Right now, all she could do was attempt to survive.

That was it.

Hands clenched into fists, she tried not to think. Panicking wouldn't get her out of here, but being in control and collected just might. It was a long shot. She was aware of that, but it was a shot she was more than willing to take.

Shock raced down her spine as soon as she heard the lock flick open. Three men rushed into the room. None of them attempted to hide their identities. All of them charged toward her, and she attempted to fight them off, punching one, kicking another, but it was the third one who wrapped his arms around her waist, hauling her off her feet.

He placed her over his shoulder, and she screamed at him to let her go, landing blows against his ass, trying to get him to stop, even attempting to kick him.

She wanted to get out of here, to be let down.

Nothing helped.

They left the room, and Milah tried to watch every single footstep so she would be able to figure out an escape.

This was what happened when her father's thirst for blood was far stronger than his love for his daughter.

Tears began to fill her eyes, but she refused to let them fall. She squeezed them closed. There was no way she'd ever show weakness. Not to her captor. Not to these men. Certainly not to her father.

She had long ago stopped crying. No man deserved her tears.

The men came to a stop, and she was suddenly dumped unceremoniously onto the floor like she was nothing. They stepped back, and Milah opened her eyes to see several men. Some of whom she recognized as her father's men. Several she did not, but she did notice the De Luca mark. Then spinning around on the floor, she came to a stop when she saw her beaten father and Damon De Luca himself, standing there looking victorious.

What the fuck had happened?

The last she knew of her father, he was planning something that would undermine De Luca's power, but she didn't know the finer details. He never allowed her to understand his reasoning or for him to be part of his plans. To her father, she was nothing more than a woman.

She hated it when he treated her as weaker than him. She wasn't.

Staring at her father now, she had to wonder what had happened because he didn't look happy. In fact, he was bleeding, and seeing him like this, he appeared broken. His men didn't have their weapons either. Only De Luca was heavily armed.

Her stomach started to twist and turn.

Milah didn't speak for fear of how she'd sound. Instead, she looked at the two men and waited.

"Will you tell her, Russo? Or should I?"

Her father wouldn't even glance at her. She'd never seen him like this. In all the years she was growing up, he was a commanding presence in her life. Someone who had always been in control, who never looked anyone in the eye with fear.

"Dad?" she asked, needing him to acknowledge her presence.

De Luca didn't look her way. Instead, he chuckled. Then he finally looked at her, but she didn't want to return his gaze.

Something had gone badly wrong.

One quick glance at him, another at her father, and nothing.

"You will be going with Damon De Luca now, Milah."

"What?" she asked.

"You belong to him."

She shook her head. "No, that cannot be."

"You will do as he tells you. You will not run. You will hold your head up high and be proud to be a Russo."

This made De Luca laugh even more. "Proud to

be a Russo? Would you like me to tell her how you sold her? How you begged for your life?"

"Dad, please, don't do this."

Her father had sold her to De Luca as if she meant nothing? No, it couldn't be. She refused to believe it. "Dad, please, talk to me."

Instead, her father stepped away from De Luca, who clicked his fingers. His men grabbed her. "Take her to my home, in the mistress's bedroom. I'll be there to deal with you shortly."

Trying to keep calm faded so fucking fast. As the men grabbed her arms to lift her, she fought them, stopping the two men with her surprise attack, but more men grabbed at her.

"No!" She screamed at them. "Let me go. Dad!"

Even as they hauled her off her feet and marched her out of the room, she screamed for her father. Anger rushed through her. It was quick and full of bitterness. What the hell had happened?

They dumped her into the back of a truck. She slammed her hands against the side of the vehicle, trying to get out. Everything was locked.

"Damn it. Let me out." She wasn't going to stop. Not for a single second. Her father had sold her to De Luca? How did this happen?

What could he have possibly done that was such a big giant screwup that put him at his enemy's mercy? She wasn't going to get any answers in the back of the truck, but she refused to go quietly.

If cops ended up following them, she'd be able to get their attention. She prayed for someone to flag them down, to bring awareness to her being kidnapped. Anything that would stop this from happening.

Her hands grew sore with the constant slapping against the metal can she was being transported in. The air was stale. Tiredness started to consume her.

She needed to get out. To get free. To finally be free of being a Russo and to be her own person.

"Let me out."

The truck suddenly came to a stop.

It was so dark, and as she tried to figure out where the truck would open, the back or the side, she kept flicking her head to the front and to the right, wanting to surprise them and make an escape.

The truck opened, and she charged forward.

Once again, shocking the men as she shoved them out of the way, she ran as fast as she could.

She'd never been the person to wear heels, always preferring sneakers and flats. Milah ran as fast as she could, hearing De Luca's men following behind her, but she had to get away. She didn't have time to take in her surroundings, and it wasn't too long before she was thrown to the ground, and a large body covered her.

No one said a word even as she kept on fighting, wanting to get away. Begging to be free. To fight. Hoping someone would take pity on her and let her go. Who would dare to betray De Luca?

In all her years of eavesdropping, she had never once heard of one of his men running away. Not a single one.

What kind of man instilled that kind of loyalty? She didn't know who it was, nor did she want to.

She was once again off her feet and being carried back toward the house. Again, she didn't get the chance to look at her surroundings as she was taken to a room. This time, she was dumped on the bed.

"There's a bathroom through there. Use it. Clean yourself up, and be warned, there is absolutely no chance of escape."

She spun around to face her captor, prepared to

15

yell at him, but he was already gone.

Of course he was.

She moved to the edge of the bed and rested her palms on her knees, taking a deep breath. Wearing herself out wasn't part of the plan. Not that she had any great ideas for escaping. She was stuck.

Getting to her feet, she assessed the room. This one had a large bed, like the last, but this time, she recognized the luxury silk sheets. A couple of cupboards were on either side, and she went to them, opening the three drawers in each, finding nothing. There wasn't a lamp, and she touched the top of each surface, wondering if a lamp had been there. She would've been able to smash it to use it as a weapon.

Nothing. There were three doors. One was the entrance the guard had exited from just a few moments ago. Another, she opened to see it was an empty closet. Again, she looked through the drawers, and they were all empty.

Next was the bathroom.

There was no mirror, and only a curtain provided cover for the shower. This room looked like it had been designed to hold a hostage.

Nothing more.

Nothing less.

What kind of man did this? Was this a happy coincidence or had he planned this?

****

Damon smiled as he watched Milah look around the room for something to fight with. The guards who'd dealt with her had already warned him that she knew how to fight. She wasn't as trained as his men, but she would cause some serious injury to others if given the chance.

He knew she'd be a wildcat. That night at her

coming-of-age party, he'd snuck in to finally get a look at the precious daughter Russo had been hiding. Damon wasn't disappointed by the woman he'd found. Then, when she was eighteen, she'd been too young for his taste. At thirty years old, he liked his women to be of age and not just on the fine border of being legal.

That one encounter had stayed with him, and for the past three years, he'd watched Milah Russo. She was nothing like her father, nor of the rest of the Russo line. For one, she showed compassion. He'd watched her with stray animals she'd found, along with people she helped, even if it was down to aiding an elderly lady walk across the street. His men captured it.

Milah wasn't cold or dead. She was full of passion and fire.

He saw it in the way she fought. Even now, she kept testing everything. His men had told her to take a shower, but she was looking for a means to protect herself. What she didn't seem to know was that her body would keep her safe.

Damon had known Russo would fuck up. The man's thirst for power and blood made him greedy. It made him believe he was untouchable, but one mistake after another this past year had brought them to this moment. To where he'd been the one to point a blade at his throat, rather than a gun. There was nothing satisfying about shooting a man. Nearly all of Russo's wealth was gone. Used up on women, drugs, gambling, and just being a bad businessman. Russo thought he was untouchable, and he had never been more wrong. The only wealth the Russo name had was owned by Milah. Her mother's trust fund that had been placed in holding until Milah fulfilled the terms set out to get it—a small fortune. Enough to make Milah a target for men, and certainly for her father who would want to marry her off.

That was what put Milah in harm's way. Her father had started to hunt for a husband for her. Someone he could control and manipulate. He'd wanted his daughter's money.

From what his sources told him, she had no idea she had a small fortune.

Damon watched as Milah stripped out of her clothes and turned the shower on. She kept her panties and bra on, not that he blamed her. She held her hand beneath the water, waiting for it to warm up.

She kept on glancing around, at one point even looking into one of the cameras he had installed.

He'd started preparing this room three years ago. From the moment he met, his intention was to take her.

Damon was known for his patience. What he wanted, he always got. And when it came to Milah, he wanted her. Not for her wealth, but to tame that wildcat.

He despised the Russos and everything they stood for, but Milah was different. Damon had taken his time. Done his research and knew she was not like her father. She was unique, and that quality was to be rewarded.

It was why he'd attacked Russo. Why when his blade was to his throat, and he was more than happy to strike the killing blow, he'd waited to see what Russo would give up to save his own life.

He was shocked when Milah's name came up.

Why would he be? The man was a coward, only interested in his own ends.

He despised that in men. Was sickened by it.

Russo would die soon enough, but first, Damon intended to take every single piece of Russo land and business. To kill all his men and make him drown in his own misery. He was going to break and destroy that man, piece by piece.

First, he was going to work on Milah.

She would belong to him.

The day would soon come when he would show her father what he'd done. How he'd gotten a Russo to fall in love with a De Luca. That would not be the only victory he anticipated. He would also knock her up, but he had no intention of marrying her.

There was no way a De Luca would ever marry a Russo. He would keep her as his mistress. Even when he found a wife worthy of the De Luca name, he would keep Milah in place, by his side, never allowing her to escape.

He waited for Milah to wrap a towel around her beautiful, curvy body before entering her room.

Damon closed the door and nodded at his guard to flick the lock into place. There was no escape.

Pocketing his cell phone, he moved toward the bed and waited for Milah to enter. The moment she did, wrapped in a towel, she froze, jerking to a stop.

He sat on the edge of the bed, staring at her.

She stood still, her hands gripping the edge of the towel as if that alone could protect her.

Every single part of this room was covered in cameras, so he would have the joy of watching her whenever he wanted. There was no weapon. Nothing to protect her. Even when he sent food in, he made sure there were no knives. Nothing to tempt her to act irrationally.

He smiled. "Hello, Milah."

"What do you want?" she asked.

"Is that any way to greet your master?"

"You're not my master. You will never be my master."

He chuckled. There would come a day when she would crawl across broken glass for him, and when that day arrived, he would fucking relish it. He would break this woman. So much spirit. So much passion. He couldn't wait to unleash it and to finally have a taste of what he'd been waiting for. His cock stiffened at the thought.

Damon got to his feet and took a step toward her. She stayed perfectly still, tilting her head back and glaring at him.

That's right, little cat, fight me. Your submission will be so much sweeter.

"Your father gave you to me."

"I'm a person. I'm not a thing to be passed around like an object."

He cupped her cheek, and she shoved his arm away.

Smiling, he gripped the back of her neck and hauled her up against him. She did have some skills, but she was no match for him. There was nothing she could do to fight him off. He was the one with complete power, ultimate control.

"You are mine, Milah. Your father gave you to me because he is nothing but a coward. He would rather sell his own daughter than lose his life."

She tried to wriggle in his hold, but all it did was dislodge the towel bound at her breasts, bringing her scantily clad body closer to his.

There was no use in fighting.

With his spare hand, he gripped the shapely curve of her ass, holding her against him. He made her very much aware of his rock-hard cock.

What saved Milah right now was that her final submission would be so much sweeter than to break her by raping her.

He held her neck, forcing her to look up at him, and he stared down into her blue eyes that so reminded him of the ocean.

She was beautiful.

He'd heard rumors of men claiming her beauty was no match for her mother's, but they were wrong. Damon had met her mother, and he'd never been attracted to her. Milah, though, she drove him wild.

She was the reason he set this plan in motion. To finally claim her for his own. Those full lips would look so good wrapped around his cock. He couldn't wait to see her body shaking with her release as she begged for him to fuck her.

All of that would come soon enough.

He didn't kiss her. Instead, he let her go and walked to the door, slapping his palm twice on the hard wood. The lock flicked open, and he stepped out without saying a word.

His guards moved out of his way as he locked the door and pressed his palm against it.

Milah would put up a fight. She was his captive, but she wouldn't submit easily. No, he anticipated a fight.

He pulled away and forced himself to go to his study, where he poured himself a large glass of whiskey. The temptation to look at the cameras was strong, but he denied himself that very pleasure. His desire for her was too strong.

Damon needed to control himself. No woman had ever made him act like a fool or a schoolboy, begging for attention.

Milah was his now, and there was no way Russo could take her back.

Sipping at his whiskey, he stared at the sofa where his father had once sat. His mother and father's deaths were the only times he'd mourned someone.

According to De Luca rumor, there was no love between father and son, but that had always been lies.

He'd been close to his father.

Damon hadn't killed him. Cancer had ravaged his father's body, weakening him, breaking him, until finally death had claimed him. As per his father's instructions, he didn't release a tear. He wasn't to cry. He was to take the De Luca name into greatness, and that didn't allow for men to show weakness. Just strength.

Sipping at his whiskey, he took a seat opposite the sofa. They had spent many hours talking about how to bring down the Russos.

It was only a matter of time before Russo was on his knees with no way out of the hole he'd dug himself into.

After finishing off his drink, he put the empty glass on the coffee table and sat back. Resting his head on the back of the chair, he stared up at the ceiling, attempting to relax.

With Milah in his home, he didn't think for a second he'd be getting much sleep. His men would guard her, but that didn't mean she wouldn't attempt an escape.

That night, three years ago on her birthday, she'd looked so fucking regal. Like she was indeed a queen. Even then, he'd been plotting Russo's demise.

She was a queen of a dying empire. The Russos would one day cease to exist.

He intended to wipe out the entire line, including all the bastard children Russo had fathered. From his sources, Milah had at least three brothers who were older than her, but there could have also been other children. No one knew for certain how many women Antonio had knocked up.

Did she know of her distant family?

He doubted it.

Running a hand down his face, he tried to clear his thoughts, but they kept on returning to Milah. The woman was already a thorn in his fucking side.

Chapter Two

Milah was going to get out. She would find a means of escape.

And so it began.

It started with breakfast being delivered at exactly seven-thirty. Not a moment before. Not a moment later. Lunch was served at twelve. Again, on time, always. Dinner was at six. Same time, all the time. The women changed for each serving, but they remained the same throughout the first week. She counted how long she had been there by the meals.

She was onto her third week, and still, Damon De Luca hadn't visited her a second time. Just that once where he'd held her tightly, letting her know without a doubt who was more powerful.

He may have strength, but Milah had a great deal of patience with nothing to do all day than sit and stare at the door, to watch who came through, to see what was on the other side. It was like watching a movie more than once. You stopped watching what was right in front of you and started to see what was going on in the background.

There were always two guards that were visible. One who opened the door, the other behind each serving woman.

Milah felt that was a little sloppy. She'd be able to hurt the first man while the second reacted, and she'd already be on the attack. It would have made more sense to have three men. Did De Luca not think she was worth a third man?

The meals were all sloppy, and none of them required a knife. It didn't take a genius to work out that De Luca had done this on purpose. She had no doubt he'd planned this.

The bedroom. The bathroom. There were no weapons, nothing for her to use to help herself. She was all alone.

He couldn't control her thoughts though.

Milah looked around the bedroom and knew there would be cameras. Only a fool would put the enemy in a room with no cameras. It was why she always changed her underwear beneath a towel. A new change of clothing arrived with her food. Always neatly folded, and again, picked with no way for her to fight back.

When she wasn't looking at the door, she moved toward the full-length doors that opened to a balcony, only they were locked. She couldn't escape from there, but the view told her she was at least three stories from the ground. Any jump would injure, if not kill her.

So, after three weeks, she had no choice but to go for the attack.

The women never spoke to her. They didn't even look at her. The food had to have been spat in, she was sure of it. She only ate what was needed to keep her strength up.

By the end of the third week, she had enough of playing the perfect captive and waited by the door, tense, counting the seconds. She heard the flick and waited as the tray was pushed inside. The only weapon was the silver food cover over her plate. While the woman pushed the cart, Milah lifted the food cover, shoved her as she came through, and then slammed the metal into the first guard's head. By the time the second one reacted, she had already grabbed the spare gun from the first guard, removed the safety, and shot the second guard in the leg. He went down, and Milah ran, jumping over him. She didn't have a pair of shoes, and so had no choice but to make her escape on bare feet.

Not the most ideal of situations, but one she

intended to do.

She heard the cry of warning, saying that she had escaped. Once she'd made it down two flights of stairs, she had no choice but to escape into a bedroom. Glancing around, she saw it was unmade, a spare room, and she didn't wait around, charging forward. She tried the doors that led out onto another balcony. She didn't understand De Luca's obsession with them, but she wasn't going to argue with them if they were means of escape. There was no way she'd be able to make the jump without damaging her body, but she saw a plant trailing up the side of the house. There was a means for her to climb down, but it also meant she had no choice but to leave the gun.

She put the safety on and threw it over the balcony. She didn't waste any time to see where it landed.

Climbing over the stone balcony, she grabbed the trellis, hoping it was sturdy enough to take her weight. She started to climb down.

She was near the ground when she heard the guards. Another alert, which could only mean the ground-floor guards had been told of what was happening.

With her feet on the ground, she had no choice but to run. She took her chances, heading toward the garden. She stumbled as she had to walk over rocks, which dug into her feet, but that didn't stop her, even as she felt one sharp edge pierce her flesh. She kept on running.

One glance over her shoulder, and she saw men had spotted her. She expected them to raise their guns to shoot, but they never did. She ran with all her might, trying to escape, to get free and clear.

She had already passed the gun but decided to

leave it. There wasn't enough time to bend down and get it. She had to keep on running.

She was close to a thick line of trees when she was tackled from the right and thrown to the ground. As she tried to fight, her arms were slammed above her head, stopping her from moving.

Screaming, she tried to push off the man who stopped her, but he held her immobile. She looked up to see Damon himself was there.

She didn't stop fighting.

"Let me go!"

"You have been a very naughty girl."

"You have no right to keep me here." She tried to push him away, but he wouldn't move. Damon was a brick wall in comparison. She tried to wriggle from underneath him, but it was useless.

"Report," Damon said.

Milah didn't look away but sensed the guards approaching.

"She shot one guard in the leg. The maid serving her lunch isn't injured. She was pushed to the floor. The other guard has a bruised face."

"Is anyone dead?" Damon asked.

"No."

Damon looked at her, his face seeming to tense as if he had a question. "You are foolish."

"Let me go." He could call her all the names he wanted, but she wasn't going to give up the fight to be free.

"Anyone else would have killed them."

Milah froze and looked at Damon.

She had never even thought about killing them. She hated violence. One of the reasons she had hated learning how to fight was the fear of hurting someone, but her mother had demanded it. Forced her to learn. She had no choice.

The guard she had shot had only been doing his job. Shooting him was an act of survival on her part, but no one deserved to die.

"Let me go."

"This is starting to sound like a broken record. After three weeks, I figured you would have started to learn your place."

"Fuck off, you piece of shit. I will always fight. I will find a way to get out of here. I will be free. You and my father can go fuck yourselves." For the first time in three weeks, Milah felt good.

She'd surprised Damon.

He gave it away with the slight widening of his gaze. It was a subtle change, but one she had seen. He hadn't expected her to say something like that.

"Sir?" the guard who had reported what she'd done spoke.

Damon didn't look away.

"I think it's time to show our guest her place in this life, don't you?" Damon asked.

Fear raced down her spine, but she didn't show it. Her mother had taught her the value of constantly wearing a mask.

Damon moved, and she was about to get to her feet, but his hands went around her neck, pulling her to her feet. She had no choice but to follow his grip, otherwise, she would have been choked.

She grabbed his arms, trying to get him to ease up. He wasn't squeezing to the point of no air, but the threat was there. She didn't want to die, but there was no way she would beg Damon to let her live. There was no way she'd beg him for anything.

He smiled at her. "You will learn your place, Milah Russo. You have had it easy up until now, but let us see how well you fare in the fucking gutter."

Damon tossed her toward the guards. Cuffs were placed around her wrists, and she stared at Damon, not caring if he saw her defiance or not. He would learn one way or another that she wasn't to be messed with. She might not land a killing blow, but she would do whatever it took to be free.

The guard wasn't kind as he marched her across the gardens. They didn't go to the house, but instead, he took her toward the left of the property, past several large trees, going up a slight incline, and she saw what appeared to be a crumbling building. It wasn't. A hidden gate waited within, and the guard opened the lock.

Milah didn't say a word as they marched her inside the cave. The stench of earth and death met her senses. She didn't see any skeletal remains, but the sound of scurrying rats unnerved her.

She refused to show fear.

The guard dumped her onto the floor. She splashed in muddy water and tried to contain her wince. She heard a metallic rattle and then the cuffs that were on her were replaced by chains, binding her wrists. The guard tested each chain, tugging at it, to see if it would give way. It didn't.

No one spoke.

One look at the men, and she saw they were happy to see her like this. To them, she was a Russo. Not worthy of being cared for.

He had locked her in a cage, close to a gutter. The stench repulsed her. She felt sick, but she didn't beg them to let her go.

She watched as they left the room one by one. With no one to see her, she flinched at the sound of the gate being locked. Alone, outside, in the dark, Milah tested how far she could go. There was nothing to protect her. No bed to offer her comfort.

Nothing.

She was all alone.

The chains only allowed some movement. Her feet were bare, and she couldn't contain her scream as something furry brushed past her feet.

Rats. He'd put her with rats.

Sickness swirled in her gut at what this could mean. Death by … what? The rats? The elements?

She sank to her knees and stared toward the small pitch of light.

Milah was afraid of the dark. Always had been.

She stared at the light, watching the hours tick by. No food or water was brought to her. This was her punishment.

The rats didn't come near her after that first one.

Tears filled her eyes as the light slowly began to ebb away, making way toward the darkness. With the dark, she had no choice but to close her eyes, to try to send herself to a happy place.

Bad shit always happened in the dark.

Her mother had always told her to take long, deep breaths and to try to think of all the good things in life. Right now, there was nothing good. Only fear.

The night was closing in, and with it, fear clawed its way within her chest, threatening to take over.

****

The maid wasn't injured.

The shot to the guard hadn't even gone through bone. She had shot the fleshy part of his leg that only needed a few stitches, and he'd be healed in no time. Milah hadn't done any lasting damage.

Why not?

Damon sat back, enjoying his medium-rare steak. It had been three days since he had sent her to the gutter.

Most people who went there stayed there to die. He'd ordered food and water to be taken to her once a day.

There was no reason for her to die. In the past, his father would have starved a person to death, or left their body to the rats. It was rare for him to do, and more often, only traitors were sent there. His father felt it rather poetic to allow rats to eat traitors.

Damon smiled, sitting back, enjoying the warmth of his home.

If Milah had given in, she would have been enjoying a fine life, but he'd seen the way she watched the door. Always assessing, and he'd been curious as to what she had been up to. He hadn't warned his guards, wondering how they would react. Damon had told them all that they were not to kill her.

Milah was to stay alive.

He took a sip of his wine, a nice red to go with the beef that was cooked to perfection. He did love fine food, and he made sure his chef was well compensated for his services.

Damon was enjoying the last bite of steak when James, the guard who was shot, came into the room. "Sir, it has been brought to my attention that Milah has not been given any food or water," he said.

Damon looked up. "What?"

"I … today, I was in the kitchen, and the chef looked at the tray of food and tutted. No maid or guard has taken any food to Milah in the past three days."

Getting to his feet, Damon ordered James to bring the guards and the maids who had been in charge of taking care of Milah. James was the head soldier he'd put in place, but with his current injury, he was on rest until the stitches had healed. Even now, he was walking with a crutch to assist him.

Within minutes, the seven guards and three maids

were brought to him. His men stared straight ahead, and the maids looked down on the floor.

"Who has been feeding Milah?" he asked.

No one raised their hand.

"What were my instructions?" He looked at his men and then toward the maids. One of the men stepped forward. He couldn't recall his name, but he was a new soldier.

"Sir, we felt it wasn't right to feed her. She injured James and has no right to live, sir!"

Rage rushed through his body. Damon pulled out his gun, removed the safety, and shot the guard twice, once in each leg. He screamed as blood seeped out onto the rug.

"When I give an instruction, I expect it to be followed. James, you will keep them all here. They will all receive punishment."

He left the room, clicking his fingers for two of his guards to follow him. Damon had no choice but to grab a flashlight as he made his way toward the cells. His father installed this many years ago. At first, it had just been a cave, but with time, he'd made sure they could hold men, subjecting them to the elements.

Damon didn't want to kill Milah. He wanted to scare her into submitting.

He unlocked the gate and charged forward, shining the light on the floor. He noticed several rats, and as he got closer, he saw Milah was on the floor with a few of the furry vermin around her.

He swatted at them, trying to clear her body.

Milah was passed out. Unresponsive.

Shining the flashlight on her, he saw she was pale. Her lips were chapped, and she was freezing cold. After removing his jacket, he spread it over her. Not that it would do much to ward off the cold, but at least it was something. He'd never had a soldier show so much disrespect. He pressed two fingers to her neck and found her pulse. It was there, weak, but she was still alive.

"Call for the doctor," he said.

He picked Milah up in his arms. Her body was nothing more than a dead weight.

One of the guards stepped forward to help, but he growled at them to step back. He wasn't in the mood to be argued with tonight. The guards heeded his warning, and they all stepped back. He quickly moved toward the entrance, taking her back to the house. The moment he entered the main hallway, he saw how ill she actually was. Her body was like ice.

He didn't take her to her room but carried her straight to his.

"Leave!" He barked out the order, and the guards left immediately. He didn't want or need any help in taking care of her.

Carrying her through to the bathroom, he had no choice but to place her on the floor gently. He quickly started to run a warm bath, constantly checking for any sign of life in her body, but there were none.

With every second that passed, his rage grew stronger. He wanted to kill that guard and the maids who dared to go against him. Their fates were already sealed. That was the problem with having young guards. They were foolish, always thinking with their dicks rather than their heads.

With the water warm, but not hot, he eased Milah into the tub, climbing in with her. Warm water surrounded them, but still, Milah didn't wake. While in the tub, he gently removed her clothing until she was completely naked. He didn't take the time to admire her body, although he wanted to.

The water was warm, and he held her close,

removing his own clothes to help provide some warmth.

He didn't speak, and all that Milah did was moan from time to time. Her body shook, and he held her even tighter.

Someone knocked on the door.

"What?" he asked, yelling toward the sound.

"The doctor has arrived."

"Give me ten minutes." He didn't want to let Milah go, but the doctor needed to see her to check on her.

She finally stopped shaking, and he climbed out of the tub, wrapping a towel around his body, then doing the same to Milah.

After carrying her toward his bed, he placed her beneath the covers and quickly changed before going to the door to make entry for the doctor.

Doctor Pierce was a family doctor and the only one Damon trusted. Letting him in, he told him what had happened. Doctor Pierce tutted but got to work, assessing her. Damon stood, watching, waiting, seeing her look so pale.

"There is a chance she might get sick and feverish," Doctor Pierce said. "For now, prepare some soup. It will help, and some water."

Damon gave the order, and Pierce continued to treat her. "She does have a couple of bites on her body. I'm assuming from rats where you kept her. There is a chance of infection. She must be taken care of over the course of the next few days." He looked behind him and shook his head. "I will return tomorrow to check on her. She will be in and out of it, but you must feed her. My bill?"

"Will be handled, and it will be doubled," he said.

"I have served the De Luca family for many years, Damon. I have never known for them to treat a woman like this, unless they intended to end her life."

"Get out," Damon said. He didn't need to be told by anyone what had happened here. This was a sign of disrespect, and if word got out that a soldier and maids dared to go against his word, there could be an uprising.

At thirty-three years old, he was the youngest person to rule the De Luca empire. Many people felt he didn't deserve the title or the role. Some had even tried to oppose him. They had all ended up dead, apart from family members he had demoted them to a lower rank within the De Luca family.

His father had taught him there was no true family. Blood was not thicker than water, but power was everything. Only those who were willing to spill blood and die for you were the ones you kept close. That was what he did, but he also knew that he needed to keep his enemies closer still.

It was a mixed balance of chaos of which he'd become the master.

Standing by the bed, he looked down at Milah. Without her scowling or guarded, she was even more beautiful.

He stepped away, going to his wardrobe where he grabbed a pair of sweatpants and one of his bed shirts. Once he'd removed the towel from her body, he eased the clothing over her and then tucked her back into bed.

Every now and then, she would let out a whimper. Sometimes she'd call for her mother. He noticed she never once begged for her father. Even in her nightmares, her father was a waste of time.

With one of the maid's help, he fed her some soup, which wasn't a lot. She was unconscious. For the first twenty-four hours, he stayed by her side. The doctor returned and didn't like the look of her. He treated the rat bites and handed him some antibiotics. Now all they had to do was wait.

He didn't like waiting. Not for this.

By the third night, James was much better, so Damon put him in charge while he made his way down toward the basement.

Many lives had been lost in this very room. He looked around at the seven guards and three maids. All of whom were in a pool of their own piss and shit, the stench revolting, and he knew more lives would be haunting this very room.

His property was always heavily guarded.

The maids were taken from the women that were sold to them. He offered them a good life serving in his home, or to be one of the whores in the De Luca brothels. Many tried to become a maid to him, but he only accepted those that he knew wouldn't take a good price. Ones men wouldn't want to fuck.

Life was cruel, but this way, they got to live, even if it meant to serve him. Most of them were strays and runaways, trying to find a better life.

"So, you thought it was a good idea to go against my decision? To starve my guest?" he asked.

"Sir, she is a Russo. She has no right to live," the man he'd shot said. Damon hadn't allowed his wounds to be treated, other than to be bound up to stop him from dying. He looked like the grim reaper was coming for him.

After going to the far wall, he picked up one of the sharpest knives. The point seemed to glisten in the lamplight. Moving to the one he'd shot, he pointed the tip against his cheek, blood seeping through from that smallest of pressure.

Drawing it back, he flicked the blade across the man's cheek. "I'll deal with you last."

With the first two men, he simply swiped the

blade right across their throats, watching the blood spill down their bodies. The third, he plunged the blade into his eye, drawing it out. This now left three more men and three women. He'd never been the kind to take pleasure from scaring women, but none of them had come to him to warn him. They knew his rules. They were not newbies. They listened to the guard rather than their master, and for that, he slit their throats one by one until all three were dead.

The other three guards were dragged out along with the one shot. His men dragged them back to the cave, where he was sure to nick their flesh so the rats would come. With them all chained up, there was no chance of escape.

As with all things, rumor would spread about what he did today.

He didn't care. This was a mercy as far as he was concerned. He could do far worse.

Locking the gate, he heard their screams. Their begs. Their pleas, but they all fell on deaf ears. They were going to die for what they did.

As Damon stepped away, he paused. Why did it matter to him that they suffer? Milah meant nothing to him. She was merely a toy to be played with.

Pushing any concerns to the back of his mind, he stepped forward and continued walking. With every step he took, the sounds of their screams started to fade until he heard nothing at all.

Chapter Three

Milah was chained to the bed.

It wasn't her bed either, but Damon's.

The breakfast maid had entered ten minutes ago and had plumped up her pillows.

"How are you feeling?" she asked.

Milah looked at the young woman and didn't know what to say to her. She felt weak and hated that she was once again at the mercy of Damon De Luca. Last night, she had heard one of the guards talking. She'd been locked away with the rats for three days.

Three days out in the cold with no food or water. She remembered the feel of the rats as they touched her. Their tiny feet digging into her body as they moved. The sharp pain of their teeth.

She had fought them off for the first day. The second was much harder. With no sleep and nothing to keep her strength up, she had fallen.

Weakness was something she couldn't abide.

She didn't know if anyone heard her scream for help, or her begs, but it had all fallen on nothing. No one had come.

For a brief moment, she had prayed for death. Wanted it.

Even now, she wanted to sink into her pit of misery at how useless her situation was, but she kept the tears at bay.

"I … I heard that Mr. De Luca dealt with those responsible for hurting you," the maid said. "They won't be here anymore."

"Why?" she asked, finally speaking.

"They're dead." The maid nodded at her.

"What's your name?" Milah asked.

"I'm simply Maid," she said.

Milah shook her head. "No, it's not. What is your name?"

"It's Glory."

"Hi, Glory," she said, holding out her hand. "I'm Milah. Milah Russo."

Glory took her hand. The other woman's was nice and warm. "I know who you are."

"Do you hate me too?" Milah asked.

"I have no reason to hate you." Glory smiled at her.

"I'm a Russo. A sworn enemy of De Luca. Trust me, you won't be the first person to hate me because of my last name."

Glory shrugged. "I guess I'm not like most people. I don't see the fight you all have."

"Why are you here?" Milah asked. Maybe if she got one of the maids to like her, that might be her key to getting out of here alive. It was a long shot, but right now, anything would beat being locked up.

The darkness. The rats. The chains. It had all been too much.

She grabbed the cuff that was locked around her wrist. Even this one was too much for her to bear. She struggled to keep her panic from rising.

"I … I … was given a choice." Glory dropped her head. "I could work here and be protected by Mr. De Luca, or I could sell my body to whoever wanted me, for however long."

Milah closed her eyes. She knew of the whorehouses. The women who were bought and sold for the profit of men. She hated it.

Staring at Glory, she knew the woman would make a nice living, but she didn't have what it took. Milah saw that.

She used to hide while her father would have

these meetings. Where women would be forced to strip naked and he'd assess them. He would grade them on their beauty, and at times, even their ability to suck cock. Not his own, but a guard's. It revolted her, but she knew the only way to truly survive was to know what she was up against.

It would seem De Luca was no different than Russo.

"Do you have any family?" Milah asked.

Glory shook her head. "No family. Nothing. Just a foster kid trying to get away from a bad situation."

Milah nodded. "I'm sorry."

There was a commotion at the door, and Glory quickly bowed her head. "I better be going. I hope you get well, Miss Russo."

"Please, call me Milah," she said.

Glory nodded and then made her escape as Damon made his entrance.

"I see you're awake."

Milah watched as Glory left before turning her attention to Damon. She lifted her wrist. "Is this necessary?"

"I cannot risk you hurting yourself." He closed the door and moved toward her, perching on the bed, by her side. "How are you feeling?"

"Like I was chained up, starved, and fed to rats. You?" she asked.

He chuckled. "I can see that even with death calling, it hasn't stopped that viperous tongue of yours."

"Why don't you just kill me? I heard the head of the De Luca empire has no shame in ending women. You are happy to kill anyone and everyone who dares to intervene with your world." In the back of her mind, she screamed at herself for being so foolish. Now was not the time to be arguing with him.

She didn't have her strength. Nor did she have a death wish.

Right now, she had to keep in control or risk dying. He had already shown that he had no problem hurting her.

"I am happy to kill anyone who is set to betray all that the De Lucas hold dear. Isn't that what your dear old dad does? It's why you are here."

She wanted to scream at him. "How is the guard?" she asked.

"Excuse me?"

"The guard that I shot. How is he?" She had thought about the man often while she'd been locked away, hoping she had been right in where she shot him. Killing someone was never her intention. She had no wish to do harm. Unlike her father, she didn't have a thirst for blood.

There were times growing up when she'd asked about love and kindness, and he'd laughed at her. Her father wasn't above slapping a girl. He took great pleasure in it too. As far as he was concerned, women had to learn their place, and if that meant hitting them, he was more than happy to do it.

Pulling out of the memory, she looked at Damon.

"You're concerned about him?" Damon asked.

"Yes. I haven't … he's not … can he…" She bit her lip, hating the worry she detected in her voice.

This was not befitting a Russo. Her mother had told her that compassion was something she could only show to those who didn't know who she was. There were so many fucking rules to abide by.

"James is healing fast. You cut flesh, and after his stitches have healed, all will be well."

She nodded. "Thank you." If she ever got the chance to see the guard, she would apologize.

41

"Your father would be proud of the way you are fighting. I'm sure the Russo name will certainly live on in you."

She glared at him. It was on the tip of her tongue to tell him she wasn't fighting for her father nor for his name, but she gritted her teeth. Damon clearly knew what he was doing. As for herself, she was struggling to keep her emotions in check.

"I am surprised you do not ask about your father," Damon said.

"I have no interest in what he does. I'm here, aren't I? That could only mean he has done something … wrong."

Damon chuckled. "Even now, chained to my bed, you're going to be stubborn."

"Do you have a thing for young women?" she asked. "They have labels for men like you."

She gasped as he leaned in close. His face was so close to hers that she felt his breath brush across her lips. She tensed up.

Not once in all her twenty-one years had she been kissed. There was no way her first kiss was going to be from this man. Just the thought of it made her skin crawl. Staring at him now, she had to wonder what he planned to do to her.

"And what would those labels be?" he asked.

Before she said anything, he smirked and cupped her cheek, running his thumb across her bottom lip. He dared to touch her.

She stayed perfectly still.

"Now, if you think to insult me by calling me a pervert, I would agree if you were barely legal, but you're not, are you? You're twenty-one years old."

"I'm still younger than you."

"Yes, by exactly twelve years. Not a very big age

gap, but trust me, Milah, I'm man enough to know how to handle you. You know, these lips are made for being wrapped around my cock. According to your father, you are pure, innocent. Is that true?"

She glared at him. How dare he and how dare her father.

"No," she said, lying easily.

Her first time was supposed to be with someone she loved. Someone she trusted. Not this … arrogant asshole she couldn't stand and wanted to kill.

Sex would never happen between them. At least not willingly. The very thought of being near him was enough to make her skin crawl. He may be a good-looking man, but he was not the man for her. She had to wonder what he was waiting for. What he hoped to achieve by waiting. Was he going to rape her? Break her? What were his intentions?

Damon chuckled. "Do you think I don't know, Milah?" He grabbed the back of her neck and tugged her close. His lips near hers but not quite touching.

He moved his mouth toward her ear. "Do you think I haven't watched you these past three years, keeping an eye on you to make sure you don't do anything stupid like fuck a random stranger?" He tutted. "I know you're a virgin. Not a single cock has been near your body. You're pure, and when the time is right, I'm going to make you beg for me."

"Never," she said, pulling away from him. "I will never beg you for anything."

"You say that now, princess, but I know differently. There will come a time when you are going to beg me. You'll crawl for my cock. Do anything I say just to feel me deep inside you. I wonder if when that time comes, I will give you what you need."

He let her go, and she tried to slap him, but he

held her wrist, stopping her from making contact. "Don't be such a naughty girl."

Damon stepped away from the bed and nodded at the tray of food. "You better eat that if you want to have any strength to defeat me. You can try all you want, Milah, but you are never going to win."

He left the bedroom, and she stared at his door, fearing he might be right. Not about her begging for his cock. That would never happen. Not in a million years, but she certainly needed her strength to get the better of him.

****

Damon sat behind his desk, glancing over the files that had been handed to him. They were from different areas of the De Luca business. He had a meeting tomorrow with the port manager about some of the containers arriving. There was also a possible business arrangement to handle with the cartel.

He looked through each file meticulously.

His father had trained him well. Taught him to read between the lines. None of these files would ever make it into enemy hands. He was to look at them, understand them, and then burn them.

There was never to be a paper trail. While he dealt with the Russo problem, these were merely updates he couldn't handle in person. With each file read, he tossed the individual sheets into the fire.

It was another cold day, and the weather forecast had warned of a snowstorm coming. If that happened, it meant he would be locked in his home until it thawed. He happened to enjoy the snow and often tried to make sure he was home when it fell. He hated city life. Always had.

Born and raised in the country, this was where his heart lay. Life in the country could become quite boring to many, not to him. His father used to make life far more interesting and playful. When his mother was alive, she didn't particularly care for the city or the glamorous life being a De Luca offered.

She'd been the kind of woman who enjoyed spending long afternoons reading in front of a roaring fire. Or in the kitchen. Damon had lost count of the number of times he found her baking away in the kitchen. She loved to cook, to serve her family.

This was where they could hide away and be natural without prying eyes. His father would only allow the guards who had sworn loyalty to him close, whereas Damon had made sure this house was heavily guarded. Once his father became ill, he hadn't taken any chances and simply did what was necessary to keep them all safe.

When his mother died, his father had been inconsolable. Much like Milah's father, he'd been set on a path of death and destruction. But unlike Russo, his own father had been intent on killing the men responsible.

The warpath hadn't brought his father peace. If anything, it had only served to make him more miserable. The men responsible were killed, and they were Russo's men. Of course, they were.

Damon had known from the start, pushing aside his grief to focus on the true act of revenge. His father had wanted swift justice. To see the Russo fall, but Damon had known that wouldn't be easy. To see Russo suffer, he had to have patience, and right now, part of his plan was already underway.

Russo would fall at exactly the right moment. With Milah finally in his hands, there was no way Damon would fail.

With the last updates burnt, Damon decided to walk outside to enjoy the fresh air. Once outside, his guards took several steps back, giving him the space he always required to think.

Shoving his hands into his pockets, he looked up into the starry night sky. Both of his parents were dead. One taken by the enemy, another by cancer. He didn't cry for them. Weakness was not acceptable in the De Luca family. He'd learned not to cry.

Damon recalled his father's warning when he was younger.

"I want you to know this is not because I don't love you. This is to make you strong. Our enemies will try to grab you, Damon. It is my job to make sure you are able to handle whatever they wish to punish you with."

Even as he took a beating from one of the guards, he had stared into his father's eyes and knew he did it out of love.

Throughout his life, he had watched men return to them, beaten, some blinded, some knocking on death's door, and he had known there was always a chance. If he ended up in enemy hands, he had to be able to take the pain. So even when his own father wasn't hurting him, he would make sure he could withstand pain.

The ink that covered his body hid a multitude of sins.

He hadn't been captured by any of his enemies, and being a De Luca, they were far and wide. He had to deal with pain though. Being shot and slashed with a knife were some of the injuries he'd sustained. His car being driven off the road. Beaten. He'd experienced it all.

Taking another deep breath, he turned around and headed back into the house. No one stopped him as he made his way toward his bedroom where the very beautiful Milah was still recovering.

No one had been down to the caves, but he had

no doubt they were nothing more than bone. The rats were very good at hiding evidence.

Once he was outside his door, he hesitated. He had tried to avoid this room for the past few days. The doctor had said she needed her rest, and he'd been more than willing to grant it.

Her time for rest would be coming to an end, very, very soon.

After opening the door, he stepped inside, expecting to come face to face with battle. Instead, he found Milah curled up on top of his bed.

He closed the door quietly, not wanting to disturb her. Even from where he stood by the door, he saw she looked peaceful. Flicking the lock into place, he took a step toward her, and another.

With her guard down, she seemed even more beautiful. Her lips were slightly parted. One of her hands lay flat beside her face. Some of her hair had fallen across her cheek, and with each indrawn breath, it moved closer to her lips before it was pushed out as she exhaled.

He couldn't resist moving some of her hair out of the way, just so he could admire her even more. At first, she didn't wake. Just moved with a little frown, but she was still asleep.

Like this, so submissive, it would be easy to control her.

Milah wanted him to think she wasn't a virgin, but he knew differently. She was innocent. No man had ever been between those luscious thighs.

He wanted to touch her. To run his hands all over her body.

Damon held himself back.

He saw her hand twitch slightly, and she moved just enough to let him know she was coming to.

He didn't move back.

Waiting.

Poised.

Her eyes opened, and she jerked back, sitting up. "You're here."

Damon watched as she quickly wiped at her mouth, and he wondered if she'd been drooling, which he found absolutely adorable. What he also was curious about was why she cared enough about what he thought to remove it.

She was an odd woman. Gorgeous, no doubt about it.

"How are you, my sleeping kitten?" he asked.

She glared at him. "You know, it's weird to stare at a woman sleeping. Kind of creepy, but I guess that is what a De Luca has to do in order to get his rocks off."

Damon chuckled. "And my little kitten has the sweetest claws, I see." He stroked her cheek, and she jerked back.

There was so much fire and passion within her gaze. He couldn't help but admire her.

"Leave me alone."

"You know I can't do that, but the more you fight me, Milah, the sweeter your submission will be."

"You're crazy if you think I am ever going to submit to you."

He pressed his body against hers, and just as he knew she would, she sank down to the bed, trying to get away from him. Milah was very easy to read.

She hated him. That was a given.

He didn't like her either.

What her last name signified was nothing but revulsion to him. A name he intended to wipe out once he used her.

Every person had a part to play, and he wasn't going to let Milah get away from hers. She would submit eventually, and he had all the patience in the world.

Milah had no choice but to spread her legs or risk them being trapped between their bodies. Doing so put his dick right against her core. The flimsy negligee she wore was no match for him.

She pressed her hands against his chest, and for her effort, he pinned them on either side of her head, locking her into place.

"Let me go."

"You're the one who wanted underneath me this whole time. I'm starting to think you like me."

"Never. You're a despicable human being." She wriggled against him, using too much strength.

He didn't want to exhaust her. The doctor had said she would be weak for some time.

Annoyed with himself for pushing her once again a little too far, he pulled away, giving her the space she needed.

"I'm going for a shower. You are quite free to come and join me." He glanced down at her lips and couldn't resist them. With a quick touch, he brushed his mouth against hers, and she gasped. He'd taken her by surprise because she'd let her guard down.

Pulling away, he smiled as he made his way into the bathroom.

He'd slid his knife from his holder before he left, without her seeing, and placed it on the bed.

Milah would use it. She'd come hunting for him.

Her need for revenge was too strong. Her hatred would make her do some stupid things.

After removing his clothes, he turned on the shower and waited for the water to heat up. Cold showers were never desirable to him. He much preferred the warmth of the water. With his fingers beneath the spray, he tested the water.

She should have found the knife by now.

He wanted to watch her, to see how easy it was for her to make this decision, but he didn't put cameras in his own bedroom. Instead, her room was heavily guarded and filled with cameras so she could never experience a moment's peace.

Tipping his head back, he heard the unmistakable sound of the door sliding open. The sudden stillness of it.

She'd fed right into his trap, and now, there was no escaping.

Milah was so easy to read. Her hatred of him would be her downfall.

Or her survival.

Damon had never been into weak women or doormats. He preferred his women to be full of fire. Milah was filled with hatred, whereas he was used to women worshiping him.

Through the stall of the shower, he saw her outline and that of his knife. He was impressed with how she held herself.

Such power.

Such control.

Some of his men didn't even show this kind of dedication. He had to wonder how she was able to fight. His men had told him that she had to be trained in some way, but he didn't know how.

Russo wouldn't allow his daughter to be trained by men. She was merely a woman. The Russos were not known for caring about what happened to their women. They were still pawns in their game.

So how did Milah do it?

Who helped her?

No one had the answers.

The door to the shower opened, and he waited, counting down the seconds before she struck.

He saw her reflection in the tile, the hesitation, and that was her downfall.

If Milah wanted to end him, she should have done it swiftly without taking a second to think about her decision. This was where she messed up.

He captured her wrist and thrust her to the wall. With his hard grip, she cried out, and the blade fell to the bottom of the shower stall between them. Far enough away from their feet that no one got hurt.

Now he had her, but what was he going to do with her?

Chapter Four

Milah had lied to Damon.

She was very much a virgin.

The men who were near her father would never betray him. Not that she'd want to sleep with any of them. The guys at school who were her own age were way too immature. She wasn't going to risk her father's wrath just to sleep with them.

"There is a chance, my sweet, that you will never marry for love. I hope one day you will be able to find love, embrace it, relish it, and hold on to it. It is the greatest feeling in the world."

Her mother had sounded like she spoke from experience, but Milah knew she didn't love her father. Her parents had been a business deal. Nothing more. Her mother had her own wealth, which she brought to the marriage.

Milah touched her hair, wishing at that moment that her mother was beside her. When she'd been talking about love, there had been a soft smile on her lips, as if she talked from the heart. The way she'd reached out to Milah, stroking her hair back as if in fondness.

Hands clenched, she looked away from the bathroom and saw the metal glint on the bed.

Crawling toward it, almost afraid of what it was, she saw it was his knife. How did it get on the bed?

He must have put it there. Or had it fallen out?

Was this a test?

Was Damon testing to see if she would try to kill him?

She touched her finger to the tip of the side of the blade. It was cold to the touch.

"You must learn how to hold a weapon."

"Mom, please?"

"No, please. Do you think anyone is going to listen to your pleas? You're a Russo. They are going to hold it against you, no matter where you go. All you can do is arm yourself."

The training had been brutal. She had to learn so much and all the while, her mother looked on, completely guarded. Almost as if she was watching something that bored her. Milah knew she did it out of love though. Love for her daughter.

That was her way of protecting her daughter against her own father. Not that her father would hurt her in that way. Never. But he would sell her, like he had done so now to save his own damn hide.

Hatred coursed through her, and this time, it wasn't directed to her enemy, but to her father. He would suffer for what he'd done.

She hoped right now he was feeling nothing but humiliation and shame for what he'd done. How his men and those closest to him would see him as nothing but weak. He'd given in to De Luca.

He would fall one day, and when he did, she hoped to watch. Even though it meant her own life would soon follow. She was a Russo.

Gripping the handle of the blade, she held it tight within her grasp and stared toward the door. She would kill him and be free. That was all she wanted. A freedom away from this life. Away from her name. She never wanted to be a Russo, preferring to be a Flynn, which was her mother's maiden name.

With the knife in her hand, she felt the weight of it. This had to be his personal knife. The one he used to maim, to kill. It was impeccable. The feel of it in her hand was … strange. She had never held anything so fine. Her mother had only been able to use generic hunting knives and whatever weapon the soldiers were able to sneak in.

This was a fine piece she held. One she imagined had seen a lot of death.

Sharp as well.

Climbing off the bed, she advanced toward the bathroom but forced herself to pause. This wasn't a good idea. She didn't have much of a chance of killing him. This would be nothing short of a death wish.

Could she do it?

Another few steps, and she opened the door and winced at hearing the slight squeak from the hinge.

Damon didn't appear, and she breathed a sigh of relief. With every step she took, she had to wonder if she should hold herself back.

She got to the shower and reached out to open the door. This was a big mistake. She knew that without even reaching for it, but she couldn't stop herself.

This was her chance. Even if she killed him now, his guards wouldn't let her live. She would have to find a way to sneak away. With the door open, she was about to step inside, but all of a sudden, Damon grabbed her and thrust her against the wall, startling her with how quickly he reacted.

She cried out as he grabbed her wrist. The pressure provided enough pain for her to drop the knife. She pulled her feet back, not wanting them to be cut.

Milah couldn't look away as she stared at Damon. He was completely naked.

She hadn't thought this through. She'd never seen a man naked before. So long as she didn't look down, she wouldn't see just how naked she was.

The shower sprayed between them, but Damon decided to close the distance, and then he was right next to her.

All she wore was a thin, cotton negligee. It

reminded her of something out of a historical period drama. There was no shape to it, but it provided coverage and modesty. With his hands on her shoulders, his body so close to hers, she wished she had some kind of armor to keep him away. There was nothing to protect her.

"You do have a death wish, don't you?" he asked.

She tried to wriggle out of his grasp, but he held her firm.

"You did that on purpose, didn't you? You knew I would grab it."

He chuckled. "You're exactly right. What I want to know is how a Russo can hold a knife so expertly."

"I'm no expert."

"You have been able to fight my men, take them by surprise, figure out ways of escaping. Climbing down the side of buildings, and now you're able to hold a knife in a way that shows it's not just self-defense. How?"

She wanted to avert her gaze, but with how he looked at her, it was next to impossible.

She couldn't tell him. This was part of her training.

"I have no idea what you mean," she said.

"They could train you to take care of yourself, but they sure didn't train you to be a good liar. You're shitty at it."

"And you're a shitty captor."

As far as comebacks went, that one was awful, and she tried not to wince. All he did was laugh, like it was the funniest thing he'd ever heard.

To him, it probably was.

Damon took her by surprise, though. Rather than call his men and order her death, or to be locked up, he closed the distance between them.

She was right.

Her negligee was flimsy and not designed to ward

off his body. Certainly a rather pointy part of his anatomy. She tensed up as his cock pressed against her stomach.

It had to be that. Or he was harvesting some kind of alien life force.

She wanted to look, but she kept her gaze on his.

This was the only way to survive.

Even as her heart raced and the desire to look down was so strong, she held it together, against all the odds. It would be so easy to look down. To see what he was … keeping alive.

"You think I'm a captor? Do you think this is some kind of romance tale?"

She glared at him. How dare he mock her? He had no idea who he was dealing with. She tried to push him away, but all that achieved was to bring him even closer as he pressed her hands above her head, locking her in place.

"I hate you."

It wasn't a great threat. He probably loved that she hated him.

"And I hate you, Milah Russo. I hate your kind. I hate your name, and one day, you will die because of it."

"Then kill me now. Get what you want."

He chuckled. It wasn't a nice sound.

"You think that is all I want?" Another laugh. This one sounded on the verge of hysteria.

Milah had no idea what he had planned, but she also didn't want to know.

He leaned in close so his lips were beside her ear. "Do you think I am a man so easily satisfied?"

"I think you're a sick, evil, twisted bastard. Just like all the De Lucas." They were responsible for killing her mother. It was why her father had been on a warpath, so determined to end every single one of them. He'd failed.

Now she was at the mercy of them.

Damon De Luca. She hated him so damn much.

"Fighting words, but if I end your life, I don't get to see you fall, do I? I don't get to watch all of the Russos fall, and that is exactly what is going to happen. I have plans for you, Milah."

He tugged her hands above her head and stroked her cheek. He stepped back, and when his gaze roamed down her body, there was no mistaking what he intended.

"You're going to rape me?" she asked.

She shouldn't be surprised. De Lucas were all the same. Monsters. Animals.

"Oh, sweet Milah, when you come to my bed, you are going to be begging for my cock."

"Never."

"No?" he asked, and within seconds, her hands were released.

She wanted to run past him, to find a means of escape, but he was in front of the door, blocking her exit, and she didn't think the glass on the side of the stall would be easy enough to break.

Milah stared at him. With the gap he'd created between them, she was able to look at him. It couldn't be avoided. He did it on purpose. There was no doubt.

His cock was hard.

How could he be hard at a time like this?

She watched as he wrapped his fingers around his length.

"Trust me, Milah Russo, when you finally come to my bed and spread those pretty pale thighs of yours, you are going to be hungry for my cock. Begging me to fuck you." He moved his hand up and down his length.

She didn't want to look but found her gaze drawn to him. This wasn't fair. No one had ever done this to her before. She didn't know what to do.

The desire to run was strong, but there was no escape.

Milah couldn't stop looking as he worked his dick.

He looked so … fierce. So large.

She nibbled on her lip and hated that she was even curious as to what he was doing. He held himself so tightly, it had to hurt. There was no way he was enjoying what he was doing, but he stayed long.

Milah was a virgin. She'd never been with a man before, but she had read a great deal, and had even watched some porn at her mother's insistence.

That had been an … experience.

Her mother had wanted her to be prepared for everything, unlike herself. She had told her that her wedding night hadn't gone to plan.

Even though she hadn't wanted to hear about what happened between her parents, she knew it had been bad.

She pulled out of the memory.

Damon's actions increased in speed, and she heard his groan as he got close.

The tension in his body seemed to mount, and then, she didn't look away as he finally came. His cum spilled out of the tip and onto the bathroom stall.

"You will beg me for my cock, and what's more, there will come a time when you'll beg to lick every single drop of spunk, and I look forward to that day."

****

Snow had fallen like the weather forecast had predicted.

A nice blanket of white covered his property. The house was freezing, and his guards and maids had no choice but to gather some firewood, to help warm the house. It was just typical that his central heating had to give out just as there was a snowstorm.

Milah wasn't in her room.

After their moment in the bathroom, Damon had decided it was time for her to go to her own room. He needed his space, and to have that, Milah had to be far away.

He'd been so close to breaking his own rules and simply fucking her. It would have been easy.

Milah would have put up a fight, but he'd seen her body's reaction to him. The flush to her cheeks, the budding of her nipples. She'd been aroused by him playing with himself. He had to wonder if she would be wet. He'd find out soon enough.

It took several hours to get the house warm, but as he stood in his office, he stared at the flames. There was no way he'd be able to get a plumber or an electrician out to the house. More snow was forecast to fall.

This was just fucking typical.

His father had told him to always be on top of the house, and that meant the barest of needs. Check on leaky roofs, the gas boiler, all of it.

He'd been so blinded by his thirst for revenge on Russo, he'd allowed the house to fall behind in its maintenance.

This house was part of De Luca blood. His family had been here for several generations. Once the snow was thawed, he would have the necessary work taken to repair it. His father would have been angry at him right now.

There was a knock at his door.

"Come in," he said.

He turned to see James entering. "Sir ... er..."

"What is it?"

"The Russo girl is in the kitchen and the staff don't know what to do."

Damon frowned. "What?"

James repeated it, not that he needed him to. With there being no warmth in the house, he had to put the guards on wood duty, chopping and gathering it.

Milah should have stayed in her room, beneath the covers, not in the kitchen.

Brushing past James, he made his way toward the kitchen, and sure enough, his staff kept a distance from her. Even the chef didn't want anything to do with her.

There was like a wall around Milah, and he stared at the woman, wondering if she cared at all that many people couldn't stand her just because she was a Russo.

"What are you doing?" he asked.

Milah looked up. She wore a large turtleneck sweater with the sleeves pushed up to her elbows. He didn't see what she wore underneath as she also wore an apron. Her long raven hair was pulled back into a ponytail, and her face that had seemed so pale the past few days was finally blooming with color. Her cheeks were a little flushed.

"What does it look like I'm doing?" she asked. "I'm cooking."

"If you plan to poison me, don't bother."

"As if I would know how to get poison. No matter what you think, De Luca, I am simply coming here to cook. My mother—" She stopped. Her lips pressed together, and he watched as she also paused in her cutting.

"Your mother what?"

He wasn't interested in what she had to say. If she didn't answer him, he'd have the guards escort her out of the kitchen.

"My mother always said that a casserole always

had the ability to warm the body. She would … make this whenever there was a snowstorm." Milah wouldn't look at him, but he heard the catch in her voice.

Damon stared at her.

She was … upset. The snowstorm reminded her of her mother.

He'd never met the woman, but sources and spies had told him she was a lovely woman. Sweet and kind. Not a good match for Russo.

"I will not intervene with your staff or your chef. I only ask for a small space, a few ingredients, and a pot. That is all."

"What do I get out of it?" Damon asked.

Milah looked up, and he saw that she'd gotten herself under control. "You don't have to worry about me running off."

"I don't worry about that anyway."

"What do you want?" she asked.

She was a foolish woman.

"You will come to my room tonight."

Her jaw clenched.

What would she do?

"Fine." She looked down and got to work.

He smiled. "Make sure she has everything she needs." He nodded toward the chef to keep an eye on her.

Milah may not be able to get her hands on poison, but there were enough cleaning products within a house to make it quite easy to harm someone. He wouldn't put it past her to try.

After leaving the kitchen, he made his way back to his office and found himself more curious than he liked.

At his desk, he pulled out his key and unlocked the bottom drawer. He grabbed the file and flicked it open. It held all the details of Milah, of her life. Where she went to school. Her grades. Even people she associated with, which were none. Milah was closed off to everything and everyone.

No one wanted to be friends with a Russo. He wasn't surprised. They were the enemy.

There wasn't enough information on her mother.

He grabbed his cell phone and dialed his man who liked to be known as Genius. Damon entertained him because so far, no matter the request, he'd been able to supply.

"What's up?" Genius asked.

"I need you to find some information for me on, Edith Russo, previously known as Flynn."

"Are you sure? The woman's dead, sir."

"I know she's dead, but I want to know everything. Every tiny little detail."

"All the dirty stuff, got it."

"Soon." He hung up and placed the phone in front of him on the desk. Milah was cooking in his mother's kitchen.

He gripped the edge of the desk and decided to go to the security room, which was located on the first floor.

His guards were all busy, and no one called to distract him.

Entering the computer room, he saw all the screens were blank. He typed in his password, and the screens came to life. Every single one that was around his property, from the front gate, through the forest, and all around the house.

He typed in the code to bring up the kitchen, and he stood, watching Milah.

No one approached her. His staff kept a wide berth, and Milah just chopped away.
She didn't get in anyone's way, nor did she threaten anyone.

One of the maids approached Milah, and he watched her look up, and for the first time since she got here, she smiled. Actually smiled, and he gritted his teeth.

Milah was beautiful. No doubt about it. But when she smiled, he felt like he'd been punched to the gut. She was even more stunning. He saw the dimples in the corner of her cheeks, and her eyes had this twinkle. She didn't look guarded as she smiled, but almost as if she was lost in her own little world.

Mesmerizing.

He cleared his throat as the maid rounded the counter, stood beside Milah, and started to help.

Was she not afraid?

Most of the staff were, especially after she had shot James and hurt others.

Damon eased out the chair, sat down, and watched her. She looked so natural in the kitchen. Like she was in the kitchen often.

She placed lots of vegetables within a pot, and the maid went to grab the kettle on the far stove. The chef glared at her, but the maid didn't stop.

She helped Milah, who stirred the hot water into her pot, and then handed it back to the maid.

He grabbed the walkie-talkie on the counter in the security room and requested the kitchen maid working with Milah to be brought to him in his office.

Milah put the lid onto the pot and slid it into the oven. She looked at the oven with such intent.

He waited until she stood back, but Milah didn't leave the kitchen. She started to clean away her mess.

Why?

He had staff to do that.

Milah wasn't acting how he expected a Russo brat to act.

Angry, he turned off the screens, shut down the feed, and then left the room to go to his office where the maid looked nervous.

"Why did you help her?" he asked.

"Pardon, sir?"

"The Russo in the kitchen, why did you help her?" He folded his arms, waiting for an answer. He could hurt her, but she hadn't done anything wrong.

"No one helped her. She only asked where the spices were, and they all ignored her. She looked ... sad, sir. I am sorry."

"What is your name?" he asked.

"Glory."

"You're not afraid of her?"

Glory shook her head.

"Why not?"

"She ... she is ... nice."

He glared at her head. The maid wouldn't look at him.

"And you're aware she is a Russo?"

"Forgive me."

Why was she bowing her head? "Look at me," he said.

Glory lifted her head, and he saw fear in her eyes. He knew why. Some maids who tried to escape had ended up dead. Anyone who tried to betray the De Luca name always ended up dead.

They had a choice.

"You are not afraid of Milah?"

"No, sir."

"Then how would you like to earn your freedom?" he asked.

"Sir?"

He smiled, and she took a step back. "If you want to earn your freedom, you are to befriend Milah. Find out

SAM CRESCENT

all of her secrets, and you are to report them to me, understood?"

"But how do I … I have my jobs to do."

"Not anymore. Your one and only task is to be by Milah's side from the moment she wakes up until I dismiss you. Deal?"

Glory looked at the hand he offered and waited. If she refused, he would have her killed.

She put her hand within his, and he was surprised by how firm her grip was. He now had someone who could learn all of Milah's secrets. The kind that were never traceable.

Glory left his office, and he made the arrangements for his men and staff to know that she wouldn't be available to them. She had a different job to do.

He was finishing up some emails when his office door was knocked on once again.

"Come in," he said.

His chef, Renaldo, entered the room. He had cooked for his parents and had offered his services to him.

"What is it, Renaldo?" he asked.

"In all of my years of service, I have never been so insulted," he said.

"No?" Damon asked, leaning back in his chair to look at the chef. "And how have you been insulted?"

He liked Renaldo.

His father had said he was the best chef in the world, and he didn't doubt that, but looking at the older man, he had to wonder if it was time to retire him.

"Having that Russo whore in my kitchen. It is an insult I cannot bear."

Hearing Milah insulted shouldn't have bothered him. She was a Russo. The name was nothing more than

65

an insult to his men and to his staff.

The Russos were vile. A name to be disgusted in having.

But hearing this man insult Milah, calling her a whore, didn't bode well with him.

"Be careful," he said. "Milah is my guest."

"Sir, she is … she should never be allowed to touch your … the kitchen…"

Damon held his hand up. "She is cooking a meal that reminds her of her mother. Would you deny a woman that right?" he asked.

"That is my kitchen," the chef said. "Your father would not stand for it."

Damon rounded the desk and looked at the chef. He'd served the De Luca family for years. His cooking was the best he'd ever tasted.

"Do you question my decision?" he asked.

"Damon?"

"It is Mr. De Luca to you, and I suggest you remember your place. If you want to continue to live, you will allow Milah to cook her mother's dish. If not, I can make arrangements for you not to be so insulted again."

The threat was clear. Damon wouldn't allow his insult to slide.

The chef bowed his head, clearly realizing what he had done. A family chef or not, he was not the boss, Damon was.

Chapter Five

"I had no idea you could cook," Glory said.

Milah was shocked to see the maid return. She expected her to be ordered to stay far away from her. The guards did, or they sneered at her as if ready to kill her. The only one who didn't make her feel like a prisoner was James. The one she shot. The only guard who should hate her for what she did, was the only one who made her feel … normal.

She heard the whispers. These people hated her. She was aware of the hatred the Russo name inspired, but she wasn't used to it being so close to her.

No one would dare speak about her or treat her like this at her home. But that was the difference. At home, she was a Russo. The people there were loyal to her. This was the De Luca home. Her sworn enemy.

"I can't cook, not really. I'm not trained, but I used to watch my mom from time to time." Her father had hated it when she'd cooked. He considered housework beneath himself and his wife. That was why they had staff to do it.

Her mother loved to cook, though, and bake. It reminded her of her grandmother. A woman Milah never got the chance to meet but had always wished she had.

"Actually, everything I know is because of her. Whenever there was a snowstorm, she liked to make what her mother would make, and obviously what her grandmother would make. It was passed down the female line, and this was it."

"It smells delicious."

Milah left her stool and went to the oven. She picked up some oven mitts, slid them on her hands, and removed the pot. Lifting the lid, she allowed the steam to escape and inhaled deeply. She was instantly transported back to a time she was a little girl. She'd been out building snowmen with her mother.

Her father was nowhere to be found.

The chef hadn't been able to make it in, but her mother had cooked for them. They had prepared this stew before going out and playing. When they got back, they enjoyed it at the kitchen counter, laughing and giggling. Afterward, her mother made hot chocolate, which they enjoyed in front of a roaring fire.

When her father wasn't around, her mother got to be the woman she always wanted to be.

Milah pulled away from the memory, gave the pot a stir, and placed it in the oven.

"If you would like, you can try it," Milah said, trying to control her emotions.

"I don't know if I could," Glory said.

She felt … deflated. Glory was a nice woman. The only one who was talking to her like she was a human being. The other staff ignored her or scowled her way.

Such open animosity surprised her.

"Of course. That is fine."

Milah sat back on the stool, waiting. She had already cleaned up all the dishes, so she didn't need to do that. She kept her gaze on the oven, not wanting to look left or right and risk seeing the hatred in the others' eyes. She had done nothing to them, and yet they despised her.

Maybe she should have stayed in her freezing cold room.

There had been no guards, and listening in on conversations, she learned the central heating wasn't working. Damon had allowed the maintenance of the house to go to ruin, and now, trapped in a snowstorm, his men were having to chop firewood.

She knew the safest and warmest place to be was

in the kitchen.

The chef left the kitchen, storming out the door, and he returned less than twenty minutes later, looking slightly pale. She had to wonder what he'd done.

He hated her, that was clear.

After another thirty minutes, when the staff were getting the meal ready for Damon, Milah went and checked on her stew. The vegetables were soft. The lentils were cooked. She picked up a spoon, tasted some of the sauce, and closed her eyes.

She could almost feel her mother's arms wrapped around her, laughing as she tasted it when she was a little girl. The joy she had at cooking.

She opened her eyes and saw Glory had come closer. "I would … like to taste some."

Milah tried to contain her joy and washed the spoon she'd used. She didn't want to ask for anything more than necessary.

Holding it out to Glory, she waited as the maid tasted her food.

"Oh, wow, that is delicious, Milah." Glory chuckled. "And you said you couldn't cook."

"Well, I'm not a trained chef. I don't know what I'm doing." She nibbled on her lip. "This is … it's just food, you know." She felt her cheeks heat. Glory was the first person she'd cooked for, and it felt good to know she liked it.

The doors to the kitchen opened, and Milah looked to see Damon had entered.

"Is your dish finished?" Damon asked.

Milah looked at the steaming pot and nodded. "Yes."

"Good, then bring it to the table. You will eat with me."

"I can eat in here."

"Consider this part of your payment for using my kitchen. You will eat with me."

Glory had bowed her head. She noticed most of the female staff did this.

She didn't want to go and eat with him, but she had wanted to cook this meal. There was no choice left to her.

Nodding, she grabbed the oven mitts, slid them on, and picked up the pot once again.

Damon held the door open as she carried her pot to the table. Would he humiliate her?

Did she care?

She had her mother's stew, and that was all it had taken. The taste had reminded her of the woman she missed daily. She tried not to think of her mother because it just made her feel so miserable.

There was a space at the table between herself and Damon. She leaned over and put the pot down on the heatproof mat. Then he opened the lid and put it on the spare oven mitt on the tabletop. After serving herself a generous portion, she sat down and watched as Damon took his seat.

Nibbling on her lip, she didn't know if she should bother to ask him or let him pick if he wanted it. There was an abundance of food on the table. She saw several steaks, pieces of chicken, potatoes, and roasted vegetables.

The chef hated her.

Most of the staff did, all because she was a Russo.

"May I try some?" he asked, holding out his plate.

She was so surprised that at first, she didn't even know what to say. "You'd like to try some?"

"That's what I said, and I don't like to repeat

myself."

She tried to contain her smile.

He wanted to try her food.

"You're not worried it's poisoned?"

"I saw you taste it, and I doubt you'd ruin your mother's dish just to try to kill me."

That was partly true. She would've made it awful so that each bite made him even more disgusted until he finally died.

Milah didn't say that, but she did serve him a small portion. Sitting back in her seat, she picked up her knife and fork, waiting for him to try it.

I don't care if he likes it or not.

He can rot in hell.

As he pressed the spoon to his lips, she waited with bated breath for what he would say. His eyes closed for the smallest second, and then a smile curved his lips.

"Do you like it?" she asked, hating the words the moment they came out of her mouth.

"That is delicious."

She ate her food, constantly looking at him out of the corner of her eye. He finished the small portion she gave him, and then when he asked for some more, she was delighted. Damon De Luca shouldn't make her happy, but he did, and to her, that was just wrong.

They ate in silence.

Milah loved every second of the meal she'd prepared. Damon didn't touch any of his chef's food. They finished the meal she'd prepared.

Glancing at the table, she knew this was going to cause her some trouble. She didn't know exactly how, but she knew she'd have to be prepared for the worst.

"Would you like to cook more often?" Damon asked, startling her out of her thoughts.

She turned toward him with a frown. "Pardon?"

"You heard me. Would you like to cook more often?"

"Your chef won't like that."

"I don't give a flying fuck what my chef thinks. I'm the boss here. He'll learn to do as he was told."

She detected the threat in his voice. Staring at Damon, his dark, penetrating gaze looking back at her, she had to wonder what he was thinking. What was he planning? He wouldn't give her anything.

His disgust of who she was was clear to her every moment she was in his company. Why would he be nice? Did he feel guilty for what happened in the dungeon or cave or whatever the hell that was?

Why would he?

He was a De Luca. They never felt remorse for anything.

"What will I have to do?" she asked.

"Keep me company every night," he said.

There it was.

"I won't sleep with you."

"Did I say sleep?"

"I won't … have sex with you."

He chuckled. "Like I said before, Milah, when I fuck you, you'll be begging me for it."

She hated him.

Cooking was a nice distraction from her current situation. From the moment she'd been taken, she had expected the worst. For him to rape her, to hurt her. He'd hurt her, not by his own hands, but by those that served him.

"Then I agree," she said. She had no intention of begging him for sex.

They were enemies. Sex would never happen between them. He would beg her before she ever allowed that to happen.

Damon smiled. "I look forward to it."

She got to her feet, reaching for the dishes.

"I have staff who do that. Go and get washed. You owe me tonight."

She clenched her hands into fists. His staff wouldn't be happy with her being in the kitchen. She wasn't going to overstay her welcome. The chef looked ready to kill her with his butcher's knife. She wasn't a fool.

The people here were her enemy. Even Glory. She didn't know why the young maid had offered to stay with her, or why she'd seemed friendly.

She wasn't going to let her guard down.

This house and all the property around was her battleground. She had to do whatever it took to make it out alive.

One day, she would live as a Flynn, and the Russo name would be a thing of the past.

****

Damon waited for Milah to arrive. Glory had already given him an update on today's progress. There was nothing to report.

This was a new friendship between the two.

He doubted Milah would trust the young maid for some time. She might share little trivial things, but for the most part, she'd be guarded, as anyone would in her situation. He couldn't blame her.

Damon sat down on the edge of the bed. Genius hadn't gotten back in touch, and with the snow falling, there was nothing more he could do.

He had his men on the outside dealing with all the necessary details when it came to Antonio Russo. The man's very name was enough to make his skin crawl. Damon despised him.

From all angles, he was squeezing him for

everything. The ports were already taken, along with the brothels.

He'd pushed the cartels away from Russo, as well as the MCs that were on his side. It was amazing how a change of thinking and perspective could make people change their reasoning. They had all become part of De Luca.

His father had taught him that loyalty was the most valuable asset, as well as fear. People tried to tame what they feared, or they hid from it.

Damon had built a reputation for being the monster in the De Luca empire, and they all should fear him.

There was a small knock on the door, and he called for Milah to enter. There was only one person who would knock so … hesitantly.

Milah opened the door and stepped inside.

"Close it," he said.

She turned her back to him and closed the door. He saw her hand rest on the wood. Did he make her nervous? He hoped so.

She wore a pair of flannel pajamas he'd supplied. They gave her plenty of modesty. He doubted she would have felt comfortable coming to him in a silk and lace negligee, or an old nightshirt that she'd worn when she was sick.

"How are you?" he asked.

Milah looked at him with a frown. "Fine. You?"

He smiled. "Do you not think that our time together could go by a lot easier if we're pleasant with each other?"

"Cut the crap, De Luca. You are not fooling me, and I doubt you'd fool any of your staff. You can't stand me."

"I don't know you."

"You don't care to know me," she said. "All you see is a Russo. Everyone does."

He folded his arms and looked at her.

Her hands were clenched at her sides, and he saw the slight tensing of her jaw. She didn't like how people saw her.

Why?

She'd been a Russo all her life. Power and privilege had come to her without any effort.

"And you don't think we can make the most of it."

"What do you want from me?"

"How about the pleasure of your company?"

"You hurt my father in such a way that you got me out of a business deal. We're never going to marry. You hold all the cards right now. You can do with me what you wish. I have no power, and yet, you're … being nice."

"Would you like me to be mean?" he asked, getting to his feet and advancing toward her.

Milah tried to stay strong and firm, but with him as her adversary, it was next to impossible. She finally stumbled back, trying to create some distance between them.

He liked that.

The wall stopped her from getting far, and he pressed his hands on either side of her head. She didn't look afraid, but she assessed him, waiting for him to attack. She was going on the defensive, which he found intriguing.

"Who trained you?" he asked.

"I have no idea what you're talking about."

A lie.

Milah was keeping her ability to fight back a secret. It was a badly kept one, but he was happy to play along for the time being.

"I think it is best I go back to my room." She didn't make a move to leave, and he didn't step back either.

He stared at her, watching, waiting, curious. Milah wasn't a spoiled bitch.

The time he'd spent with her in the maze had been short and sweet, but the encounter had stayed with him for the past three years.

He'd met spoiled bitches. Fucked plenty of them in his time. They were used to getting what they wanted with the simple snap of their fingers. On her birthday, with all gazes on her, she'd run away.

"You are to keep me company tonight. Have you forgotten?" he asked.

"You want to talk in riddles and questions."

"Do you not have any questions for me?"

"I have nothing I want to say to you," she said.

Damon stepped back. "Then let us merely enjoy each other's company without the pressure of talking." He moved back until he was perched on the edge of the bed. "You can't leave, not yet. I will have to punish you."

"Why?"

"You asked for something, I granted it. If you don't make payment, there are always consequences."

"And a De Luca always expects payment?" she asked.

"Only a fool wouldn't."

Part of him wanted her to go to the door, to make a run for it. Not all punishments ended in a dungeon with rats. Some could be quite pleasing.

Instead, she moved toward him and sat down on the edge of the bed, her hands poised in her lap.

Not a word was spoken. Silence fell between

them, and Damon watched her.

She took a deep breath. It was slow, calming.

He watched her chest rise and then slowly fall. She did this several times. Her palms went from gripping her thighs to resting with them up. She kept looking around the room and not at him.

He waited. Damon was used to silence.

Milah tilted her head from left to right. Rubbed her hands up and down her thighs, glanced around. Looked at him. Quickly looked away.

He couldn't help but chuckle. She wasn't fooling anyone. Least of all him.

Damon waited.

Curious.

"What do you want?" Milah asked.

"I take it you don't want to sit in silence."

"I'm not an idiot. I know you can do whatever you want to me, so why wait? Why not get it over with?" she asked, shooting her accusatory glare his way.

He reached out and stroked some of her hair back behind her ear. "And why would I do that?" he asked. "Your begging will be so much more enjoyable."

Milah sank to her knees, clasped her hands together, and raised them. "Please, let me go. I am begging you. This fight is not between us. Your problem is with my father. Please, just let me go."

Now this was a sudden turn of events he didn't anticipate.

Sinking to his knees in front of Milah, he cupped her face, tilting her head back to look at him. "And why would I do that when I can have so much fun with you?" He ran his thumb across her lips and leaned in close. The temptation to kiss her was strong, but he held himself back, wanting to make her wait.

Part of the pleasure was the anticipation.

Milah would relent eventually.

All he had to do was wait. He could make her life difficult or easy. It was up to her. Personally, he wanted it to be all pleasure, but he knew Milah would fight him.

He looked forward to it.

Damon moved his lips toward her ear, and he felt her tense up. The neck was such an erogenous zone. He wondered if she felt arousal. Was her tight pussy soaking wet? He'd find out soon enough.

"It's nice to hear you beg, but have you ever thought that it might be amazing between us?" he asked. "Your tight little cunt sliding up and down my cock. I could give you the world, Milah. Show you how good it can be between us. All you have to do is give in."

"Do you have to force all the women you sleep with?"

He chuckled. "They beg with me entering the room."

"You sicken me."

"One day, you're going to want me. Let us see if I will still want you then." He grabbed her arm and moved her toward his door. He pushed her out with enough force to make her stumble. "Take her to her room."

Milah shot him a glare, and for her effort, he gave her a wink.

It was going to take more than a few glares to anger him.

After closing his door, he moved toward the balcony. The night was cold, but he didn't care. His cock was rock fucking hard, and there was no way he was going to be able to satisfy his craving for that woman with anyone else. The only woman he wanted was Milah. He didn't care about the age gap between them.

Age was just a number.

Milah would belong to him.

He could just fuck her and be done with it. Force her to take his cock, but of all the bad things he'd done in his lifetime, rape wasn't one of them.

Damon refused to be tarnished with that brush, even if previous De Luca generations had been known to do it. His father hadn't. Neither had he. His grandfather, however, that was ... different. Damon knew of the tales of his grandfather trapping young women. Especially those who didn't desire him. Not because of his wealth or looks. Grandad De Luca had been a wealthy, handsome man back in the day. The women who rejected him didn't want anything to do with the De Luca name. It was one of the reasons the De Lucas and Russos were at war.

Damon didn't like the tale.

His father said it wasn't exactly accurate, but apparently there was a young Russo woman. Eighteen, beautiful. Considered to be the most beautiful woman in the country. His grandfather wanted her, but the Russo patriarch of the time denied him. There was no way a De Luca and a Russo would ever marry.

So, because she wasn't given to his grandfather, she was taken.

This was where the tale twisted. Some believed she died on the way to his grandfather. Others said she was taken to his grandfather where he raped her repeatedly until he drove her crazy and she took her own life.

Damon knew his grandfather was evil.

The bastard had a thirst for blood that his son didn't quite inherit. With the Russo girl's death, the war between the two families spilled out. There was no chance of peace. After Russo killed Damon's mother, De Luca had finally sworn to put an end to the violence by simply wiping out the Russo line.

Not only was he going to do that, but he was also going to make sure Milah Russo bore him a son. He would raise that boy a De Luca, and Russo would know that his own grandson would have De Luca blood running in his veins.

Milah was part of his plan.

What he wanted more than anything was to see her fall.

She was a Russo, and making her fall in love with him, then shattering her world, was also part of his plan. He had inherited some of his grandfather's evil, but rather than allow it to fester, he would release it.

Chapter Six

Milah was twenty-one years old.

Playing in the snow was for children.

Damon had finally rectified the problem within the house, and the rooms were warm. Glory had told her that several parts of the house had been closed off to help sustain the heating.

She hated that she loved this old house. The only bad part about it was the fact it was owned by De Luca. Men and women from that family had been born and raised here.

The house was more … homey than the one where she lived. Her father wouldn't allow her to leave home, even though she had tried to do so many times. He didn't believe in daughters going out on their own until they were married. It was such an archaic way of thinking, and she had laughed at him, which had earned her a slap for her troubles.

For all of his ranting on tradition and what was expected of a Russo woman, he'd given her up to his enemy.

She and Damon were never going to marry. This wasn't a love match. Was it even a business contract? Damon got to play with Russo's daughter for an extended length of time.

Milah needed to understand the full ramifications and terms her father had agreed to. She had no idea how she was going to do that without speaking to her father. Or would Damon tell her?

She doubted it. He would want to keep his power over her by any means possible.

She was all alone.

Wrapping her arms around her body, she snuggled into the thick sweater Glory had brought with her, along with the rest of her clothes. She wasn't allowed to have any clothes. The bedroom was always bare apart from the bed. Glory was the one to bring her clothes in the morning, and she assumed at night as well. Every night, she left Damon's room, escorted by a guard to her own room. The lock was always slid into place, only to be removed when Glory entered.

The first day she made it down to the kitchen with no one to stop her had surprised her. She expected there to be guards all over wanting to kill her. There were still guards, but they were assigned different jobs.

Staring out the window, across the gardens, it was hard not to be mesmerized by the fallen snow. She didn't want to marvel at its beauty, nor take a walk outside, but she … couldn't look away.

Even as a girl, she'd loved the snow. Hearing it crunch beneath her feet, and as she walked, seeing it glisten on the ground.

Her mother liked the snow whenever Antonio wasn't around. There were a lot of things her mother enjoyed doing when he wasn't near. She missed her mother dearly right now. No amount of holding herself was going to rid her memories or her wishing for her mother.

Milah spun around as she heard the door being thrust open. This morning, Glory had told her to wait in her bedroom. The house was in a little bit of chaos, but De Luca wanted her to remain here.

Her first instinct had been to make a run for it. This might be her only opportunity to get free, but as she'd gone to the door, intent on opening it, and finally embracing the chance of freedom, she had stopped herself. What if … this was a trap? What if Damon expected her to make a run for it, and as punishment, Glory suffered?

She didn't know Glory all that well, and she doubted they would ever be besties. It didn't for a second mean she wanted the young woman to suffer.

Rather than push open the door, she'd stepped back, sat on her bed, and waited. There would be a time and place for her to make a run for it. Damon would lose his guard, or something. She had to keep on hoping for some kind of miracle.

Anything.

What she wouldn't do was use someone else, an innocent, as a means to make her escape.

Damon stood before her now, his gaze focused on her. Did he expect her to run? Had she passed his stupid test? What was he thinking?

Rather than ask any questions, she dropped her hands by her sides and greeted him. "Hello," she said.

He smiled. "Are you liking the snow?"

She glanced behind her at the view. There was no point in denying the appeal. "It looks beautiful."

"That it does." He nodded his head in agreement. "Very beautiful. How would you like to take a walk with me?"

It was on the tip of her tongue to refuse, but then she stopped herself. Why would she refuse him?

"I'd like that."

His brows went up, and she took a step toward him. "I don't have a jacket."

He snapped his fingers, and Glory entered the room.

She smiled at the young woman, taking the jacket from her.

This wasn't what she expected, and when Damon offered her his arm, she was tempted to refuse.

Sliding her hand around his arm, they walked out together, making their way downstairs. The corridors were large enough to accommodate two people side by side.

She couldn't resist taking quick glances. Every now and then, she looked at him, curious as to what was going on in his mind.

The rumors that circulated about the De Lucas always made the women fearful. They knew of Damon's grandfather who had no problem with stealing women, raping them, bringing them to the point of death, and at times, even killing them.

She had expected Damon to be the same.

Only, he was different. He hadn't forced himself on her.

If anything, other than the dungeon, he'd been a perfect host.

"You keep looking at me like that, I'm going to wonder if I've got something on my face," he said.

Then he'd say things like that, almost teasing. There was a smile on his lips, and she didn't know what to say or think.

"You have nothing on your face and you know it."

"Then you're admiring my face?"

She rolled her eyes. "I wouldn't do anything of the sort."

"You know a lot of women would love to be in your position."

"Locked away. No freedom. Fearing for my life. Surrounded by people who despise me. I see the appeal."

He chuckled. "Now that you put it that way."

"I have no desire to be here, Damon. You know that. You don't want me here."

"Oh, but I do," he said. "This is where you're going to stay."

"Is this part of your punishment?" she asked,

coming to a stop before they even got to the garden. "To lure me into a false sense of security. Will you kill me?"

He patted her hand and leaned in close. "I have no interest in killing you. You haven't betrayed me."

"And you only kill people who betray you?" she asked.

"No, but that is usually the case within this house."

She wanted to argue with him. "I'm a Russo. My very name tells you that you should hate me."

"I don't hate you."

"Why not?"

"I have no reason to."

That was a lie. Milah refused to be pulled into tricks.

The doors to the garden opened, and she was tempted to go back to her room. To run and hide, but instead, she felt the chill against her cheeks.

It felt so good compared to the chill around the house. This was crisp and fresh, and a little exciting.

She stepped forward, following alongside Damon as they made their way outside. The sneakers she wore were no protection against the ice. Her foot gave out, and if it wasn't for Damon, she'd have fallen to the ground, but he caught her, keeping her balanced with his thick, strong arm wrapped around her waist.

Milah chuckled. "I'm sorry."

"I should have known to buy you some boots. Those shoes are no match for the cold weather."

They went to move again, and Milah burst out laughing as her feet skidded across the thick patch of ice. Damon had no choice but to haul her up against his body, and she gasped. Their faces were so close together.

"I think it is easier if I carry you off this ice."

She didn't want to touch him, but she also didn't

want to fall on the hard ground. Hating herself for showing any kind of weakness, she slowly wrapped her arms around his neck, holding on to him as he carried her the short distance to the snow. The porch had become nothing more than an ice hazard. Any other day, any other time, far away from De Luca, she would have enjoyed the ice.

With his arms on her, she found it hard to focus. De Luca was her enemy. Her sworn enemy because of their last names. She wouldn't give in to him.

Milah remained tense in his arms, refusing to give in. He placed her on the ground once they were in the thick snow. She tried to remain angry and indifferent toward him, but with the snow coming nearly to her knees, she refused to ignore the joy racing through her body.

Letting go of Damon, she held herself steady, trying to lift her legs, and as she did, more snow seemed to gather around her ankles. She couldn't stop laughing, especially as she stumbled, falling flat onto the snow.

Without Damon's help, she got back to her feet and smiled at him. "Are you not having fun?" she asked.

She grabbed a handful of snow and tossed it his way. The ball landed against his chest. Not too hard, but playful.

"You want to go there?"

"You brought me out here, I'm guessing to have some fun. Let us have some fun." She gathered up another snowball but cried out as Damon was already there, snowball in hand, and he threw it at her.

She quickly turned, and it hit her back. Smiling, she moved fast, throwing her new ball toward him. This one hit him in the stomach.

It didn't stop Damon as he threw his, and Milah cried out as it hit the base of her neck. Again, not hard, but the cold leaked beneath the collar of her jacket and sweater.

She didn't have time to pick up another one before he was throwing another her way. Milah attempted to make a mad dash for it, trying to run away, but with how thick the snow was, there was no chance of escaping.

Damon also wasn't about to let her go free so easily. He charged toward her. She tried to pick up snowballs, most of them missing their target, and when she thought she might be able to evade him. Damon wrapped his arms around her waist. Before she knew what was happening, they were on the ground. The snow buffeted her back as she landed with Damon on top of her.

Her legs were open, and he was between them. The hard ridge of his cock pressed against her core. His jeans were a little thick, but she felt him. The thickness of him as he was right next to her.

Damon was aroused. She had done that to him.

"I've got you," he said.

She felt it. Licking her lips, she tried to think, but no words came. She stared up at him, hating that she could admit he was handsome. Scary as fuck. Even with him wearing a high neck sweater, she saw the ink just peeking from beneath the band.

Damon was heavily tattooed. She'd seen him in the shower. His arms, chest, back, even some on his legs. All of him was covered in some form of ink.

Biting her lip, she stared up at him. Many women would not mind being trapped between the snow and his body. They were not her.

This man was her enemy, but she refused to spoil the day by saying something rotten. "You may have me right now, but you don't own me," she said, showing him a smile to let him know her words were not bitter.

Damon chuckled. For a change, the sound wasn't ugly. He closed the distance between them so that his lips were against her ear. "Are you sure about that?"

****

"Come in," Damon said, calling toward the knock on his office door.

Ever since Milah had been in his house, he'd noticed an increase in knocking on his door. He missed the times of complete silence and peace where he could catch up with work.

Glory entered his office. Her gaze was on the floor, not daring to look up.

He'd looked into her background and learned she'd been brought from the streets. A runaway with no will to live. She hadn't been addicted to drugs, but he'd also sensed an air of innocence around her. She might have fetched a pretty price, but sending her to the brothels had been out of the question.

"What do you have to report to me?" he asked.

For the most part, Glory's job hadn't been enlightening. Milah didn't give anything away. She talked about the day. The weather. Sometimes cooking. Since he'd given her permission to use the kitchen, she rarely used it.

At the thought of the kitchen, he had a sudden desire to eat, and he glanced toward the time to see it was getting close to dinner. He was starving. Walking out in the snow was hungry work. Especially when he had such an energetic guest occupying his thoughts.

"Milah wants me to attempt to get a message to her father," Glory said.

This was news. "What kind of message, and look at me when you're talking. I have no desire to see your fucking head."

SAM CRESCENT

She jerked her head up and he saw the fear, but he didn't care. People were meant to fear him.

"She wants to know how long she is meant to stay here. She ... wants to know the full details, and also what exactly he agreed to."

Damon nodded. "Okay."

"What do I do?" she asked.

"Find out why she wants to know."

"I ... I did. She wants to know what is expected of her." Glory pressed her lips together and then continued. "She is ... scared. She told me that she doesn't know what to expect. Every time she sees you, she expects you to kill her. She said that she knows everyone here hates her and would love for any excuse to kill her. They all hate a Russo, but then she said, as if she didn't understand why... I ... I..."

"What?"

"It's nothing."

"Tell me."

"I think she is ... lonely and she's afraid. She doesn't know what to do. How to act. I get the sense that she has always known how to deal with things back at home. I don't think she always had an easy life."

And he had yet to hear anything from Genius.

Milah had a sharp tongue on her. It was nothing he couldn't handle, but he was curious. She was used to knowing ahead of time how to react. How to be, and why? Was it because of her father?

Antonio Russo would never win father of the year, but then most of them here would never win it either.

"Thank you," he said. "You can go."

"What do I tell her?" Glory asked.

"Give it three days. Tell her you are doing your best, and I will give you a response."

89

Glory nodded and then left his office.

One way or another, he needed to figure Milah out.

A guard came to his door and informed him dinner had been served. When he arrived at the dining room, Milah was already there, sitting in the same chair she'd been in the past few nights.

He sat down as the chef brought out their food. This was a new occurrence, the chef paying such close attention. He doubted the man enjoyed his food being left the other day, but it simply hadn't been as good as Milah's.

Nodding at the man, he watched as his food was placed in front of him. Steak with roasted vegetables, and a thick herb sauce. One of his favorite meals. It was a meal his mother had made him many times.

He smiled.

Glancing toward Milah, he saw her hands clench, and then she reached for the knife and fork. She rarely finished any of the food that was brought her way. He watched her now as she took the tiniest slice of steak and put it in her mouth.

Milah tensed up, and he noticed she closed her eyes, and her lips seemed to go into a stern line.

"What is it?" he asked.

"Nothing."

"Do you not like the food?" He took a bite of his steak.

"It is delicious." She took another taste and then another.

Figuring she was struggling with the enjoyment of the day, Damon enjoyed his meal, noticing Milah didn't finish hers.

"You need to eat," he said.

"I'm not hungry." She put her napkin down.

He snapped his fingers and dessert was brought out. Damon noticed her shoulders seemed to slump, and he frowned. What the fuck was going on?

When Milah's dessert was put in front of her, she lifted her spoon and hesitated in scooping out some of the chocolate mousse.

"Enough," Damon said. He lifted his spoon and leaned over.

"Sir, your own dessert," the chef said.

Damon took a spoonful and placed it at his lips. Milah's gaze was wide and as he tasted it, he had no choice but to grab his napkin and spit it out.

"Has your food been like this all the time?" he asked.

"It's fine."

"He has used fucking salt and vinegar in your mousse, Milah." He shoved his chair back. "What did he put on your steak?"

"Damon, it is fine."

He looked toward the guards. "Get me all the kitchen staff, now!" He yelled the order. Out of the corner of his eye, he saw Milah shake just a little bit. She'd had to deal with inedible food. For how long?

She hadn't gone into the kitchen, and he had figured she was being a little stubborn, but trying this food, why would she? If trying to recreate the single memory of her mother had caused this, he doubted very much she would have wanted to keep on cooking.

His guards rounded up the kitchen staff, bringing them to him. He looked at them, one by one. All of them staring at the floor, quivering in fear.

"What did he put on the steak?" Damon asked. "What has your chef been doing to Milah Russo's food?"

The chef fought against the hold one of his guards had on him. "Do not answer that!" the chef yelled.

Damon walked over to the chef, pulled out his own knife, and slashed him across the cheek.

Cries rang out in the dining room.

"Salt, and he sometimes made me put on flowers from the garden," one of the women said.

"He ... he wanted me to gather dog shit to use on her plate." This came from another woman.

Each woman who spoke sank to their knees, begging for forgiveness.

Anger rushed through him. His chef had cleaned her plate in dirty water, not fit to drink. The same with her water, it was taken from the dog bowls where they drank. Not that he had any dogs, but he knew strays wandered on the property from time to time, but rarely ever stayed.

"And no one thought to report it to me?" he asked.

No one spoke.

Milah had been suffering in silence. She'd been eating food not fit for human consumption, and he had figured she was just being testy. He couldn't believe this.

Staring at the men and women before him, he nodded at the guard to take them away. They were not to be given food or water, and then he looked toward the chef. "Take him to the basement," he said.

"You cannot do this. I have served you and your father, and your grandfather. I am to be respected."

Damon grabbed his shirt and pulled him toward him. "Do I look like my father standing here? Do you think he would have allowed you to walk free after nearly poisoning my guest?"

"She is a Russo whore!"

He slammed his fist in the guy's face, instantly breaking his nose. Blood spilled down his face, and he threw him toward the guards, making them take him away. He would deal with him later.

Wiping the blood from his knuckles, he glanced toward Milah. She hadn't moved an inch. Her body shook.

He grabbed her arm, and she flinched, but didn't look away.

"Come on," he said.

Marching her into the kitchen, she tried to fight him, but he had hold of her hips and got her moving until she rounded the counter and stood in front of the stove. "Cook yourself something."

"Damon, it is fine."

He pressed his back against hers, banding an arm around her waist and pulling her against him. "It is not fine." His lips brushed against her neck. "You will eat something, and the next time food is served to you, do not eat it."

"I … I … I'm a Russo, Damon. They don't like me."

"Do I look like I care? You are my guest and you will be treated with respect." He kept his hand on her stomach, admiring the curve of her neck. Imagining how good it would feel to have her so close.

It wasn't time yet.

Milah had to warm to him for his plans to work. This might just be the start he needed. "You know how to cook."

He didn't want to let her go, but to allow her to cook, he needed to. Removing his hands from her body, he didn't like how disappointed that made him feel to let her go.

He rounded the counter and watched her.

At first, she stared at the stove, not moving.

If he had to, he'd force-feed her something, even if it had to be raw.

Milah suddenly moved, going to the fridge, and he watched as she grabbed some cheese and butter. She rummaged through the kitchen and came back with some bread. She spread some bread, added a slice of cheese, and then spread the other side.

He wondered what she was doing, but she put the bread to one side, and then went back to the fridge.

Within a matter of minutes, she had some shallots, celery, and garlic sizzling in a pan. Next, she added in some tomatoes, fresh, and some from a can, bringing it together with a small splash of vegetable stock.

With the tomato mixture bubbling away, she got to work looking through all of the cupboards and came out with a stick blender. She removed the pan from the heat, placing it on a metal rack, and then, she added in some whole basil leaves before putting in the blender and blitzing.

The scents were amazing.

She blended up her mixture. Put the pot back on to boil, and then got another pan. She heated it up, put the sandwich with the butter side down, spread the other side with some more, and then after a few minutes, flipped it.

"Grilled cheese and tomato soup," he said.

Milah smiled. "A firm favorite when you're coming in from the cold."

She put the sandwich on a chopping board and ran her knife through it. Then served up a ladle full of the soup. "Would you like to try some?"

"I've ... yes," he said.

Milah handed him the plate, and he was about to question her, but she was already making another sandwich.

Within minutes, she served herself another bowl

of soup and moved toward him. She took a seat beside him, dipping her grilled cheese into her soup then taking a bite.

This woman could cook.

The food was good, and he hated to admit it was even better than the steak he'd just consumed.

Chapter Seven

The following morning, Damon demanded that she make herself breakfast, and so she had decided to do some savory eggy bread. Milah had noticed last night the bread she used felt slightly stale, so it wasn't a hardship turning it into something that would make it edible.

Damon was in the kitchen. Last night, he'd made her a little unnerved by how he'd dealt with his kitchen staff.

The day after she'd made her mother's lentil stew, she had noticed a change in the taste of the food. She'd known the chef hated her for interfering. The fact Damon had eaten her stew, rather than his, had upset him.

Milah hadn't gone into the kitchen to cause a problem for anyone. All she wanted to do was cook the food that reminded her of her mother. The woman who helped her to feel comfortable when her life was in so much turmoil. Glory had told her this morning that she was doing her best to get word out to her father.

She wouldn't let Glory be hurt for doing this. She would do whatever Damon asked, so long as Glory didn't suffer. It was a big risk, trying to contact her father. Part of her didn't want to. The man was a complete and total bastard and had no regard for anyone but himself.

But she needed to know how to deal with everything. Without knowing what to expect, she felt very much like a fish in open water.

As soon as she knew what was expected of her, she could adapt accordingly.

With Damon's gaze on her, Milah finished frying two slices of the bread and served him up. She already had another two slices soaking up some egg mixture.

Damon looked at the bread. It was one of her mother's favorites. Milah had loved it when her mother went into the kitchen. Her father had tried to stop it, but her mother always found a way.

"What do you think?" she asked, placing her slices into the pan, loving the sizzle. Home cooking always helped to soothe her soul.

It was so basic and yet so … comforting. In the kitchen, there was a great deal of rules on safety and in cooking. Sometimes she liked to break boundaries, but for now, she was happy not to experiment too much.

"Delicious," Damon said.

He finished off his two slices before she had even finished cooking her own. He held his plate out, and Milah served him the two she had originally planned to cook for herself. Making up some more egg mixture, she got to soaking the bread and cooking some more. Damon looked tempted to ask for the two she had cooked, but he put his knife and fork down, and instead, drank his coffee.

"Have you never had eggy bread before?" she asked.

"Not for a long time."

"You could have asked the chef for what you wanted." She wanted to know what had happened to the chef. She had been starving the past few days. She hadn't eaten much of the food. Spending more of her time pushing it around her plate than eating it.

Damon didn't say anything, just sipped at his coffee as she finished her food.

Once she was done, with her coffee drank, she got to her feet and was about to clean away.

"I have staff for that," Damon said. "Follow me."

She wanted to argue with him but knew to do so would be futile. Damon always got what he wanted.

Putting the plates down, she followed close behind him. She expected to see the kitchen staff, but the only people they passed were guards.

She had yet to apologize to James properly. There had never been a right time to bring it up. How did you go about saying sorry to someone you'd just shot?

Two guards stood at the French doors overlooking the yard. Jackets were held in their hands, and Damon took hers from the guard, helping her into it. He pushed her hands out of the way when she tried to do it up, sliding the buttons inside the holes, one by one.

He grabbed the hat from the guard and put it on her head, and then some gloves. She pushed her hands inside, but Damon made sure they went on properly. She wanted to ask him what he was doing, but he turned away, putting a jacket on himself. He didn't bother with a hat or gloves.

They stepped out into the freezing temperature, and Milah enjoyed it.

Damon took her hand, and together, they walked straight down to the steps. She noticed the main porch had been gritted, and she couldn't help but smile. Did he do that for her?

They walked together. The sun was high up in the sky, not that its warmth was felt. The ground was way too cold. This time, he'd allowed her to have some boots. They'd been with her clothes that very morning.

Last night, Damon hadn't requested her to come to his room. She remained in her bedroom, and Glory had told her he was dealing with the kitchen staff. Glory had also asked why she hadn't told her about what was going on.

The truth was, she had a feeling Glory was trying to get close to her to spy on her. It was the only explanation for why Glory was being nice to her. To earn her trust. She wanted to believe more than anything that she was wrong, but she doubted it.

People always betrayed the Russos.

Glory was owned by Damon. There was no way she would help her, but she couldn't help but wonder if there was a chance of it.

Damon had put her up to it, but why? What did he hope to achieve?

She hated the number of questions she had when it came to this man. Like, why was he being nice? Why was he eating the food she cooked?

Pushing them all away, she decided to take one problem at a time. For now, she needed to enjoy being outside, enjoy the cold air.

Damon was silent. His grip on her arm was tight, and neither of them said a word.

Milah didn't know his home very well. The view she had from the bedroom window only gave a small view that overlooked his gardens.

They came to a stop toward a large outbuilding. Milah glanced up at Damon, who looked at the building. His hand on her arm slid down to take her hand, and then he walked with purpose toward the building.

She noticed three guards were waiting outside.

Milah had attempted to count all his guards, to assess the situation, but it was impossible. There was no set routine to any of them. One day, two guards could be out in the hallway, the next, one, another time, four. The numbers kept changing, and so did the hours that they changed.

It wasn't an accident.

She knew Damon did it on purpose. Not because of her, but for all of his enemies. By not having a set routine, it made attacking him even more impossible. The only way to take him out would be to go at him head-on, but at the same time, that was also unfeasible. No one knew definitely how many men were on the property.

The men rarely showed their faces. Unless someone could recognize faces alone, they might have a shot at figuring out a weakness. So far, she hadn't found a single one.

The guards stepped out of the way, and Damon moved her in front of them. They walked into the outbuilding, and after one look at it, she saw it was a large gym. In the center were several mats pushed together. She spotted a treadmill, weights, a bike, and several other pieces of equipment.

She should know them. Her mother had ordered her to use them all.

The gym mat was the easiest to detect, seeing as it took up most of the room, and that was where the men had trained her. Not in this place, obviously, but back home. When her father was away on business.

Damon stepped away from her.

She heard the door to the building close, followed by the bolt sliding into place. They were locked inside.

"What is going on?" she asked.

"You'll find a set of gym clothes there." He pointed off to the left. "Change into them."

Milah hesitated but knew there was no point in arguing with him. Damon got what he wanted. She realized that quite quickly. She looked at the gym clothes and then tried to find somewhere to change into.

"Change there," Damon said. "No one is here to see you or take pictures."

"You're here."

"And I won't look."

She didn't want to be out of her large clothes that swamped her body, but now was not the time to fight

SAM CRESCENT

him.

Without looking at him, she put the clothes down and did a quick swap, changing into the gym gear. The shirt wasn't as fitted, which she was thankful for. The yoga pants and bralette fit like a second skin.

She appreciated the shirt she could slip right on over the top.

Damon was already on the mat when she finished, and she didn't want to join him, but she had no choice. There was nowhere for her to run to.

Damon looked at her, and she stared back at him.

What was going on?

His gaze ran up and down her body, but he wasn't looking at her like a woman, but as an opponent. Her mother's guards had taught her to assess body language, including the way someone looked at her as well. The key to survival was being able to read each situation. To know how best to fight.

She didn't want to fight Damon.

He charged at her, and Milah had two choices, allow him to hit her or to attack. She tried not to respond, but it was instinct. She didn't like pain, so she blocked his hit. He came at her from the side. She ducked down and thrust her leg up, connecting with his stomach, and he pushed back.

Damon chuckled. "So you are trained."

She stood up and folded her arms, keeping him within her sight. "I have no idea what you're talking about."

"They said that you moved like you had some training. Not like a panicked woman. The way you fight, you know what you're doing."

"Your men clearly lie to you. They don't know what they're talking about."

Damon moved fast, and Milah tried to react like

someone who hadn't been trained, but Damon didn't give up. There was only so much evading she could do.

When he nearly punched her in the face, Milah had no choice. She attacked, spinning around, jabbing his ribs with her elbow, and then hitting him in the face.

She spun around, and this time, she attacked him.

Her mother had told her to defend herself. To never show what she could do, but with Damon right now, she was tired of him. Once she went on the attack, Damon had no choice but to defend. As she took him by surprise with her actions, he also tried not to hurt her.

Damon was treating her like a girl.

It wasn't long before she straddled his waist, with her hands locked around his neck. "If I had a knife right now, you would be dead."

She gasped as he grabbed her hips and moved so that she felt the hardness of his erection. His grip was too tight. She couldn't move away from him, and he knew it.

His chuckle made her angry.

"And you, my little kitten, have some of the sexiest claws I have ever had the pleasure of feeling."

She tried to get up, but Damon used her annoyance against her, spinning them around so she was flat on her back. "Get off me."

"Who trained you?"

"That is none of your business." She had fallen into his trap and now, she had to find a means of escape before he fucked everything up.

Damon grabbed her hands and pressed them to either side of her head. With her legs spread open, there was no getting away from his hardness. She hated that the feel of him made her feel warm. "Let me go."

"Not going to happen." He smiled. "Why would I let you go now when I know so much already?"

She gritted her teeth.

SAM CRESCENT

"Who trained you?"

He pressed his lips to her ear. "Do you think I won't find out? I wonder what your father will say when he finds out that his daughter can fight."

Her mother's guards were still alive. She couldn't allow anything to happen to them.

Fuck.

He'd pushed her into a corner, and she'd fallen for it. If she hadn't reacted at all, he wouldn't have the upper hand.

"My mom taught me!" she yelled. She closed her eyes, hating how easily he had manipulated her.

"Your mom?"

"My mom's guards." She opened her eyes and stared at him, glaring, defiant. "She knew this world wasn't fair to women. To help, she ... she made sure that her only daughter knew how to fight. How to take care of herself, and so she trained me. Without my father ever knowing. She got her men to teach me everything I know, which is why I know how to fight."

****

Damon had no intention of ever telling Russo what he knew about his daughter. His only mission when it came to that man was to bring him down, begging and pleading for his life.

Only then would he be satisfied.

Milah fighting, that wasn't a bad thing as far as he was concerned. Her ability to defend herself made a whole lot of sense to him. This world wasn't kind to women. Milah was living proof of that.

Her father had told him he could have anything he wanted, but not to kill him. He'd asked for Milah. Not for marriage, but for his daughter. He'd given her to him without batting an eye.

After their session in the gym where Damon had

103

asked her to spar with him, they'd returned to the main house. Milah left to get washed and changed, and he'd gone to the basement, where his chef was chained up.

He hadn't attended to him last night, dealing with the staff. Three of the women were dead. Two more he'd made sure they never defied him again, sent to one of the street whorehouses. They would earn their keep one way or another. Not with the rich cock, but with cheap dick.

The small light of the basement was lit, and he stared at his chef, his body limp as the chains held him up.

"How the mighty does fall," Damon said.

"You can't kill me. Your father offered me protection," the chef said, coughing.

"And you think he's alive somewhere to see that you are?" Damon asked. He laughed. It was sinister.

He used to like the chef. Not as a boy. He'd hated him. The man was cruel and would often swat at him if he even dared to sneak into the kitchen to steal food. It was strange he hadn't thought of that time until this very moment.

His father had always said the chef was just looking after his domain. The kitchen was his responsibility, and it was up to him to serve them all good food.

Damon stepped in front of the chef. "You never stepped out of line. Even after my father died. You were always sure to do as you were told. Never making waves. Until now."

"She has no right to sit at your table. To cook in my kitchen."

"That kitchen is mine!" Damon yelled. "It was never yours, and you thought to poison my guest."

"It would be a kindness to her."

Damon picked up one of the chef's knives. He'd

watched him use it as a boy, striping the skin from fish. It was sharp, with a nice point, and also flexible.

"You see this? I wonder if it will do the same trick on human flesh as it does to fish."

The chef's screams filled the basement. With his body wriggling, Damon took large chunks of flesh off the man's body.

The pain got too much for him, and he passed out.

Damon didn't stop though. Unbeknownst to his father, he had learned the fine art of torture from his grandfather. He continued to take more pieces until he was bored. Some of his guards were in the room, waiting. They were the ones with the strongest stomachs.

When he was a young boy of about eleven, his parents went away on a honeymoon, leaving him at home with his grandfather. Now, his grandfather was a cruel man, but to his grandson, he wasn't. Damon liked his grandfather, even if he didn't agree with the man's methods most of the time, if at all. The De Lucas always had enemies. Not just the Russo, but far and wide. One night, the house was attacked. Some of the guards had turned against his grandfather because of his cruel treatment of them, and it had put them all in danger.

Damon had nearly been killed, but his father had shown him how to hunt, and killing had been natural to him.

His grandfather had been proud to see the men who had attempted to kill him dead on the floor. As a reward, he got to see what they did to the enemy. It was the first time he watched his grandfather torture.

"To survive in this world, Damon, you need to be willing to do the unthinkable. To be willing to hurt those who would take from you. The more people fear you, the greater you will become."

After Damon threw a bucket of water onto the chef, he came to, screaming, gasping, begging.

Damon wasn't done teaching this man a lesson. He didn't want to think about why he was so angry. Why it bothered him that this man would dare to serve a Russo dog shit or poison. Milah had nothing to do with this.

With every passing hour, it was hard to think of her as a Russo. Her actions didn't scream of it.

Anyone else would have allowed her mother's guards to be killed. Her father would be furious to know what she could do. He had no doubt. Russo hated powerful women. It was why none of his closest allies were women.

Damon didn't mind a strong woman, even a powerful one. Milah being able to hold her own against him was something he greatly admired.

He stared at the chef, and with a final slash across his throat, he ended his miserable existence. He waited and watched the life slowly drain out of him before he stepped back.

After stripping out of his bloodstained clothes, he washed his hands in the sink and then grabbed a fresh pair of pants and a shirt to change into. His men were already dealing with the body.

He left the basement and went straight to his office to pour himself a drink. Taking the first sip, he moved toward the sofa as his cell phone rang.

Damon reached for it as he took a seat, seeing Raoul on the line. Raoul was his closest friend and ally when it came to his initial takeover after his father passed. He was the one who helped sniff out all the possible traitors, intent on taking his position, and there had been a lot of them. More than Damon cared to remember.

"What do you have for me?" he asked.

"Russo is trying to reach out to your enemies. He is attempting to overthrow your power. I've also heard word that he is trying to get a message to his daughter about the instructions he wants her to do while she is with you."

"And what are those instructions exactly?" Damon asked.

"To find your weak spot. To worm her way into your heart and to expose you for the weakling he believes you to be."

Damon chuckled. "Really? Do we know who will be the messenger?"

"That is where I'm having difficulty. I'm not sure exactly who it is. My sources don't know either."

Damon tensed up. "Someone in our guards."

"That's what I'm figuring."

This was … infuriating. He looked at his office door, and now he had to deal with a potential in-house traitor. This pissed him off.

Sipping at his whiskey, he tsked and leaned forward to put the glass on the coffee table.

"Anything else?"

"Sources tell me he's trying to figure a way of breaking into her mother's inheritance. Milah Russo is a very rich woman, but until she reaches the right age and circumstances, no one can gain access to those funds."

"Do we know what age and circumstances are?"

"No. No one does."

"I've got Genius working on the finer details of everything." Not that he needed the money, but he had to gain ultimate control of everything that once was owned by a Russo. Her mother had gained the name through marriage, and he doubted it was a happy one. Still, her assets were a potential liability to his plan.

"I'll keep an eye here. I will have more

information for you in a few days." He didn't hang up but hesitated for a few seconds.

"What is it?"

"How … is she?" Raoul asked.

Damon gritted his teeth as he thought about the wildcat staying in his home. "She is … everything I said she was."

"And you still intend to go through with your plan?"

"Nothing is going to stop me."

"You do know you can stop this whenever you want. All you've got to do is take control. No one is forcing you to do this."

"She is a Russo."

"From what my sources tell me, Milah was never a Russo. Not in spirit, but by blood, that was all."

Damon had heard enough. "Call me when you know more." He ended the conversation and leaned forward, resting his elbows on his knees. Exhaustion swept over him as he thought about the coming few months.

He needed everything to fall into place before he ended Antonio Russo, and he couldn't wait to be the man to finally kill him. Then his family would be able to rest in peace. There would be no more retaliation.

Getting to his feet, he left his office and made his way toward his bedroom. He'd already asked for James to collect Milah for him.

He wasn't in the mood for much discussion, but he liked looking at her pretty face.

After stripping out of his clothes, he tossed them into the laundry basket, not caring that he'd only worn them for a short time. He stepped beneath the shower's spray of cold water, not allowing his mind to drift or focus on anything but the present.

Antonio Russo had someone here, watching and waiting. He should have known. Some men didn't have the strength to resist temptation, but the question was, what? What could he bribe his men with? Irritation gnawed at him.

He wanted to fucking kill Russo. The temptation was strong. It would be so easy. Just the swiftest swipe of his blade, and he'd be dead.

Ended.

So easy.

So quick.

But he needed to make sure no one else would rise up. Antonio hadn't been a faithful husband. There were bastard Russos running around, which he would have to deal with if they posed a potential threat. Milah didn't know she had a brother the same age as her, or a few that were younger. He would have to deal with them all.

Chapter Eight

Milah stared out her bedroom window for the hundredth time or what felt like that long. Glory had gone to ask Damon if it would be possible for her to go enjoy the last of the snow.

In the past few days, she'd rarely seen Damon. He only called for her at night, and because of this, she'd been confined to her room. Even her meals were delivered to her bedroom. There was a guard on the door, stopping her from leaving.

She didn't have the means to escape Damon's property, she knew that. It would be next to impossible.

When a situation like this arose, she remembered her mother's guard telling her to play it safe. To never draw suspicion but to always be ready to make a move. This place was highly guarded. Damon had spared no expense when it came to protection.

This was a De Luca home.

He lived here where his father had lived before, and his father before that. There was a great deal of history, and she hoped within time, he'd let her explore. There were so many rumors and lies when it came to their combined families. Her mother didn't always know the truth and would often refuse to spread nasty gossip as she didn't believe it. Her mother, at times, was too good for the Russo. Milah had often thought it.

The marriage had been a sham. A farce. She couldn't believe her maternal grandparents had even allowed it to happen. Their thirst for power must have driven them to it. Although the couple she had met as her grandparents hadn't struck her as the kind who cared for more money. They were already extremely wealthy people.

Milah was pulled out of her thoughts by her door

opening. Glory walked inside.

"Is that good news?"

"Yes. Damon said you can walk the grounds, but you must have a guard with you at all times."

"Oh." It wasn't exactly the freedom she was hoping for.

She looked past Glory's shoulder to see James, the man she had shot. Guilt consumed her as he held up a pair of walking boots and a jacket.

"Mr. De Luca doesn't want you to freeze. Those were his exact words."

Milah chuckled and went toward him. She stopped when she got close enough. "I'm sorry." The words just blurted out before she could stop them. She winced. "I ... I didn't hurt you too badly, did I? I didn't want to kill you or anything."

James held his hand up, stopping her. "All is forgiven."

She forced a smile and then, she did the unthinkable, she hugged him.

James tensed, and she heard Glory gasp.

"You can't do that," James said, pushing her away.

"I know. I know I'm a prisoner here, and I ... I've been worried that you were hurt or sick. I'm sorry."

She picked up the boots and jacket and quickly pulled them on.

"Show no weakness. They will only use it exploit you. These animals are good at doing things like that. Never let your guard down."

It was hard to see these people as animals. They were human.

This feud with the De Lucas was tiring. She didn't know if she was going to be able to keep it up.

After wrapping the jacket around her arms, she

tightened it up, and then looked at Glory and James.

"Please, tell me you're coming with me," she said, looking at Glory.

She knew without a doubt Glory worked for De Luca. Glory would have to report everything to him. Not a moment of her life was safe, but she liked to pretend just for a short time she had someone on her side.

"Glory will be joining us," James said. "Damon has already given me permission to escort you two ladies outside."

Milah smiled and glanced at Glory.

Every now and then, she saw the guilt flash in her gaze. The other woman wasn't always comfortable being her friend.

What Milah didn't know was if it was the guilt of pretending to be her friend that upset her or the fact she had to actually spend time with her, which made her feel like a traitor to the De Lucas.

Either way, Milah was happy to have some form of a friend, even if it was fake.

She had no secrets to spill, so talking to Glory was never an issue. Being a woman, she wasn't allowed to know any secrets of the Russo empire. That was all to her father.

Stepping out of her bedroom, Milah followed Glory down toward her own quarters, which was far across to the other side of the house. Her room was small, and Milah glanced inside to see not too many belongings.

This was the life of a … what? She didn't exactly know what Glory was.

"She's a slave," James said.

Milah turned toward the guard. "What?"

"Bought and sold."

"No. I don't believe it."

Glory grabbed her jacket and changed her shoes for boots. All of the maids working in Damon's house wore the same clothes. Their hair was also the same, pulled back into a ponytail.

To Milah, it seemed rather old fashioned to have maids or servants, but she knew her father was also of the same mind.

Aghast, she covered her mouth and felt even more like a fool. The people working for her father didn't have a choice. At least not the women. The soldiers were men who trained to fight to kill, to work for the Russo. The women were captured.

How could she not have realized this?

If De Luca didn't send the women to the brothels, then he kept them to work for him. Tears filled her eyes as she looked at Glory. The woman was so sweet and kind, and she didn't ... no woman, no person, deserved to be a slave.

Sickened, she stepped back, about to go and confront De Luca with this atrocity.

"Before you go and attempt to save Glory, you should know that she is in fact happy here," James said.

Milah spun toward the guard. "Is that what you tell yourself? She has no life but to serve that ... him?" She didn't want to cause any hatred between herself and James. Insulting Damon might not be the best way to go about it.

Anger rushed through her entire body.

"It's what I know. I'm not saying every single woman here is happy with the life she leads, but Glory's past is not the same as anyone else's. For the first time in her life, she is safe. She is cared for. Damon doesn't allow any harm to come to the women who serve in this household, or indeed who work for him."

Milah threw back her head and laughed. "This is

ludicrous. You're talking absolute crap."

"No, you are acting like a foolish girl. This is the way the world works. Regardless of if you were born into it or not, this is what it takes to survive!"

They stopped talking in their whispered tones as Glory came toward them.

Milah wanted to protect her. She took hold of the woman's hand, and together, they left her room and made their way out into the cold.

James stood close beside them. The paths were still gritted so neither of them fell as they made their way across the ground toward the gardens.

"Do you like the snow?" Milah asked.

"Very much so. It is always beautiful when the snow falls."

She had so many questions to ask Glory, but she didn't want to make the other woman uncomfortable, and she feared she would.

"So, er, how are you?" Milah asked.

"I'm very good, Miss Russo. You?"

"Please, call me Milah. Calling me Miss reminds me of my mother, but you know with the M-R-S, not the other one." She groaned. "Sorry."

"It's fine. Do you mind me saying you're very different than what I imagined?" Glory said.

"No, I don't mind. I didn't know you knew about me."

"Everyone knows of the Russo's daughter. You're a beautiful woman."

"Thank you." She didn't feel beautiful. She took a deep breath. "So I'm not what you imagined?"

"No."

Milah glanced toward Glory. "Is that a good thing?"

Glory smiled. "It is a very good thing. Antonio

Russo does not have a good reputation and so, I imagined someone cold and cruel, and spoiled. Before you arrived, many of us were worried that you would … hurt us."

"And I did so anyway." Shame flooded her.

"No, not in the way you think." Glory gave her hand a squeeze. They were still holding each other's as they walked across the grounds. "We thought you would be cruel, possibly even attack us, and beat us, just for fun. Lie about us. There were a lot of rumors."

"I guess it's why the kitchen staff took great pleasure in serving me disgusting food, yes?"

"I didn't know about that, Milah. I would have gotten it stopped."

"There is only so much you can do. I know that." She sighed. The incident was over, but she couldn't help but feel guilty for the men and women who were hurt. "Do you know when the chef will return?"

Glory turned her head away, and James cleared his throat.

"The chef will not be returning, so you don't need to worry."

Milah stopped. "What?"

Glory's lips were pressed together, and she kept on looking back at James, all nervous.

"What is going on?"

"It is nothing to concern yourself with."

"He killed them, didn't he?" Milah asked.

Glory whimpered, and Milah gasped.

"Oh, God, that was because of me, wasn't it? I…"

"No," James said. "Their own actions caused them to lose their lives. Not you. You had nothing to do with it."

"But they are dead because of me," she said.

"No, they are dead because they failed to follow

115

instructions. They believed they were above Damon De Luca, and they decided to do what they wanted. You are a guest."

"A hated prisoner, more like."

"Either way, he gave a list of instructions for them to abide by, and they failed. You can call it what you will. This has nothing to do with you."

Milah shook her head, and tears filled her eyes. Glory tightened her grip on her hand.

"I ... I need to walk."

"Milah, you will not do this alone. Do not feel guilty for their deaths. It is not right."

She wanted to scream at them. How could they see it like that? If she hadn't been at this stupid house, it wouldn't have happened.

"Come on, let us enjoy the snow. The chef was a horrible man, anyway. He always felt that he was to be protected," Glory said. "It's why he would hit us if we didn't do what he wanted. Even if we did, he'd find a reason to harm us, and none of us would tell Damon."

Milah looked at Glory in shock. "He'd beat you."

"Yes," Glory said.

She didn't know if it was a trick to get her to calm down. People had died because of her. There was no way she was going to be able to forget that. Death wasn't so easy. She hated it.

They continued walking, but for some time, Milah couldn't speak. She had tried to hide the bad-tasting food. Of course, it meant she was starving for the most part, but she had tried to play it safe. They'd died anyway.

What had been the point?

"Have you heard any news about ... what I asked?" she asked, aware of James close beside her.

"No, Milah. I haven't. Nothing new has come just

yet."

Milah stopped. The snow outside was not soothing her thoughts. If anything, it was making her more miserable.

"I think it is time—" She stopped as she heard an animal cry. "Do you hear that?"

It came again, and James held his weapon tightly. She hated the sight of guns but had learned as a child to accept them. Her father demanded similar security around his home.

The cry came again.

Milah spun around, detecting the sound and heading toward it. Letting go of Glory's hand, she followed the sound, and as she drew closer, she saw a puppy. It was so small in the snow.

On instinct, she removed her jacket, but James moved in front of her, and she feared he intended to kill it.

Throwing herself in front of him, she quickly gathered the cold pup in her arms.

"Milah, put it down. It could have diseases."

"Do not be so fucking cruel," she said. "I will not let you harm an innocent animal. Not now. Not ever."

****

"She found a stray dog?" Damon asked.

"Yes, a puppy," Glory said.

"I attempted to kill it, but she was like a wild animal, sir, I couldn't kill it."

Damon sat back in his chair. "Where is she now?"

"In her bedroom," Glory said. "She is … she would like the vet to come and check it over."

He shook his head. "I'll go and deal with it," Damon said. "You may leave. Glory, I need a word."

James left the office after giving a lingering look

to Glory.

She didn't look in James's direction. Damon made a note to keep an eye on that situation. The maids in his service were all protected. He'd ordered the men to never cross that line. When he was a boy, his father had been furious after one of his guards had raped a woman. She had attempted to kill herself, and because of this, his father made an example by chopping off the man's dick and allowing him to live. He had to serve in the brothels, always being close but never allowed to touch.

The man was still alive to this day, serving women he could never have.

"Yes, sir."

"How ... is she?" Damon asked.

Glory looked up at him and then quickly bowed her head.

"You can look at me."

"She seemed distressed when James went to kill the small pup."

"It was out in the cold, and it would probably die anyway."

"Milah is ... she's not happy about the death of the kitchen staff."

"She knows?"

Glory nodded. "She asked when they would be returning."

"Of course she did."

"I don't think she is anything like her father or the Russo men, sir." She bowed her head again.

He was starting to see that, but he wouldn't make the same assessment quite yet. The Russos were known liars and manipulators.

"She has asked about her father again. About what he has said."

"She has?"

"I don't know what to tell her."

"Tell her that her father's message is to see me," Damon said, getting to his feet. "You're dismissed."

Milah had fast become a thorn in his side.

He made his way out of his office and went straight to her room. Milah looked up as he entered. She lay on the bed, a huge bundle by her side, and he saw her wrap her arms around it protectively.

"You brought a mutt into my house?" he asked.

"It was cold. I would like a vet, please. I … she…"

"Enough of this. Give the damn vermin to me."

"No," Milah said. She pulled the dog into her arms. "I'm not going to let you kill her. She has done nothing wrong. I won't let another animal get hurt."

Damon frowned. "Another? I have not killed an animal."

Milah looked up at him, and he was surprised to see tears in her eyes. "It's nothing."

"Tell me."

"Why? So you can mock me? So you can laugh at how stupid I'm being over an animal?"

"So I can decide if I want you to keep the fucking thing!"

"My dad killed my last puppy!" Milah screamed. Her face screwed up as the puppy in her arms started to shake. "I'm sorry. I'm sorry." She cleared her throat, kissing the top of the puppy's head and then looking up at him. "My mother had gotten me a puppy as a birthday present. I was ten years old. My dad didn't want me to have one, and he was furious. He … beat my mother for going behind his back, but in the end, I was able to keep it. She was a beautiful Labrador, so happy with life, and one day, we were playing, and I don't know what happened. He came outside where we were laughing and just having fun and right there in front of me, he shot her," Milah said. "And then he tossed her in the trash as if she was nothing. I couldn't do…"

Tears fell down her face and he witnessed real pain. This wasn't a trick. The tears were real. Milah's heart was breaking as the seconds ticked on by.

"I'm not going to let you kill this girl. She has done nothing wrong. She wants to live, I can see that. Please, let me keep her. I will do anything."

Damon knew he had what he wanted. The first part of his plan, which wasn't how he intended it to happen. Her finding a stray animal and being willing to protect it wasn't part of any of his plans, but he also wasn't going to pass up an opportunity to exact his own kind of revenge.

"What will you give me in return?" Damon asked.

Milah lifted her head. "What?"

"You heard me. Nothing in this life comes for free. If I get you a vet and that … puppy lives. What do I get out of it?"

"The pleasure of knowing you helped save an innocent?"

"I don't care about that, Milah."

"What do you want?" she asked.

He smiled. That was what he wanted. Her at his mercy. "You."

"You have me."

"Not completely. You, naked, in my bed, whenever I damn well please, and you cannot come as a victim, but as a woman who wants to be there. You have to beg me for it."

"You'll get your way eventually," she said.

"All the fucking time."

Milah looked down at her puppy and nodded.

"Fine."

This did surprise him. "You'd do this for a pup?"

"Yes."

Milah had surprised him again. "But you must have the vet here today, and this pup must survive," she said. "Otherwise, it is only for one night."

"Deal."

Even if he had one night, it was all he needed.

He called out to James to arrange for a vet to be brought to the house immediately. Rather than leave, he took a seat in the only available chair in the bedroom.

"You're not leaving."

"I'm going to make sure this pup lives."

Milah snorted.

She looked at the animal in her arms with so much love. Damon had never seen such true affection on her face. Not even when she was cooking the meals her mother loved. Milah was usually so heavily guarded.

The pup had awakened something inside her. She wasn't cold.

"Would you like to see her?" Milah asked.

"It's not a child."

"No, but it is a precious little pup. She is so … sweet."

He hated that he felt even a twinge of jealousy for the dog. This wasn't like him.

James came back two hours later with a vet.

Milah had no choice but to let the pup go and take a step back. Damon used the opportunity to pull her into his side, taking hold of her hand and watching as the vet got to work.

Damon didn't have the first clue what he was doing.

He'd never owned an animal outright. His father kept dogs in the kennels, which had been empty for the past couple of years. With his father's death, the dogs had mourned their master. When they passed away from old age, Damon didn't have it in his heart to train new dogs.

The vet finished his assessment and came toward them.

"She is … a very healthy little puppy. I don't think she was too far from home. She is very young."

"Wait," Milah said. "You think there are more?"

"There is not too much damage. Warmth, food, and tender loving care will see this one bouncing off the walls in no time. I believe there are more pups somewhere."

Milah looked toward James. "Please get Glory for me." She stepped toward the vet and threw her arms around him. "Thank you. Thank you so much."

Damon glared at the vet, and the man instantly moved away from Milah's embrace. So she would go around hugging any random stranger but he had to manipulate his way into her bed?

This pissed him off.

Glory arrived seconds later as the vet was making his way out.

"Before you leave, I want to just check. If she hasn't gone far, that could mean there are more pups out there, right?" Milah asked.

"No," Damon said.

Milah moved toward him. She grabbed his hand. "Please, don't be cruel. I will take care of them."

Damon pulled her close, gripping the back of her neck and placing his lips near her ear. "You're mine. No argument. No fighting. Willingly. Every single time."

She tensed, but he felt her head nod in agreement.

Milah turned to Glory. "Please, stay here. Take care of her. I need to go and check."

"You don't even know where they are," Glory said.

"I have to try."

She wasn't acting like a Russo. Damon followed her as she rushed out of the bedroom. Some of his men stepped forward as if to intervene, but he gave them a warning to stop.

He wanted to see this side of Milah. The one that wasn't guarded. The one intent on saving animals.

This was so … odd.

He saw her hands shaking as she grabbed her jacket and then rushed through his home. Damon followed, taking a jacket from one of his guards and sliding it on as he followed her.

She took off, and he had no choice but to chase after her. His guards were on high alert. He had ordered them to be so for two reasons. One, there was a traitor amongst them. Two, he hoped by having them on high alert, the traitor would make a mistake.

Milah stopped and panted for breath. "This is where we found her."

There was nothing else around.

She took a deep breath, closed her eyes, and listened.

There was no sound. Seconds passed.

"They are not here."

"You heard the vet. They have to be."

"Why is this so important to you?"

"Because … they have done nothing wrong."

"And so you keep saying," Damon said.

"Why does there have to be a reason for doing something good and kind? Why can't you see that I care? Why does it have to matter?"

"You're a Russo!"

She screamed. "Enough with that. I get it. My

father is a Russo. That makes me one as well, but guess what, that doesn't mean I'm like him. I have my mother's blood running in my veins as well. It might be a hell of a lot stronger than his. Have you thought about that?" she asked. "Have you thought that I might be innocent? That I might not follow in his plan of death?" She growled and stomped her foot. "What is the point? You two are exactly alike."

"I am nothing like that scum!"

"No?" she asked, rounding on him. "You keep women that you stole off the street. The ones who won't make a decent price are kept here to serve you, but you delude yourself in thinking you're giving them a good life."

"I am giving them a good life."

"What about freedom?" Milah asked. "What about the right to come and go as they please? To think of owning a house one day? Of having a family?"

He couldn't help but laugh.

"Go ahead, laugh at my stupid thoughts. It's just women, right? What could women want other than to have a man between their legs? To serve men and to never think of owning property. And you think you're not like my father. The De Lucas and the Russos are all the same."

He didn't like her attitude.

"Do you want to hit me?" she asked. "Another comparison point right there. Do you think I don't see it? You both use fear and manipulation. You would make the perfect couple. It's a shame you're so intent on killing each other."

"I am nothing like your father."

She took a step toward him and glared. "Prove it."

He was about to say something else, but they both

froze as whimpering filled the air. There was no mistaking the sounds of dogs.

Milah didn't wait to finish their conversation. She took off. They came across a small log that was hollowed out, and sure enough, six tiny pups, and one distressed-looking mother, funnily enough, a Labrador, was inside.

"Hey, sweet girl," Milah said. "You're missing one of your pups. Don't worry. Don't be afraid."

A growl sounded, and Damon grabbed his gun, ready to kill if it so much as attacked Milah.

She had infuriated him, but that didn't mean he wanted her to die.

Chapter Nine

Seven pups in total.

Four girls.

Three boys.

And a very tired mother. The vet had stayed to check on them and had promised to come the next day to make sure there was no sudden setback.

Milah was in love.

The pups were the cutest things and the mother, she adored her. The mother had already been scanned and there was no chip, nor did she have any tags. From her fur, it didn't look like she had any collar.

The vet had suggested she might have been roaming wild.

He'd taken some blood and started them on some antibiotics and treatments.

"I wonder how long she was out there," Glory said. "She looks like a young dog herself."

Milah agreed.

Damon hadn't called on her last night. They did have their agreement, and she would honor it.

He hadn't killed the dogs.

James was inside the room, and she smiled at him. The mother had wandered over to him and sat at his feet.

"We're going to have to name them," Milah said. She had the little girl she had found first in her lap.

"Yes, we are," Glory said.

"Damon will not keep them in the house," James said. "There are kennels outside."

"Dogs shouldn't be kept outside. It's way too cold, and these are so cute."

"And they're going to grow up to be big."

"Can you seriously not look at the girl at your

feet?" Milah asked. "See the way she looks at you."

James glanced down and cleared his throat. The mother dog was staring adoringly up at him. "I do not need a dog."

"But they are so easy to love." She kissed the pup's head. "And this one, I'm going to call Snowy."

Glory chuckled. "Sounds appropriate."

"Where is Damon?" she asked, wanting to go see him.

"He is in his room," James said.

Milah looked toward Glory, who smiled at her.

"I … I am going to go and see him. They've had their medicine and feed for the night," Milah said. They were staying in her room, at her insistence.

"I'll stay a little longer," Glory said. "If that is all right?"

"Yes, of course." Milah realized she didn't have the authority to say yes or no and looked at James.

"It is fine. I will stay also."

She reluctantly got to her feet and left the pups. There was another guard outside that she didn't recognize.

Damon had changed his men once again. She realized he did it regularly. It was all part of his protection so no one would be able to find a weak spot.

Maybe that was his weak spot. The constantly changing men. Even as she thought it, she didn't entirely know how. Not that it would matter. She had made a deal with him, and she wouldn't back away.

She would keep her word, even if it meant sleeping with Damon.

Arriving at his room, she lifted her hand to knock and hesitated. What should she do? She had lied about not being a virgin. Did he think she was a woman who knew what she was doing?

Drawing her wrist back, she forced herself to continue, even though sex wasn't something she knew anything about.

Damon asked who it was.

"It's me," she said, calling out to be heard and wincing at how weak she sounded. Clearing her throat, she repeated the words and hoped there was something firm in her voice. She didn't want him to know that she was terrified.

"Come in."

She stepped forward, not daring to glance back at the guard.

After opening the door, she slid inside and closed it.

Damon sat on the edge of his bed, staring right at her.

"Hi," she said.

Could that have been any more awkward?

He chuckled. "How are the dogs?"

"They're fine. I think. Mommy dog has taken a shine to James. He's playing hard to get right now." She was babbling.

"And now you're here," he said. "To keep your end of the bargain."

"I will keep my word." She clenched her hands into fists, trying to show she wasn't afraid. Being in a room with him wasn't so scary. It was easy.

Damon chuckled. "I'm going to ask you again." He stood up and stepped toward her. "Are you a virgin?"

One moment he was by the bed, the next, he was in front of her, making her nervous. "Why do you want to know?" She tilted her head back to look at him.

"Because I want to know if I can go fast or slow."

"Why does it matter?" she asked.

Damon pressed her against the door. "And I have

my answer."

"I have no idea what you're talking about."

"A woman who has felt a cock deep inside her for the first time would know why going slow would be best."

"I'm not a virgin."

"I think naughty, lying women should be punished."

She gasped as his body pressed against hers. His body was so much bigger and harder than hers. Milah felt the hardness of his cock as he rested against her stomach.

"Do you know what I do to lying women?" he asked.

"Kill them?" It certainly put a dampener on her arousal.

"No. I put them over my knee and smack their plump ass. Now, I will ask you one more time. Are you a virgin?"

She wanted to lie, but the idea of having her ass smacked didn't appeal. Pain wasn't something she sought. "Yes," she said.

Damon pulled away, just far enough to look into her eyes. "Good girl."

"You already knew."

"Of course I did, but that is what has saved you tonight."

Before she could ask him what he meant, Damon slammed his lips down on hers. At first, she didn't respond as she didn't know what to do.

On instinct, she pressed against his chest, but then, she remembered the deal. She had to be willing.

The kiss wasn't … awful.

She didn't want to enjoy the kiss, but Damon knew what he was doing. One of his hands moved from the door to grip her neck. Milah hated how much she liked this. Feeling him surround her. His lips locked on hers.

Milah whimpered.

Desperate.

Hungry.

She pressed her hands flat to his chest and slowly slid them up his body to wrap them around his neck, her body moving closer to his.

He growled. The hand on her neck slid down her body, and then both of his hands were on her ass, drawing her closer.

Milah couldn't fight her reaction. Kissing him was intoxicating.

She'd never kissed a man before and Damon, as he traced his tongue across her lips, set her body ablaze. He pressed her against the door. One of his hands moved down to her thigh, lifting it and pressing it over his hip. This brought his cock closer to her core, and she whimpered, not wanting him to stop.

He grabbed her ass again, and this time, he lifted her. She circled her legs around his waist as he carried her toward the bed.

Damon dropped them both down. He broke the kiss, and she immediately protested.

However, he trailed his lips down her body.

Milah gasped as he grabbed the old ratty shirt she wore and tore it straight down the middle, exposing her body. She tried to cover herself, but he captured her hands, pressing them to the bed, not letting her hide.

"You never hide from me," he said. "That's an order."

Her pussy was so wet with his growl. She watched as he leaned down, and through the lace of her bra, he sucked her nipple right into his mouth. It was even better than she had read about. The tug at her breast sent an answering wake between her thighs, consuming her.

Crying out, she couldn't contain her pleasure for a moment longer. It felt so good.

She needed to be touched between her thighs, but with how he was between them, she couldn't close them.

Damon kept her hands locked to the bed as he moved between her breasts, going to the second nipple.

It wasn't long before he let her go, and then he flicked the catch at the front of the bra, leaving her exposed to his gaze.

She stared at him, wondering what he was thinking.

He cupped her tits, pushing them together, and then his mouth was on them once again, kissing between the valley. Alternating between sucking on her nipples and tonguing the hard buds.

His touch heated her flesh, making her ache. This was so unfair. She wanted to tell him to stop, and then to not ever stop.

Milah was no longer in control of her body. Damon was. He knew what buttons to press. How to make her ache for more.

"Please," she said, hating herself for even relenting a little bit.

Damon didn't stop in his torment. He kissed down her body, his lips setting a fire as he went down.

Milah lifted onto her elbows and gasped as he tore the sweatpants from her body with so much ease. He tossed them aside and then placed his hands on her knees. The panties she wore were a matching set to her bra. He slid her thighs open, and she was nearly naked while he was still dressed.

Her face was on fire.

He slowly traced his fingers up, and Milah felt

like she couldn't breathe.

"Has anyone ever told you how fucking beautiful you are?" he asked.

She shook her head.

This was a position she had never been in. Damon got to the edge of her panties, and Milah held her breath, waiting.

The tips of his fingers stroked the edge of the fabric, teasing.

She waited. He didn't rush, prepared to wait.

He slid her finger beneath the fabric and then gripped the lace in his fist. Milah gasped as he tugged hard. The sound of it tearing filled the room. Her pretty pair of panties were ruined as he threw them across the room.

Naked.

Exposed.

At his mercy.

Milah waited, not sure what to do.

"I have never cared for a virgin. They have never appealed to me. I like my women to know what is coming."

With each word he spoke, she felt herself recoil. Why was he saying these things?

"But when it comes to you, Milah, I don't want another man's leftovers." He pressed a kiss to her thigh. "Any man who dares to touch you, I'll fucking kill." He kissed her other leg. "You are mine, and I am never going to give you back."

"I'm a Russo," she said.

She wasn't trying to dampen the mood, but he couldn't forget that. They were enemies."

He laughed. "No, Milah. You're mine."

She screamed as pleasure rushed through her body. His mouth went between her thighs, and she knew what all the books had spoken of was true. This was real pleasure. This was worth fighting for.

Milah couldn't believe her first time was going to be with her family's sworn enemy. A man she should despise. A man who was making her ache in all the right places.

His tongue danced across her clit, stroking around and over, consuming her with need. It just didn't stop. The pleasure was instant, intense, and Milah cried out, begging for more and not wanting it to end.

Damon's hands went beneath her body, gripping her ass, squeezing the flesh, and tightening his grip. She loved the sharp bite of possession, and with the way he lapped at her pussy, she felt the waves of her orgasm starting to build. Her body no longer felt like her own. She shouldn't feel this way because of who De Luca was, but there was no holding back. The feel of him was almost too much and at the same time not enough.

"Please," she said, desperate and begging.

He growled against her flesh. Then he sent her over the edge, and she couldn't stop his name from falling from her lips as he took her to the stars. She had never felt like this. Not ever.

She didn't want it to stop, but slowly, even before her orgasm was over, Damon released her. He stepped back, and she watched, a little dazed as he started to undress.

Milah pressed her thighs closed, but he merely tutted. "Keep them open."

She had no choice.

He was the one in charge. She wanted to continue touching herself to prolong the pleasure his wicked tongue had caused. Excitement filled her as she watched him undress, revealing his heavily inked body.

Even as she hated him, she couldn't deny the

sudden hit of attraction. It wasn't right or normal, but at that moment, she truly didn't care.

All of her focus was on this moment. Of feeling Damon.

He wasn't the man she wanted, but she was determined to enjoy this. Damon hadn't raped her. He hadn't used force. There was manipulation, and he'd used her concern for the pups to get what he wanted. She'd already begged.

Damon knelt on the bed, nudging her thighs open with the sheer size of him. He stared down at her, and she looked up at him, waiting.

"This is going to hurt," he said. "I can't change that."

She licked her lips and nodded. "I know."

Her heart raced as his hand moved down. She hadn't looked at his dick, too afraid to. She waited, staring at him, curious and wondering how painful it would be. Would he be too large for her to handle?

She felt him between her thighs, and just as he tensed up, about to take her, there was a knock at the door.

Milah looked toward the door before glancing back at Damon. No one had ever interrupted them before. Why now?

"Sir, there has been an attack."

****

Damon made his way into his nightclub, Toxic. Anger filled him after being interrupted as he was about to take care of step two of his plan. Milah had been willing, waiting for his cock. He intended to fuck her raw, to fill her full of his cum and hope she got pregnant.

She'd been so responsive.

He'd never bedded a virgin before, so this was a first for him. James's interruption had pissed him off, but he needed to be notified of any attack. Especially one that had also taken civilian casualties.

His men within the law enforcement had brought him up to speed on the details. Three of his nightclubs had been attacked. Toxic, he was currently in, as well as two others, Wicked and Burn. Raoul waited for him.

Milah followed close behind him. He'd been tempted to leave her back at the house, but with a traitor in his midst, he wanted her close. Russo wasn't going to get a chance to get near his daughter. Not on his watch.

"Where is it?" Damon asked.

Raoul looked toward Milah. She stood with James by her side as she looked around the office. He liked large spaces. It was one of the many reasons his nightclubs thrived. People loved the space, the freedom to go crazy.

"Would you like her removed?" Raoul asked.

"She is mine. Show me the footage." He snapped his fingers, bored with having to ask a second time.

Raoul placed the laptop he'd been carrying under his arm. The cops were not aware of the tight security he kept. They were only privy to the most basic of cameras he let them know about. De Luca wasn't a fool. The best way to stay in control was to be one step ahead of the game, and that was making sure his enemies didn't have a place to run.

With cameras everywhere, they couldn't hope to take them all out without being seen first.

Staring at the screen, he watched the multitude of live feeds. Raoul pressed some keys, wiping out several of the cameras and bringing into focus the main dance floor, the bar, as well as the bathrooms.

He then forwarded it, and Damon watched as his *staff* started to attack the people.

The bartender had a gun stashed under the bar,

and he began shooting at the bar. The attendant in the bathroom took out three people using the room.

"Where are these men?" Damon asked.

"Chained up and ready," Raoul said.

"I will deal with them."

"This is Russo," Raoul said.

Out of the corner of his eye, he saw Milah tense. He noticed anyone who used her last name always created that kind of reaction.

"I know."

"How?" Milah asked. "How do you know?" She glared at him. "You have plenty of enemies. It could have been anyone."

James went to grab her.

"If you lay one finger on her, I swear I will break your entire fucking hand, and your legs for good measure," Damon said. He got to his feet, rounded his desk, and approached her.

She went to take a step back from him, but he watched as she squared her shoulders and faced him directly on.

He liked that.

He hadn't been able to finish what he'd started in the bedroom, but there was going to be plenty of time to explore her body. Patience was a great virtue, and he intended to enjoy every second of her.

"You don't need to threaten him."

"Do you think it's a good idea to question me?" he asked.

She glared at him. "You don't know this was my … father."

"Do you think your father is a good man?"

"Hell, no, but you cannot assume everything is his fault."

Damon chuckled. "He begged for his life. He told

me I could have anything I wanted. I told him the price for him to walk away was you. Do you think he hesitated?"

"I don't care," Milah said.

"Innocent people died tonight, Milah. I will get to the bottom of this."

"If my father is not responsible, you need to let me go."

Damon threw his head back and laughed.

"You can laugh all you want, I don't care. You and I, we're toxic together, and nothing good could come of this. Let me go, and you can have war with my father."

"Milah, I'm going to have war regardless of if you're with me or not. I don't make deals like this. You're mine. Deal with it." He took her hand and led her out of the nightclub. No one dared to stop him. Not even Raoul. He'd never taken a woman along with him to question men responsible for killing people who frequented his club.

His men hadn't been injured, but the news of the attack would spread, and it would be bad for business. The people who knew what he was associated with as well, like his brothels and casinos, would also suffer. Even some of his restaurants. There would be ripples.

There was no one else other than Russo responsible.

Behind the scenes, Damon had been taking control of all of Russo's assets. Stripping him down piece by piece until he had absolutely nothing left. He had Russo's daughter, which stopped him from being able to sell her or merge with anyone else.

This was retaliation.

"Where are we going?" Milah asked.

He climbed into the back of a car, keeping Milah

beside him. Then he waited as Raoul and James climbed in the front and drove them across town to where Raoul had set up a special house that was safe enough to deal with traitors.

With Russo as their enemy, using warehouses had been out of the question. Especially as during one of their more vicious spells, Russo had torched several of their warehouses with people inside.

He had to be careful.

"Answer me."

Damon stayed silent. She tried to wriggle out of his grip, but there was no use. He was the one in control, not her. She had to give up.

She released a heavy sigh, not at all happy with conceding. Soon, she would learn that she'd have no choice but to give in if she wanted to survive in his world.

They didn't like traitors or anyone associated with them.

They arrived at the safehouse without any problems. He had no doubt Russo watched his every move. He wouldn't put it past the bastard to attack even with her by his side.

The man didn't love his daughter. He only cared about himself. Even the men who swore loyalty to him were nothing but fodder.

When it came to Russo, he knew nothing but rage.

Once they were securely in the building, Damon helped Milah out of the car and walked her out of the main garage. She came to a stop when she saw the three men responsible hung from chains that were attached to the ceiling. Two were around their wrists, and another wrapped around their neck.

Bound up.

Bleeding.

Bruised.

Already in pain.

Milah gasped, putting a hand to her mouth. "What are you doing?"

"Do you know there are many ways to get a confession? The longest, I think, is through seduction. Earning their trust, only to turn on them when they least expect it. Then you've got the ultimate betrayal of invading enemy territory. My personal favorite is torture," Damon said. "Pain and fear is a good mix of getting people to talk."

"How can you know they will tell you the truth?" Milah asked.

"It's quite easy." He looked at the three men.

His men had stripped them down to their boxer briefs. There were no tattoos or marks that showed who they belonged to. They were trained though. He saw that from the footage. All three of them knew how to shoot, but Russo's mark would have made his life easier.

Now he had to battle with them, not that he minded. He was great at getting what he wanted.

Each man had a weak spot. The question was who the weakest was.

Staring at all three men, he went to the one in the middle. This man had already pissed himself and was visibly shaking. His gaze kept going to his men and trying to find an exit.

"Who do you work for?" he asked.

The man continued to vibrate, and Damon smiled at him.

"Please, don't kill me."

"I'm going to kill you. There is no doubt about it, but I need to know who you worked for."

"I have a wife. Children. Please. Please. I beg

you."

"We won't tell you a fucking thing," this came from the man on the right.

Damon stared at them and smiled. "Let's see who will cave first."

He went to Raoul, who held out a knife for him. It was a nice length with a sharp point, one his grandfather once owned, and he turned back to the middle man, who screamed.

"It was Russo! He told us we had to attack your nightclubs. Tomorrow night it will be your brothels."

"Shut the fuck up!" The men started to wriggle free of his chains, but Damon had heard enough. He nodded at Raoul, who grabbed Milah, covered her eyes, and spun her away as he slashed the knife across the three men's necks.

Dropping the knife to the floor, he took over from Raoul, dragging a panicked Milah from the room.

The moment they were out of sight and sound, and the door closed, he let her go. She rounded on him, lifting her hand to slap him.

He captured her wrist. She growled, pulled back, and tried again, but he stopped her.

Milah was good, but he was better, and tonight, she wasn't going to slap him.

"Let me go."

He kept hold of her wrist and pulled her close. "James is going to take you to a room. Get changed and make yourself look pretty."

"How can I do that? I didn't bring any clothes with me," she said.

He smiled. "Do you think I wasn't prepared for that?" He nodded at James, who had followed him out of the room. Before they left his country house, he'd told James that he was to stay close by Milah's side. He wouldn't put it past her to try to escape.

"Do you think it is wise bringing her along for … this?" Raoul asked, minutes later after he appeared.

"Russo will not expect me," he said.

"He'll expect retaliation."

"And he will get it. Just not in the way he thinks." He turned to Raoul. "I want the ports all closed. Anyone associated with him that continues to do business, I want them sent my way. His brothels, I want full control. There is no way I want him to escape. He has just lost whatever shred of dignity he has left. I will make him suffer."

"What about his daughter?" Raoul asked.

"What about her?"

"She can be a target as well. With her life, people will think there is always a way for Russo to come back fighting."

"It's not going to happen. Russo will die with her. I have something even more special in mind."

"Do you think this is … wise?"

He looked to Raoul. "What?"

"You … you had one brief meeting with her three years ago, and it set you on this course."

"This is my revenge, Raoul."

"Is it, though? Are you sure this is not obsession for a woman you cannot have?"

Damon grabbed Raoul's jacket, hauling him up toward him. "What the fuck did you say?"

"Do you think I'm not used to this, Damon? I've never seen you react like this to any woman, but this one. Your plan, do you really think it is best?"

"You think I've fallen in love with Milah Russo?" Damon asked.

"No, but I think you're obsessed with owning her."

"Trust me, Raoul, Milah is all part of my plan. There is no way I would ever love a Russo," he said.

Someone cleared their throat, and Damon turned to see James there with Milah. She had dressed in a tight-fitting black dress. Her hair fell down, and they were natural waves.

Milah had heard what he said. He saw it in the way her hands were clenched, the tightness of her jaw, but also the worry in James's gaze.

"It's time to go."

Chapter Ten

"There is no way I would ever love a Russo."

Milah tried to ignore the sharp pain that pierced her chest. It wasn't like she cared what Damon De Luca thought anyway. She didn't love him, nor did she crave any affection from him.

He was a monster. No, he was worse than any monster. He was a fucking De Luca.

As if she would ever want him either.

Staring out the window, she refused to look at him. Silence fell in the car. James and the strange man who'd been close with Damon when she arrived downstairs to hear his confession were in front once again. Damon was on his cell phone.

She missed Glory. She missed the puppies. Above it all, she missed her mother.

She was all alone right now. No one gave a shit about her. Not her father. Certainly not Glory or James. Even though she rescued the puppies, if they found loving homes, they would soon forget about her.

Her throat felt tight.

A Russo. That was her. A person to be hated. Unloved.

Sinking her nails into her palm, she counted to ten and tried to stop the hit of tears that was so fucking close. She'd never been the kind of person to have a pity party. This was life. Her mother had told her that she wished for a different kind of life for her daughter, but it was never going to come.

All she could hope for was to prepare her daughter to fight for herself. Her father was responsible for killing those people and the men he'd hired to do it.

So much death. So much bloodshed and all because of two families who were exactly the same but never saw eye to eye. They were intent on destroying each other. Damon would kill her. Of that, she had no doubt.

He was going to use her first, but for what? What did he hope to achieve?

The car came to a stop, and she glanced out the window and gasped. They were at one of her father's nightclubs. She recognized it because he'd named it after her, *Milah's*.

The glowing blue light looked a little garish, but it was there, shining brightly for all to see. She saw the queue wanting to get inside.

"Why are we here?" she asked.

"I think it is time we had some fun, don't you? You've been cooped up in my house for way too long."

This was a ploy. What was he plotting?

Damon climbed out of the car, and all Milah wanted to do was run. This wasn't good. Her father had attacked his nightclub, and yet they were here. Why? What good would it do?

He held his hand out to her, and Milah had no choice but to place her hand within his as he helped her out of the car.

She glanced down at the line of people before turning her attention to the men guarding the entrance. The looks they sent her way were full of hatred. As if she had any choice in her date.

Her father had handed her over to the enemy to save his own skin. There was no love here. No betrayal, and yet as she entered the nightclub and felt the music piercing the walls, almost vibrating in the loudness of it, she felt herself shaking.

Damon was doing this on purpose. Showing her father's men who he owned.

He held her hand and led her straight to the bar.

She didn't say anything, not even asking for a drink she'd actually enjoy. Damon ordered for her, a cocktail that sounded utterly ridiculous. She didn't drink. Not cocktails, not wine, not champagne. She never got the taste for it.

Her mother had always told her to sip water and tea, but never alcohol. She had to constantly keep her wits about her.

The barman placed their drinks in front of them. Damon picked it up, sniffed it, and chuckled. "Your father doesn't even stock decent whiskey," he said.

"Can we leave?" she asked.

"Why? I thought you'd like to be here. Enjoying the nightlife."

Milah glared at him. "What are you hoping to achieve right now?"

"In all honesty, I want to dance." He put the drink down without taking a sip. Milah didn't even bother glancing at her drink. She wouldn't enjoy it anyway.

He grabbed her arm, and without so much as an invite, he dragged her onto the dance floor. His hands immediately went to her waist, drawing her indecently close to him. There were couples that were closer still, nearly crawling into each other's flesh, but this, after him being between her thighs, it seemed a lot more intimate.

The music was so loud she couldn't hear herself think.

She'd never been to her father's nightclub before, and this one, it was … disappointing. How could he even name this place after his own daughter?

Damon nudged his leg between her thighs, his hand going to her ass, and the other reached up to sink into her hair. He pulled her even closer. His lips brushed against her ear. "Have fun."

"Why? You're not here to have fun," she said.

"You're right. I'm here to show off his sexy-as-fuck daughter who belongs to me. He thinks he can destroy me, Milah. Take a look around, I will bring this place and your father to his knees."

She clenched her hands into fists, wanting to pummel his chest. With how close they were, no one would see her anger.

"Why are you doing this to me?" she asked.

"Because I can, and because his men need to see how far he has fallen."

Milah frowned.

Damon could have ended her father a few weeks ago. He had him right where he wanted him. His life had literally been in Damon's hands, but why hadn't he? They were sworn enemies.

She pulled back, and with Damon's grasp on her, she couldn't fight him as he tilted her head back. Then he slammed his lips down on hers.

The kiss took her by surprise.

Milah was frozen. Unsure. His lips were hard, and she stared at him. Damon looked at her, and as he traced his tongue across her lips, she gasped. The moment she did, he plunged inside, and her hands, which had been clenched between them, flattened out.

She touched his chest, feeling the rock-hard muscles beneath. The hand at her neck tightened, and he deepened the kiss.

Against her better judgment, she let her eyes fall shut, and slowly, she wrapped her arms around his neck, kissing him back with a passion that shocked her.

She hated Damon. She despised all things De Luca, but his kiss was everything.

Her pussy began to grow wet. Her nipples hardened, and even as she tried to deny her feelings, she couldn't stop. Damon made her ache.

Was this because they nearly had sex back at his home? Was it because he'd given her her first orgasm?

Milah had no answers. She wasn't a woman hungry for male attention. She never cared about that, but this, it was … heavenly.

Even with her father's men close by. She had no doubt her father would be notified of this moment. It wasn't as though he ever liked her anyway. This shouldn't disappoint him.

Damon pulled away from the kiss, and if he hadn't been holding her so tightly, she would have stumbled.

The music was slow, erotic, and rather than be annoyed by it, she let go, feeling it awaken her body. With her arms wrapped around his neck, their bodies flush together, she was transported to somewhere else. Where she wasn't a Russo and he wasn't a De Luca. They were two strangers within the night, attraction bubbling between them.

He cupped her ass with his leg wedged between her thighs, and as he touched her pussy, she gasped, feeling an answering quake inside her. She was so wet, and she couldn't resist gyrating against him, feeling his hardened cock against her stomach.

Damon was just as affected by her as she was by him.

This shouldn't be happening, but Milah didn't care.

He was using her. Just like her father had used her.

De Luca and Russo were going to paint the streets with blood, but Milah didn't care. She followed his lead, giving in to temptation for the first time in her life, and she hated how freeing it was.

Glory had told her that her father's message was

to simply ask De Luca what he wanted. She hadn't asked him yet and had no intention of doing so. He was the enemy. There was a high chance he still could lie. She couldn't trust him.

Milah didn't want to think of all those thoughts right now. Not with how good his leg felt between hers.

He let go of her neck long enough to stroke down her back and cup her ass. His lips brushed across her neck, and she gasped as he flicked his tongue over her pulse right before nibbling it with his teeth.

She gasped again. An answering heat flooded her body.

She didn't want him to stop touching her.

"Do you know what I wanted to do to you in my bed, what I still want to do?" he asked.

She still couldn't believe it had only been last night when she'd been so close to losing her virginity to him. Sinking her teeth into her lip, she tried not to show just how desperate she was.

Giving in to him was the last thing she wanted to do, and yet, it felt like she didn't have much of a choice.

The way he touched her. Damon was in command of her body. No one else.

She could tell herself not to want him, but her body had other ideas. It was like she was working against herself, which was infuriating.

"Please," she said.

Milah didn't know what she was saying *please* for. Begging him to tell her? Or begging for him not to ruin this for her? Which one could it possibly be? Even she was confused. Did she want him to stop or keep going?

With the grip he had on her ass, she felt an answering fire deep inside her. With the way his leg rubbed her, she wanted to give in. To cave to him.

He chuckled. The very sound was like sin.

"After I took that cherry, Milah, and felt your precious innocence break on my cock, I would've fucked you, hard, and show you how a real man took what he wanted to. I would have you screaming for the rooftops. Not a moment would go by when you weren't begging for my dick."

She wanted to refute him, but the truth was that she'd wanted that too. What had happened to her?

De Luca was her enemy.

She needed to start chanting it, but as he held her closer, one of his hands moved from her ass to settle between them. His palm was flat against her stomach. She tried to jerk out of his hold, but he wouldn't let her.

Then, right on the dance floor—she didn't know if he discreetly did it, or he simply didn't care because this was her father's nightclub—his hand was between her thighs. The dress she'd worn had been like a second skin, but she refused to forgo the panties. Damon simply nudged them to one side as if they were nothing more than a pest. Then his palm was flat against her pussy. The tips of his fingers teased around her entrance, making her tense and gasp at the same time.

Damon moved the hand at her ass to the back of her neck once again, and this time, he slammed his lips down on hers, kissing her as he rubbed at her clit with his palm. Those fingers were so close to her entrance, but he didn't once penetrate her.

Milah didn't know if she could survive his touches, not on the dance floor. Not anywhere, but as he fingered her pussy, she didn't know if she was ever going to be able to survive. Then, without her even suspecting it, he shoved her right over the edge, the pleasure instantaneous.

He swallowed her pleasured moans and accepted

her sinking fingers in his hair. There was nothing more he could do.

They were surrounded by people, and once again, Milah realized that her body, at that very moment, was not her own. She belonged to Damon. No one else.

He held her still, drawing every single last pleasure out of her body before withdrawing. Damon kept a firm grip on her though. If he hadn't, she'd have fallen easily. Her legs felt like jelly.

"I think it's time to take you back to the hotel room." He pressed another quick kiss to her neck, and she gasped, arching up, wanting his touch.

Damon moved her in front of him, walking her across the dance floor, toward the exit, but she came to a stop when she caught sight of her father. He stood at the edge, looking at her with disgust.

How dare he look at her like that?

What the fuck did he want?

She'd never loved her father. Milah realized it at that very moment. He had sent men to kill innocent people in Damon's territory. He was a snake. A filthy, slimy snake, and now she knew why her mother made her train so damn hard. It wasn't because of the potential men she'd encounter, it was because of her father.

This man, he was her enemy.

Then what did that make De Luca?

****

Damon hadn't intended to make Milah orgasm on the dancefloor of her father's nightclub. That hadn't been part of his plan.

Rubbing it in Russo's face that he owned Milah, that had been part of the plan. Showing the old bastard that he didn't have any real power over them, that was what he wanted to show him. Milah, in that tight dress, and looking so … angry at him, he couldn't resist.

The woman back at the house had been so ready for his cock. He had no doubt if they hadn't been disturbed, he'd already be the proud owner of bloodied sheets and the captain of her virginity.

Milah was so innocent.

She could be the perfect woman for him. Begging for his love and attention. Only granting it when he felt she deserved it.

Milah Russo could be at his beck and call. Even as the temptation was strong, he refused to give in to it. This was not the time to give in to petty fantasies. He already had an important job for Milah, and he wasn't going to stray from that path, not for anyone.

Seeing her father waiting for them on the edge of the dance floor had helped to bring him back into focus.

No one was going to take the true pleasure away from him. Wiping out Russo, raising a son to one day fight by his side.

"Russo," he said, as they were shown toward the main office.

Damon had already figured out the best exits and clocked all of Russo's men. To his surprise, there were not that many. Only three men were close to Russo, which must mean his sources were, in fact, correct.

He was losing the fight to keep his soldiers intact. Some of them had tried to come to his side, but he'd pushed them away. No way in hell was he going to accept them.

Milah sat in her father's office, her hands clasped together, not even looking at the man she called a parent. Antonio didn't look at her, which seemed to piss Damon off.

He didn't understand the family dynamic between the two of them. Even though his own father had been the head of the house, Damon still missed him and would have traded anything to have more time with the old bastard. He loved him that much. The same went for his mother as well.

The Russos were nothing but strangers.

"Don't you think your daughter looks beautiful?" Damon asked.

"She looks like a slut," Antonio said.

Those hands clenched. He saw the distinctive whitening of her knuckles.

"Be careful, Russo," Damon said, standing up. "Do you want a repeat of last time? I don't believe you have anything else to bargain with. I already own your daughter."

"And you're not going to marry her?" Russo asked.

Damon chuckled. "That wasn't part of the deal, remember?" This was a good time to let Milah see exactly what her father was made of.

He rounded the chairs and put his hands on her shoulders. She tensed up at his touch but still didn't look at her father.

"Should I tell her exactly what you bargained for? What you were willing to allow your daughter to become, just so you could live your sorry excuse for a life?" He leaned in close to Milah's ear. His breath fanned across her flesh.

Milah was aroused by him. He had some semblance of power over her. It was only minimal, but it was there, and he intended to exploit it from every possible angle he could.

Even if it meant her nipples showed her attraction to him, or the subtle way she tried to press her thighs together.

When he wasn't in Milah's company, he spent a great deal of time watching her. The art of winning was to know what his opponent's next move was and to read them. He'd been reading Milah, and she was a fascinating book. One he enjoyed immensely.

"I don't think you know exactly what your father was willing to have you do, Milah."

"Enough," Russo said.

"He begged me for his life, and I told him that if he wanted to live, then he was going to have to give me something precious." He chuckled. "He told me he had nothing. I said to him, what about Milah?" He kissed her neck. "He laughed at me and said no one wants my daughter."

She turned her head away. He cupped her face, forcing her to look at him so she saw the sincerity in his eyes, even as he tormented her father.

He had more men on the dance floor having fun than Russo had to protect him. It would be so easy to end this dance here and now, but Damon didn't want to put a premature ending to this.

He intended to enjoy watching Russo fall. Seeing him suffer every single step of the way. That was the real part of his plan.

"But I wanted you," Damon said. "I looked him in the eye and said I wanted Milah Russo to serve me. To be at my beck and call. To be my mistress. Not my wife, but my little plaything. To fuck, to tease, to be all mine. There is no escape for you, Milah. I made it abundantly clear that once he gave you to me, there was no going back. You are mine, and your job is simple—to worship my cock. That virgin cunt will know no other dick but mine."

He turned to look at Russo.

"Leave!"

He raised his voice loud enough for the door to open, and then, at his command, his men took Milah out of the office, so it was only him and Russo. After extracting his knife from his jacket, he pressed the tip of the blade against the desk.

Russo attempted to look unaffected, but Damon watched him, knowing he unnerved the pathetic loser before him.

The one and only Antonio Russo was nearly at his knees. Already drowning in debt. Each of his revenue sources had dried up. The men no longer respected him. Why would they when the first real test of strength had shown how weak he was? Begging for his life. Seeing him give up his precious daughter just so he could live.

He could have come in, killed a bunch of people, made it look like Antonio had turned on them all. He could have brought one of his few surviving businesses crumbling, but instead, he was going to make sure the men spread the word.

Milah Russo was in De Luca's arms. She was at De Luca's beck and call.

De Luca was the fucking king, and soon, Russo would fall. Just like he had planned.

Piece by piece, his plan had fallen into place, and by the end of tonight, he was going to have his seed deep inside Milah's cunt. There was no getting away from it. He wanted Milah pregnant, and soon.

"I think it is time for you to leave."

Damon threw his blade, and it was embedded in Antonio's shoulder. The man fell against the wall, a scream leaving him.

No men came running to him. There was no one.

Russo was so fucking broken. The stubborn bastard refused to fucking see it, but Damon was going to make sure he had no choice.

Shoving his fist into the man's stomach as he approached, he grabbed the hilt of the knife out of his shoulder, relishing every scream.

"You're going to wish you had died that day," Damon said.

"You're going down, De Luca," Russo said. "The arrogant never succeed."

"I'm not arrogant, but let's see how you can keep on fighting me." He sniffed the air. "Because I believe I just saw a rat. A big fat city rat, scurrying across Milah's."

Antonio sneered.

"I wonder how many people will come running to Milah's with that piece of information." All it would take was one call. "The next time I see you, Russo, you will die." He slapped the man's face, almost affectionately.

Then he stepped back and found two of his own men still waiting for him outside of Russo's office.

"I want you to torch the bathrooms," Damon said, pulling out his cell phone. He dialed Genius's number.

The man answered less than two seconds later. "What can I do for you?"

"Do you not have anything better to do?"

"Oh, you mean apart from saving your excellent ass? You know me, I'm married to my computer. It won't leave me. It will occasionally give me the cold shoulder for an upgrade, but let's face it, she has never cheated or lied to me. Can't say that about a woman."

"Have you ever had a woman?"

"Ha, ha, ha, very funny. I might write that one down. Keep looking over it because it is so funny. What do you want?"

"A sudden sighting of a big fat rat at Milah's," Damon said.

"Reported, sent, and guess what, that piece-of-shit nightclub is going to go down." Genius let out a maniacal laughter. "Oh, wait, what is this?"

Damon made his way outside toward the car.

James waited outside, but Damon paused. "What?"

"According to this, in the past few weeks, there have been some mysterious overdoses occurring outside of Milah's nightclub. They don't know the source, but let me do a little digging."

Damon waited and climbed into the car, giving James the signal to take them back to the hotel.

Milah stared at Damon but didn't say a word.

"Well, this is a heroin overdose. Looks like a pretty nasty batch."

"Any touch mine?"

"Nope. This is in Russo's territory only."

"Keep an eye on it," Damon said.

He closed his cell phone and looked toward Milah.

Damon had closed down Antonio's drug connections. He'd arranged deals himself, so most of the product was being run through De Luca hands. Antonio's situation was desperate. Would he be stupid enough to try to sell cheap drugs that ran the risk of killing his own clients?

"What is it?" Milah asked.

"It's nothing." He put his hand on Milah's knee.

The drugs were a problem for another time. It wouldn't take much to find the fucker who was dealing with Russo.

What he didn't want was for a bad batch to get mixed up in De Luca's brands. Shit that killed was bad for business. Was that what Russo hoped for? To fuck with his business even as he struggling to hold himself together?

He wouldn't put it past Russo to do that. Or was this just desperation? Genius would have the answers for him soon enough. Genius had already told him he might have some news, and he wanted it and hoped it was what he was looking for.

The drive to the hotel didn't take too long. The woman at the reception desk gave him a warm welcome, which he ignored.

Going straight to the elevator, he reached out to put a hand on Milah's hip, to pull her close. She was tight within his embrace, but he didn't let her go.

As he stared at their reflections, he noticed how her tits pressed against the confines of the dress. They looked ready to spill out. His dick began to harden as he thought about having her completely naked and at his mercy again.

She had a body made for sin. And he wanted to show her every little piece of it.

Would she be a good little student?

The elevator opened, and he took the lead, going to his room. He pulled out the card, but James moved in first.

"We don't want to take any chances in Russo territory," James said.

Damon agreed, but Milah snorted. She tried to pull out of his arms.

"Now what is the problem with you, my little wildcat?" Damon asked.

"Are you just trying to mock me? I saw it. You don't have to rub it in."

"Rub what in?"

"My father is powerless. He would never go anywhere unless he had at least ten men at his disposal. I counted, three, four at best." She snorted again. "Trust me, he doesn't have the firepower to deal with you all."

This made him chuckle. "Are you disappointed?"

"I'm nothing."

He ran his hands down to her ass, drawing her close. "You're not nothing, baby," he said.

She tried to wriggle out of his hold, but he wasn't going to let her go that easily.

"Leave!"

His men didn't need further instruction. They all left, quickly, and he was alone with Milah.

"Is that all you have to do? Give one-word grunts like a damn neanderthal?" she asked.

He chuckled. "No, I usually have to give my boys respect, but they know who I am dealing with."

Damon bent down and picked her up. She screamed and he carried her through to the bedroom.

The hotel was luxury, and no matter where he stayed, he always liked to have only the very best.

After dropping her to the bed, he stepped back and removed his jacket.

"What are you doing?" Milah asked.

"I'm finishing what I started. Or do you just want to keep getting that pussy taken care of?"

Her cheeks were bright red.

With his jacket gone, he removed his shirt. He'd already dealt with his holster. No matter how far Russo had fallen, Damon didn't intend to take any chances on the bastard.

He'd find a way to squirm free. Of that, Damon had no doubt. Antonio Russo was used to getting out of tight spots. The man was a master manipulator, and even though he'd broken him, he hadn't shattered yet. But there would be time for it.

Damon pushed thoughts of Antonio Russo out of his mind. He didn't want to be thinking of that cowardly bastard when he was balls deep in Milah's pussy.

"I'm not sleeping with you," Milah said.

"Sleep is the last thing on my mind."

He removed his pants, then his boxer briefs.

Milah crossed her arms beneath her breasts, but he saw the hard points of her nipples as they pressed against her dress. She wanted to seem aloof to him, but her body was a bad liar.

"Give me your hand," he said.

She hesitated for a second, but then she held out her hand. He placed it on his dick, wrapping her fingers around his length. "That's it, baby, now hold me tightly." He showed her exactly what he liked.

Milah didn't look at him, but he didn't mind. He showed her with his hand exactly what he wanted. Stepping close, he wrapped his fingers in her long, raven hair, tugging her head back so she had no choice but to look at him.

"Are you telling me that your pussy is not wet for me right now?" he asked.

"No."

The defiance in her eyes was a real turn-on, but he saw the lie.

"How about we have a deal? I will feel your pussy, and if you're bone dry, I won't touch you tonight. If you're soaking wet, then not only will I take your virginity, but you will suck my cock and fucking enjoy it."

She glared at him.

Was she willing to risk it?

He fucking hoped so.

When it came to Milah, he intended to enjoy her.

Chapter Eleven

Milah didn't know what to do.

If she took the deal, then she was at his command.

You're at his command anyway!

What was the point of this deal? Was it to humiliate her?

No one but the two of them was there to witness it. If she backed away now, he'd still know she had something to hide, and that just … annoyed her even more.

There was no way he was going to win this. Not today.

She didn't know what she could do to help herself. Maybe nothing, but she wasn't going to back down from this.

"Deal," she said.

The moment she said it, she felt like she heard the nail in the coffin.

She hated Damon De Luca with a fiery passion, but her body hadn't got the fucking update. Even as she hated him, there was still attraction.

Gritting her teeth, she stared at him defiantly.

His cock was hard, thick, and soft to the touch. She liked how it felt in her hand, and again, it was another reason to hate what he was doing to her.

Why was Damon doing this?

Was this all part of his plan?

To make her suffer because of what her father did? She wouldn't put it past him. Hatred rushed through her, but it wasn't completely true, or was it?

Damon pushed her hand out of the way.

He pressed against her shoulders so she had no choice but to lean back, falling. He had her dress pushed up around her waist in a matter of seconds. She looked at him, waiting as he pressed his palm against her pussy. The frown that had strengthened across his brow smoothed out as he smiled.

His fingers touched between her slit, and like a victor, he held them up for her to inspect. "I think it is fair to say that I won." His fingers glistened from her arousal.

Milah glared at him. She hated him so fucking much.

"I think someone owes me those lips." He pressed his mouth to hers in a quick, fleeting kiss, then stood.

It wasn't fair that Damon De Luca was a fine specimen of a man. She didn't want to be aroused by his heavily inked body or by the blood that she knew covered his hands.

This man was her enemy.

Within seconds, the dress that had been impossible to put on was off and in his hands. He flicked the catch of her bra, and then the panties she wore were gone. He gripped her neck, lifting her off the bed and pulling her in close. Their bodies were flush against each other.

She couldn't look away as she stared into his eyes. They were so dark, but as he looked at her, she got a sense that they were filled with warmth. Was she trying to find it? Did it really exist?

He's the enemy.
Do not fall for any of his tricks.
Ignore him.

There was no time to as he slammed his lips down on hers. The grip on her neck loosened as he started to move down and took her ass in his hands. He pulled her close, and she felt the hard ridge of his cock as it pressed against her stomach.

A moan slipped from her lips, and then all too soon, he pulled away. His hands were at her shoulders, and this time, he pushed on them. Milah had no choice but to sink to her knees before him.

Now, on the floor, at his mercy, she stared up at him, waiting, curious, wondering what was going to happen next.

"I like you this way. On your knees."

She licked her lips, feeling her mouth was so dry.

"Open your mouth."

Milah reluctantly did as he asked.

He groaned.

"Push your tongue out."

She did so and watched as he moved forward. His hand went to the base of his cock, holding his dick stiff and firm, and then, he placed the tip against her tongue and slid it into her mouth.

Milah watched him as she closed her lips around his thick length.

He growled. One hand still rested at the base, but he once again, fisted her hair.

"Suck it. Don't use teeth, just those precious lips. That's right, baby, slowly. Fuck, that feels good."

He moved in and out of her mouth, and Milah hated that she wasn't … repulsed by it. She should hate him. She wanted to, but he felt nice.

When she tried to close her eyes, he gripped her hair even tighter, not allowing her to close them.

Damon had control.

She watched him as she began to rock into her mouth. At one point, he pressed quite deep into her mouth that for a few seconds, she thought she was going to choke, but he stopped himself from going too deep.

He rocked in and out of her mouth, going deep, but not too far, but all too soon, it was over, and Milah hated that she didn't want him to stop.

Damon lifted her, and she was back on the bed, but this time, Damon didn't go to her pussy. His lips were on her mouth, and his hands held hers above her head.

She watched him as he moved both of her hands beneath his, and his free hand went between his thighs.

This was it.

"I can't stop this from hurting."

Milah didn't know what to say.

"But trust me, once this is over, it is going to feel so much better."

She cried out as he tensed up, and then she felt his dick as it tore through her pussy, slamming in deep. The pain was sharp, instant, and not unbearable, but it took her breath away. Her initial instinct was to push him away, but Damon held her hands firm.

Under the weight of only one of his hands, she couldn't push him off, even though she wanted to. He kept a firm grip, and then, both of his hands were free and his cock was balls deep within her.

Tears blurred her vision. She hated the pain.

Damon was her first.

She ... did she hate it?

He held perfectly still within her.

This was a De Luca, and he was being kind, which went against the very nature of his being. They were monsters.

He didn't say anything. Didn't offer any soothing words or help her to understand what was going on. He just ... he was ... what was he doing?

He kissed her lips, brushing across her jaw, then down to her neck, but he didn't move.

Why wasn't he being a complete fucking bastard and forcing her to take his dick? Instead, he was giving her time. Kissing her tears away, touching her body, and forcing her to accept that she wanted him.

She didn't know if she hated him more at that moment than ever before.

She watched him, waiting. Time seemed to freeze between them.

The pain slowly faded, and all that was left were the two of them. Her body was on fire with need, and then Damon started to slowly fuck her.

He took his time, pulling all the way out of her and then pressing inside. She expected him to be hard and rough, but he wasn't. Then she realized Damon wasn't fucking her. He was … making love to her. Slowly. Intimately, their hands locked together as he worked his cock inside her.

She didn't want him to stop, and the pleasure was intense.

He took his sweet time, the pain nothing more than a distant memory.

Something she was soon going to forget, and then, he lifted and his thrusts sped up, becoming a little more erratic. She looked up at him in time to see him lose complete control.

He came, and she felt the answering pulse inside her as he filled her with his cum.

It kept on going. Pushing inside her.

When it was over, he didn't collapse over her.

Damon stared down at her.

Neither of them spoke. Words failed her.

Should she say something mean?

He was her first.

Damon made the first move. He lifted off her, and she didn't know what to do as she pressed her thighs together, feeling him spill from between her legs.

This was awkward. Damon didn't say anything as

he left the room. Milah hated the weak tears that filled her eyes. There was no point in being depressed. Damon De Luca was the enemy. Someone she should hate.

You didn't wear a condom.

She hated herself. They hadn't been careful, and the last thing she wanted was to get pregnant.

These were not the best circumstances in which to raise a child. Damon hated her, just as she … didn't like him.

There was no way they could bring a baby into this world. It would be too cruel.

Her mother had always asked her that if possible, to try to find someone she liked and who would make a wonderful father. Thinking about her mother right now made her miss her so damn much.

Life wasn't fair. This wasn't fair.

Damon returned, and without a single comment, he reached for her.

She let out a squeal, not wanting to be the first one to speak between them, but she had no choice.

"Put me down!" She tried to pull out of his arms, but Damon held her even tighter.

"Stop being a baby."

"Ugh, I can walk." She didn't like how nice it was to be in his arms.

Now wasn't the time to be enjoying the enemy. She knew that.

"And when I want you to walk, that is exactly what you will do, but not today."

He carried her through to the en-suite bathroom. Damon surprised her even more by slowly lowering her into the bathtub.

"Relax. Do not move or I swear I will fucking paddle your ass." He pointed at her and then left the bathroom.

The warm water was nice.

Milah glanced around at the luxury bathroom and slowly breathed out a sigh of relief. Leaning back in the water, she suddenly jerked upright and kept her gaze on the door. Damon had claimed her virginity, but that didn't mean anything. They were still enemies.

She refused to give in to him, even though, much to her shame, part of her wanted to. They had only had sex.

It meant nothing.

Nibbling on her lip, she kept her gaze on the door.

Damon took some time, but he soon reappeared. Milah didn't know if she should be happy about that or not. He didn't say a word as he stepped into the tub on the opposite side of her.

She tried not to look at him.

You didn't use a condom.

"We're going to need to stop by a pharmacy," she said.

"Why?"

"I … there was no…" She looked at him, hoping he would get the general idea of where she was going with this.

He merely stared at her. Was he playing dumb on purpose?

"I will need the morning-after pill," she said.

"Not happening."

"Damon, this isn—"

"I said no."

She glared at him. "I don't want to have a child with you."

"Who says there is going to be a child?"

"I'm not stupid. It only takes one time."

"And that means you could already be pregnant,

and I'm not going to take that chance."

"You're being unreasonable."

"That is what happens when you fuck with a De Luca."

Anger rushed through her, and she tried to hit him, to attack, but Damon grabbed her hands and turned her attack into his advantage, moving her legs to either side of his waist. He pressed her hands behind her back, and now it looked like she wasn't attacking him, but instead, offering up her breasts.

"Now this is so much better," he said. "Don't you think?"

"I hate you."

"Good. You can use that hate, because the sex is so much better." He ran his hand up her stomach, going between the valley of her breasts, and chuckled. "So pretty."

He licked one of her nipples, and even though she was so fucking mad at him, she couldn't deny the sudden hit of attraction that filled her. She wanted him.

Life was so unfair.

****

Damon stared at Milah's naked ass.

They hadn't stayed in the city.

Genius had discovered where Russo was getting the drugs. It was from some backyard, high school science kid who was playing with chemistry. Desperate times clearly called for desperate measures, and Russo was allowing bad shit to go on the streets. All he wanted was quick money.

What he really wanted was access to Milah's funds.

It had been a week since the attack on his own nightclub. He had already made sure the victims' families had been compensated accordingly. So far,

Russo hadn't attacked him again, however, the cheap drugs were doing the rounds in all the nightclubs.

He had to deal with Russo soon.

As for Milah, every chance he got, she was being filled with cum. He hadn't given her a chance to get used to it. Even sore, he'd fucked her long, hard, and deep, flooding her pussy. He had ordered Glory to keep an eye on her menstrual cycle, and he was to know the instant she missed one.

He also had the doctor on standby to do the necessary tests to confirm her pregnancy.

Every part of his plan was falling into line, just as he knew it would, but there was one tiny little hiccup he didn't like. The feeling of guilt that swirled in the pit of his stomach as he looked at Milah's sleeping form.

There were bruises on her waist, ass, and hips from how hard he held her. The blanket lay between her legs, curling up around her back. All he saw was one rounded ass cheek and juicy thigh.

His cock hardened at the sight. He wanted her again.

This was another problem.

When it came to women, he was used to being the one in control. Always. No one had the upper hand. Just him.

But as he looked at Milah's sleeping form, and his dick wanted inside her once again, he knew she was different.

This was only supposed to be basic. Milah was a means to an end.

Sure, she was fucking beautiful, and her body was made to be worshipped. On paper, this was only supposed to be part of a business deal. An arrangement that put her at his mercy. But the reality was far harder to comprehend.

Milah moaned softly, her legs moving, and then she snuggled in deep. He didn't like that. When she slept, he wanted to be part of her dream world, just as he filled her reality. There was no room for any reprieve.

After opening his robe, he wrapped his fingers around his stiff prick and approached the bed. He let go of his penis and put his hands on her thighs, turning her over so she was on her stomach.

Milah didn't wake up but let out a soft protest.

That ass was so fucking juicy.

He gave a ripe cheek a squeeze, and then a small slap, jolting her out of her sleep.

She glanced over her shoulder at him. Even waking up, she looked sexy as fuck. Her hair was a mess, and it looked like she'd been fucked into oblivion, which was so fucking right.

"What are you doing?" she asked, moaning.

"You look way too good to leave."

He pressed his hand between her legs, cupping her pussy. She was sodden. "Were you thinking of me?"

She gasped, thrusting her pelvis onto his hand. He stroked over her clit before sliding down to push inside her.

Last night, he'd filled this cunt three times. Each time he did, he hoped he got her pregnant.

His seed would take root soon enough. He was sure of it.

Adding a second, then a third finger, he began to rock inside her, feeling her pussy tighten around him. He didn't want to fuck her with his fingers, but to feel that tight heat on his dick.

Pushing her to her knees, he moved into position behind her. As he gripped her ass cheeks, he spread them apart and looked at her anus and tight opening.

Her cunt already glistened.

It would be so easy to fuck her, but now he wanted to claim her asshole as well. No other man was going to go near her.

Just the thought of his guards looking at her filled him with jealousy, and he didn't like those feelings.

Running his fingers through her slit, he pressed them inside her, watching her push against him, hungry for him.

With his digits slick from their combined arousal, he drew them back to rub against her asshole, getting her nice and slick, ready to take his cock.

She moaned as he did this, but as soon as he pressed his finger against the tight puckered hole, she tensed up. He wasn't going to fuck her ass tonight. Not until he was guaranteed she was pregnant. Only when he knew she carried his kid would he fill her asshole with his cum, but that didn't mean he couldn't have some fun.

Grabbing his dick, he placed it at her entrance and pushed inside for a couple of inches, spreading her ass cheeks wide so he could watch his dick disappear into her sweet abyss. She was so tight. Even after he'd been taking her multiple times a day.

"Oh, fuck me, you feel good," he said.

"Please," she said, moaning.

He held her hips and fucked inside her. Holding her tightly, he gave it to her rough, just as he knew she liked it.

Her hands sank into the blanket, her knuckles white as she tried to contain her moans.

After a few sharp thrusts, he stopped but kept his dick balls deep within her.

"Damon?"

"Shh," he said.

She whimpered and tried to rock back against him. For her trouble, he gave her ass a nice little slap, stopping her from moving.

She whimpered again, but this time, he kept her in place, not wanting her to move. "If you want to be allowed to come, then you are going to hold still. Do not move."

"Damon? Please."

"When I'm good and ready." The truth was, he didn't want to hold back. He was addicted to the feel of her cunt. How good she felt around his length. It was like she was made for him and him alone.

What man in his right mind would want to give that up?

Milah was fucking perfect. They were amazing together.

With his fingers still slick, he moved them back to her asshole. She tensed up but didn't try to move away.

"Trust me, Milah."

He was the last person she should trust, but she didn't try to get away.

Rubbing against her anus, he pressed on the puckered hole, and she gasped. Her muscles were tight, but he was determined, and he filled her asshole.

Her pussy squeezed his dick even tighter, and with there still being no condom between them, he felt her get even more aroused as he pushed inside her ass.

She cried out.

Damon used a single finger, pushing in and out, taking his time and allowing her to get accustomed to it.

Reaching between her legs, he started to stroke her clit, rubbing that tender nub, and Milah went up in flames, just as he knew she would.

He wanted to take the time to explore some more, but he was so close.

Pulling the finger from her ass, he held her hips

and fucked her long and hard, watching his cock. His length was covered in her arousal, and he soon joined her, falling over the peak.

Damon pushed as deep as he could get, wanting every single drop to soak her womb.

He closed his eyes, loving the feel of her mini-orgasm. Each time he came, it seemed to set her off, and afterward, they collapsed onto the bed.

Milah always tried to create some distance between them, but to make sure his cum had the best chance, Damon kept her locked against him, touching her.

He had soon come to realize that Milah didn't have enough affection. Her father was cold, and he imagined he'd never truly cared for his daughter, and her mother was dead.

There was no one for her.

Glory had told him that she believed Milah was lonely. Being in this house, surrounded by people who hated the Russo, it made her loneliness even worse.

"Don't you have some work to do? People to kill?" Milah asked.

"They can all wait." He kissed her shoulder. "You never said if it was hard to see your dad."

She let out a chuckle. "You want to make small talk?"

"It's what we do."

At the start, he had simply held her, but as the days changed, he had started to talk to her. Enjoying the soft, subtle tones of her voice as they filled a room.

"Why are you being nice to me?"

"Do I have to have a reason?" he asked.

"No, I guess not, but it does seem odd that you would."

He kissed her neck. "Nah, it's not."

"I'm a Russo, and our trip made it very apparent that you cannot even stand to be in the same room as one of us."

"Are you a Russo?" he asked.

"Of course. I carry my father's blood. Don't I?"

"Yeah, but that doesn't make you one of them. Would you die for him?"

Milah was silent.

"Do you love him?" he asked.

"I…"

"We're friends here, Milah."

"Stop it. We both know you have enough friends. I'm not important to you. I never have been." She growled, "No."

"No, what?"

"I would never die for my father. I cannot stand him. He's a … bastard, and you know that."

He saw her jaw clench. There was no mistaking the tension within her body. Milah struggled with her anger. She suddenly started laughing. "You know the crazy thing?" she asked.

"What?"

"I was trying to get out of it."

He frowned.

"The night you attacked my father head-on and he decided to use me to save his sorry neck, I'd been about to leave. To never look back. I never wanted to be a Russo. My mother … I know about the inheritance she left me. She told me all about it, and she said if I ever found a chance to get away, to take it. So I was doing exactly that when you arrived. I didn't get very far."

He had no idea about that.

Genius had been onto something, a false identity and some records, but Damon hadn't been sure what they meant at the time.

"You hate your father?"

"So fucking much. Do you think it is easy for me to keep the Russo name? I hate it. I hate everything it stands for, and what is worse, I hate the man who gave it to me as well. He is a bastard of the highest order." She sniffled. "I need to use the bathroom."

Damon didn't want to pull out of her, but he had to give her the space to do so.

He watched her go.

Her head bowed.

Milah intended to get away all along. The woman at the party, she had been so fucking proud. A true Russo, but it must have been a lie.

There was a knock on his bedroom door, and he wasn't welcome of the interruption right now.

Going to it, he saw James on the other side.

"What is it?" he asked.

"Antonio Russo is attempting to flee the country," James said.

Damon listened as James gave him a rundown of what had happened within the last twenty-four hours. With the health inspectors closing down Milah's and Damon taking out the drugs, Antonio's funds had dried up almost immediately. There was still no way Russo could access Milah's trust fund. It also meant old allies had soon shut their doors on him, and he was left with absolutely nothing.

It was exactly where Damon wanted him.

"Hold him," Damon said.

James nodded, giving him the location where they were holding Antonio. After closing the door, Damon moved toward the bathroom and found Milah taking a shower. He removed his robe and stepped into the stall.

She turned toward him, not hiding her gorgeous

body from him, which he happened to adore.

"I've got some business to attend to. I'll be back the moment it's done."

"Okay." She nibbled on her lip.

"What's the matter?" he asked.

"Er, be careful. Not that I care or anything."

He cupped her chin and forced her to look at him. "You can tell me anytime you care about me."

"I just … I'd hate for something to happen to you, and you'd leave me sitting here forever, waiting. It's self-preservation."

He smirked. "You've got nothing to worry about." He pressed a kiss to her lips. "I'll be back before you know it. Take some time, relax, enjoy." He brushed his lips toward her ear. "Because the moment I come back, your pussy is mine."

Damon loved that spark in her eyes, but he couldn't linger. He had business to attend to.

Entering his bedroom, he paused as he looked at the bed.

Milah no longer had a separate bedroom. She stayed with him. He'd also given her free rein around the house. She could come and go as she pleased. His men knew not to allow her to actually leave the grounds though. She still belonged to him.

Staring at the bed, he recalled the night he'd taken her virginity. After he'd put her in the bath, he'd gone back to deal with the sheets, but he hadn't been able to let them go. He'd wrapped them up, and now they were in his safe.

Milah was his. No one else was going to know how perfect her pussy was.

He wasn't letting her go.

His plan was moving along perfectly, and he couldn't have asked for it to have gone a better way.

Even as he dressed, he didn't like that giant pit in his stomach at what he was doing.

Chapter Twelve

One month later

Milah held herself up over the toilet as she vomited.

She'd been doing this for the past couple of days, and each time she did, Damon was nowhere to be found. At least there were small mercies. She didn't want him to see this. He probably knew about her sickness anyway.

In the past few weeks, she'd tested Glory, and each time, she had proven her right. Her suspicions had been raised from the moment Glory had started to be near her. She rarely did any housework, and she saw the other staff were not impressed. Whenever Milah was, Glory wasn't too far away.

Milah had needed to know.

Suspicions were exactly that. Without evidence, she didn't know who she could trust. So the complaints had been subtle.

The first was so stupid. She always suffered from cold feet and she absolutely loved warm, fluffy slippers. The kind that made her feet feel pampered in their own right. Within a day, Damon had mysteriously presented her with a pair she had talked about in great deal to Glory.

The second was even easier. She remembered her mother talking constantly about a Bakewell tart she had while staying in the English countryside. As a little girl, Milah recalled trying one, and so she talked about it. The truth was, she hadn't thought about a Bakewell in so long. The crumbly pastry, with a layer of jam and an almond cake layer on top, finished with white icing, and a single glace cherry. Delicious.

That evening, a Bakewell was served.

She requested books, and they of course arrived.

Glory wasn't her friend. No, she was a spy. Damon's spy.

She had also witnessed Milah throwing up on two other mornings, and this one was no different as she walked into the bathroom.

"You're sick," Glory said, dampening a towel, like the two other times.

"It's fine. I probably just ate something that didn't agree with me." It was lies. All lies. The only thing that didn't agree with her was Damon's penis.

She was pregnant.

They'd been having sex for five, possibly six weeks. She hadn't menstruated since, and now she was vomiting. It wasn't a coincidence. Damon didn't use condoms, and she'd never been on the pill. With no boyfriend, there was no point in getting on a pill she didn't need. What made matters worse, her cycle was like clockwork. It never failed to arrive on time.

She was late. A couple of weeks late.

She had insisted on Damon wearing a condom, but the moment he touched her, all thought and common sense went right out of the window. His touch shouldn't be able to affect her this way, and yet, it did.

"Could you give me a minute?" Milah asked.

"What do I do?"

"I'll have some toast with jam." She wouldn't raise Glory's suspicions. "My mom always gave me toast and jam when I felt sick." The lie fell easily from her lips. She didn't want Glory running off to Damon and telling him.

He probably already knew, but she wanted to be sure herself.

"Do you know if there's…" She stopped asking and shook her head. "No, it's fine."

"Please, tell me. I want to help."

"It's nothing, honestly. I'm fine." She didn't trust Glory.

"I'll be back with some toast and jam."

Milah nodded and watched Glory leave. The moment she did, she collapsed in a ball on the bathroom floor, her heart breaking slightly as she put her hand on her stomach.

Now was not a good time to be pregnant.

She moved her hand off her abdomen and then immediately put it right back on.

Did she want a child?

It didn't matter. Child or not, she would protect her baby. She wanted to sob, but this wasn't a time to show weakness.

Damon De Luca had a plan and she didn't know what it was. She had to figure it out.

As she got to her feet, the sickness passed as quickly as it arrived. Milah quickly brushed her teeth and made her way into the bedroom, changing into a dress as Glory arrived. She didn't have the tray.

Jam on toast was gross. Milah hated it but it was the first thing she thought of.

"Mr. De Luca is waiting for you in the dining room."

"Oh, okay."

"Your breakfast is waiting for you."

She smiled at Glory, who took the opportunity to disappear.

Damon was home.

This was … new.

In the past month, he'd only been home late at night. They rarely shared dinner together. He always waited until they were alone before he showed her any kind of attention. Glancing at her reflection in the mirror, she tried to assess herself as a stranger. Did she look sick?

Her cheeks were red, and she placed her palms flat on them, hoping to make it an all-over pink, but she gave up as slapping herself wasn't exactly fun.

"Get your act together." Hands clenched at her sides, she made her way down to the dining room.

She nodded at several of the guards. Most of them ignored her. Some couldn't control their sneers, but she refused to let them get to her. If she was pregnant, she was going to have to be at the top of her game.

Damon sat at the head of the table when she entered. No one was around, but the scent of bacon and eggs was heavy in the air. She also detected a hint of coffee, and she put a hand to her stomach, feeling it turn.

This wasn't good. Every single sign so far indicated to her being pregnant.

Rather than panic about it, she took a seat beside him, being sure to reach for a piece of fruit. A nice, heavily scented orange.

"You wanted to see me," she said, feeling so damn formal as she said it.

They'd been fucking like rabbits just last night, and here she was, treating him like some kind of boss.

Damon didn't answer. "How are you feeling?" he asked.

"I'm fine." Did she say it too fast?

Glancing over at him, she forced a smile. So long as she breathed through her mouth and didn't detect the coffee, she'd be able to get through breakfast. What she needed was a plan though. How could she get to a pharmacy without him knowing the reason for the trip?

Damon rapped his knuckles on the table and tutted. She watched as he reached into his jacket pocket, and on the plate, he dropped a ring. She still held the orange quite close to her nose as the scents made her mouth water, but that ring, she recognized it.

It was the same ring her grandfather and his father passed down the line of each ruling Russo. The eldest son.

Her father had told her that she would never get to wear this ring. Only men could. Men were the only people worthy of ruling the Russo line.

He'd never take off the ring. Not unless he had a true son. The man he called an heir.

"What is this?" she asked.

"Your father attempted to run," Damon said. "My men caught him at the docks, trying to leave."

She put the orange down and picked up the ring, turning it over to see the Russo crest embedded in the ring. He'd been so proud of this ring, never giving it up. Always wearing it with pride. If this ring was on her plate, it only meant one thing. He was dead. That was what he'd said to her so many times in the past. No one would get this off his finger unless his body was dead and cold.

The ring was too big, but she had no desire to slip it onto her finger.

Her father was dead. She didn't need Damon to tell her this.

Milah nibbled on her lip and stared at the ring, not exactly sure how she should feel.

Should she be angry? Disappointed? Upset?

Her father had been a horrible human being, but he'd still been her father. Tears filled her eyes. Both of her parents were now dead and gone.

"Did you ... have you killed his ... other children?" she asked.

"No."

Milah looked up at him then, shocked. "You haven't?"

"No."

"Why?"

He didn't speak.

"I … I never got the chance to meet them. I know they exist. I think he had a son, but because it was with a woman … he called her a whore, he would never claim him, nor would he allow his name to be given to him. He should have this."

"Milah, that is your ring."

"No, it's not. I'm not even the eldest, Damon. I'm not anything. I was a daughter. He often called me a waste of space."

"Yeah, but you soon came in handy when it was saving his neck."

"It doesn't matter. It doesn't change anything." She put the ring on the table. What little appetite she had disappeared. Just like her father to ruin even the comfort of food.

"Milah, it's yours, and I won't be seeking anyone else out to wear it."

"But you will seek them out to kill them?" she asked.

"Take the damn ring."

She had to get this conversation to stop. "I think I might be pregnant."

Damon went silent.

She stared at her plate for the longest time, but that wouldn't tell her what he was thinking. Lifting her head, she stared at Damon, waiting.

His gaze was on her.

"Did you hear me?"

"How do you know?" he asked.

She chuckled. "I don't know, maybe it's the morning sickness. We've had unprotected sex. I haven't had a period. Name your reason. I want to go to a pharmacy." She pointed at the ring. "This isn't important to me."

"Milah, he was still your ... father."

"Does it matter? He died at your hands, and I can't bring him back. I'd like to go to a pharmacy." She got to her feet but felt a sudden wave of sickness wash over her. Damon was on his feet, and if he hadn't been there, she would've fallen.

"No pharmacy. I'm going to call a doctor."

"Normal people go to the pharmacy. They have perfectly capable tests."

"We're not normal people."

"No, you're not a normal person. You're a De Luca, and me, I'm no one."

"You're Milah Russo."

"No, I've never been a Russo, and I never will be one."

Damon lifted her in his arms and carried her back up to his bedroom. At that moment, she didn't want to be in his room. "Take me to my room."

"No."

Glory was there within minutes.

"Call the doctor," he said.

Glory left without a fight.

Damon lowered her to the bed, and she tried to pull away from him. "I'm fine. Leave me alone. I don't want to be here."

"You can cry."

"I'm not going to cry."

"When my father died, I locked myself in his office with a bottle of whiskey. I will allow you to do that but only when we have the results. Until then, cry."

"I'm not going to cry."

"You can fall," he said.

She pressed her lips together, feeling her eyes

flood with tears, and they made no sense at all.

She hated her father. There was no love lost between them. They meant nothing to one another, and yet, the tears fell.

One by one, they spilled down her cheeks, and she hated them as well as herself.

"You won't catch me. Not ever."

"I will always catch you. Make no mistake about it, Milah. I will always be on your side." He stroked her cheek, and she couldn't believe he lied to her.

"I'm a Russo."

"I thought you once told me you were a Flynn."

Milah covered her face with her hands, and even as she hated doing so, she sobbed. She sobbed for the man she called father, and the mother she missed so much.

What did she do now?

Damon had finally achieved what he set out to do, and she didn't know what the hell to do now. Her life had no meaning. She had focused for so long on escaping, but now that she might be pregnant, what did it all mean?

The Russo ring didn't belong to her. That was her father's, and now it would be either her half-brother's, one of the guys her father had sired.

Damon stroked her hair.

They were never going to work. Never.

What kind of parents would they be?

****

Milah was pregnant. The doctor confirmed it after a blood test. Damon had no doubt she was pregnant since Glory had reported to him that Milah had morning sickness. Sitting in his office, he stared at the generous shot of whiskey he'd poured himself.

The color was dark, and he'd waited to drink this

to celebrate his victory. Russo was gone. His entire empire had fallen, and now Milah was pregnant.

His plan hadn't worked exactly as he hoped because Antonio had been an unpredictable player.

Now he owned all of the Russo territory and had their nightclubs, everything they had once owned. Antonio Russo had signed everything over to him.

Apart from the ring. He'd requested it be given to Milah. Shocking, considering the bastard had sold his daughter for his own personal ends.

Damon stared down at the ring.

Milah didn't want it.

Every time he tried to give it to her, she left it abandoned.

The Russo ring was a very important piece of their heritage. It normally went to the firstborn son.

Damon paused and stared at the ring. He was aware of the bastards Antonio had sired, but Antonio hadn't once acknowledged any of those children. Only Milah. It was the one part of tradition Antonio had kept.

Tapping his fingers on the glass, Damon picked up the ring and turned it over. This was done on purpose.

Any child he had with Milah wouldn't ever be a true De Luca. Damon gritted his teeth. He'd told Antonio in those final minutes that he had knocked Milah up, and Russo had laughed.

"Doesn't mean you're ever going to be a good father to it. After all, it will forever be a Russo!"

Those had been his parting words.

He couldn't allow that to happen. No child of his would ever be a fucking Russo. Grabbing his drink, he took a long swallow and relished the burn as it ran down his throat. He opened the bottom drawer of his desk and tossed the ring inside.

It meant nothing.

Russo wasn't going to win this.

Leaving his office, he made his way toward the kitchen. The new staff was busy preparing some food for dinner. He and Milah had eaten breakfast at different times. She hadn't been in the kitchen for a couple of days, and he figured that was because of her morning sickness.

Glory had advised him that Milah didn't want him present when she threw up. He had yet to install cameras in his own room, but he did want to be there.

Milah and his … relationship was not love. They had good sex. No, great sex, but he shouldn't care what she was going through. This was her punishment as much as it was her father's. Being a Russo, by extension, it made her part of it all.

She's nothing like him.

Damon left the kitchen and asked a guard if he'd seen Milah.

"She's headed out into the yard with that Glory maid."

It was freezing cold outside.

Annoyed, he glared at the man, turned on his heel, and made his way out into the yard. There was no sign of her, but the guards were very much aware of who he was looking for, and they pointed in the direction where he needed to go.

He was so fucking pissed off. Glory should have known better.

He had guards stationed at different points, and each one held a finger in her direction.

Damon looked up ahead and sure enough, there was Milah, kneeling on the ground, her hands clasped together. A few feet away from her was the small cemetery. He hadn't been here in several months.

Seeing the names of his father, mother, and

grandparents. It was all just a little too much for him.

He stepped on a twig, drawing attention to his presence.

Glory immediately bowed her head. He saw the way her hands were clasped in front of her.

"Leave us," he said.

She walked as fast as she could while Milah got to her feet, brushing off the dried, crumbled leaves.

"What are you doing here?" he asked.

"I came to pay my respects."

"You have no right to be here."

She lifted her head, and he saw her eyes were swollen red. "I have every right to be here."

"What gives you that impression?"

"You're unbelievable."

"What is with this attitude? When I left you this morning, you were fucking sated from taking a pounding from my cock!" he yelled.

Milah lashed out, her hand slapping him right across the face. "No, this morning when you left, I ran to the bathroom to fucking throw up because I am pregnant. I am having a De Luca, and you know what, I'm fucking terrified. All my life, my father has been completely against everything you have ever stood for. He is dead. Gone. His last piece to give to me, the Russo ring. You don't even have a clue what he said to me in that message!"

"That he knows you're going to be pregnant and give birth to another Russo heir."

"I hate you right now."

"You only stop hating me when you beg me for more."

She went to hit him again, but he captured her wrist, drawing her closer.

"I allowed the first hit. Don't think you'll get

away with another."

Milah tried to pull away from his hold, but he had a firm grip on her. There was no escaping it until he let her go, and she knew it.

"Let me go."

"No."

"I hate you."

"You can hate me all you want to, princess. It's not going to change the fact you're pregnant with my kid."

"And I bet you're loving this, aren't you?"

"Do you think I'm happy about this?" he asked.

"Yes. I do." There was fire in her eyes. "You can't tell me this isn't part of some wicked plan of yours. The great Damon De Luca always has some twisted scheme to play. If not, then you are foolish because this is what happens when you have unprotected sex!" She yelled the last part while also pointing at her stomach.

There was no sign of her being pregnant yet. Apart from the morning sickness and her mood, no one would be the wiser.

He stared at her, a little … annoyed.

"We need to get married," he said.

The words shocked him, but he was able to hide it a lot better than Milah.

"No."

"I'm not accepting no for an answer."

Milah folded her arms and shook her head. "Then how about hell no. Fuck no. Take your pick."

"You're carrying my child."

"Exactly, that is all I'm carrying, but don't for a second think I don't see the disdain in your eyes. Hear it in your voice. No matter what happens between us, I will always be a Russo in your eyes." She growled. "Why not send me and my child away? Isn't that what happens to mistresses? That's all I am because I wasn't good enough to be a wife to a De Luca."

"I've just said you're marrying me."

"And I said I'm not marrying you. I already belong to you because of my father, but that is where it ends. You and he are not going to take another thing I was looking forward to."

Damon stopped and watched her as she tried to leave. He grabbed her hand before she could take another step and pulled her in close. "What the hell is that supposed to mean?"

"None of your business."

"Milah, you have no secrets from me."

"You don't think I don't know that?" she asked. "But this time, you will never find out what I want."

When she pulled out of his hold, he let her go. His gaze followed her until she walked out of his sight, and even then, he couldn't look away. He didn't want to. Milah was a fighter, and he loved that about her.

Damon froze.

He didn't love anything about her.

She was a Russo. There was nothing to love. She meant nothing to him.

Glancing back at the cemetery, he didn't want to go and see his parents, but while he was here, he didn't have much of a choice.

Walking away without showing respect would gnaw at him.

Fucking Milah.

Why couldn't she be someone he found infuriating? Instead, he had to deal with a passionate, caring, and considerate woman.

The perfect woman to be his wife and the mother of his children.

He opened the small gate and stepped through.

He glanced at the stones of his grandparents, but went straight to his parents. Resting against each other. Mother and father.

"Hey, Mom," he said. "Hey, Dad."

No response.

"So, I did it. I got everything we had ever hoped for. Russo is no more. His empire has fallen with no way of rising up. We win."

Silence.

"So why does it feel … wrong? I have a bitter taste in my mouth. Milah Russo is pregnant with my kid. You're going to be grandparents." He didn't know what his father would say if he was right in front of him. "Her child will be a Russo if I don't get her to marry me."

He took a deep breath. "I guess Russo was one step ahead of me. He knew what I'd do with his daughter. This is his … counter fight, isn't it? I didn't ask for Milah's hand in marriage, so, she is now going to be so fucking stubborn. What do I do?" he asked, looking at his parents' graves lying side by side.

They had defeated the odds. Turned an arranged marriage into a love match. He had flashes of memories from birthdays to holidays. When his mother was alive, their house had been filled with love and laughter. It didn't matter the fight that was going on outside or the war constantly raging between the Russos and the De Lucas. So long as they had each other, they could face everything.

Love.

That was what he needed.

He smiled. "So you still have all the answers for me, don't you, Pop? Love. I've got to make Milah fall in love with me. Marry her, and then every single child she has will be a De Luca, and Russo will cease to matter."

It felt right.

There was only one problem. He didn't have a clue on how to make a woman fall in love with him. He was used to them falling all over themselves for him. He never had to put any effort in.

This was … this pissed him off. He had no fucking idea what he was going to do.

Running a hand down his face, he realized he'd won one war only to start another.

Chapter Thirteen

It started with flowers.

Beautiful arrays of colors that stole her breath.

Then came the jewelry. Magnificent pieces with rare and precious gems. The kind that Milah had no idea which was which because she'd never been interested in jewelry. Next, chocolates, from all over the world.

Again, she didn't have an overly sweet tooth, and when she did want to enjoy something sweet, it often came from home baking.

Since becoming pregnant, she missed her mother so much. Being in the kitchen while the staff was preparing food, suffering morning sickness was … difficult. She feared throwing up everywhere.

Which was why, after Damon had come to bed, he made love to her, and this time, it had been love. He'd taken his time, drawing out every single moan and plea she had to offer before finding his orgasm.

She loved being with him.

The sex was incredible, and it was the only time she didn't feel she had to be on guard. They were having sex, which went against all rules that were associated with being a Russo and De Luca. She was tired of that never-ending fight.

Glory had asked her what it was she wanted, and Milah knew it was a direct order from Damon. He wanted to know the final thing her father wasn't going to destroy.

Beating the butter and sugars together like crazy, she got all her aggression out in the mixing.

Since learning she was pregnant, her temper had been at an all-time high. Where she once could ignore Glory's presence and pretend the woman was her friend, she wasn't in the mood to continue it.

She was protecting her unborn child. The doctor had already taken his time to call her, giving her all kinds of advice, and there was a prescription that all pregnant women should take, folic acid. She couldn't recall exactly why she needed to take it or if all pregnant women were indeed forced to take it.

Once the cake batter was made, after finishing up with the flour, she found an ice cream scoop and started to measure them out into the cupcake cases she found. The oven was already pre-heated, and she'd just put them in the oven when Damon's growl met her ears.

"What are you doing?" he asked.

Milah turned toward him, and in the cold of the night, his hair was a mess. He hadn't bothered with a shirt, leaving his heavily inked body on display. She smiled at him. "I'm baking cupcakes, and next on my list is some cookies."

She'd been craving them for so long, she needed to have one, like right now. Cupcakes were a must though. She wanted the buttercream. Actually, now that she thought about it, she wanted to eat two cookies with a cupcake wedged between.

What the hell was wrong with her?

There was no way cravings should be starting already.

"It's after one, Milah. Come back to bed."

She shook her head, weighing out some more butter. "Not happening. I want to bake."

"You can bake in the morning or whenever you want. It doesn't have to be now."

Milah looked at his offered hand. "I can't in the morning, and I'm not going to push the kitchen staff out of this room."

"Damn it, Milah, you are pregnant. You can't just wander around at night. Bake when there are other people around."

"Ugh, you're not listening. It's because I'm pregnant that I can't bake with other people around, okay? The smells in the kitchen are too much. With all the garlic and coffee and onions. I tried and I ended up vomiting. I couldn't stop it, so no, I'm not going to come into the kitchen when everyone is doing their thing. It's not … right."

"Milah?"

"I want to bake something, okay? Is that so hard for you to understand? My mom would do this when my dad wasn't around. You know this." And now she felt the tears starting to fill her eyes. This wasn't what she wanted.

She didn't want to cry in front of Damon.

"Milah, please, don't."

"I don't expect you to understand. I'm pregnant. With your baby. Do you have any idea how hard it is to know that I am hated? That you hate me because of my last name?" She spun away from him, not wanting him to see her tears. They were driving her crazy.

Tears didn't help any situation, and she was never one to cry about her problems.

Damon surprised her as he rounded the counter and pulled her into his arms. "I don't hate you."

"Yes, you do. I'm a Russo."

"You're nothing like your father." He kissed the top of her head. She wanted to believe his sincerity, but it was really hard for her.

"I … Damon, you need to stop sending flowers."

"Not going to happen."

"What are you trying to prove?"

He sighed, letting her go.

She liked his arms around her, but she wasn't going to beg for more. Milah expected him to leave, but instead, he grabbed a chair and sat down at the counter.

"What are you doing?"

"If you want to bake, then go ahead and bake, but I'm not going to let you be alone."

"Why?"

"We're going to have a child together. We're not doing anything on our own. Not anymore."

"Are you trying to get me to marry you?" she asked, her suspicions rising with every second.

He rolled his eyes. "Milah, baby, I could be married to you by the end of tomorrow. I wouldn't even need you to say the official *I do*. I've got men who would be willing to do anything I wanted for a price. When we do marry, it's going to be your choice. You're not going to want to back out."

"You do realize you're making all of this up, don't you?" she asked.

He laughed. "You do realize, one day, you're going to have to eat your words. You want to bake, then bake. I don't mind."

She stepped toward the counter and got to beating again, aware of his gaze on her, and she was cautious. "I don't ... trust this."

Damon chuckled. "So long as you're not poisoning my child, I don't care."

She rested a hand on her stomach. "I'm not."

"Good."

She started to work on the cookies, and the scent of the cupcakes wafted toward her. She dropped everything on the counter and went to the cupcakes. They were not brown yet, but the tray did need turning, which she did, breathing out a sigh of relief as she spun it around.

Damon was a distraction. She had to stay focused.

With the cookie batter made, she was sure to add more vanilla than she needed along with lots of chocolate chips, because that was what she wanted.

Once the cupcakes were out of the oven, she slid the cookies inside.

After a few minutes, she moved the cupcakes to a cooling rack and then got to work on the buttercream frosting, which was the most important part of the entire process.

"What do you hope for?" Damon asked, pulling her out of her thoughts.

"Huh?"

"We've never really talked about the baby and what we'd like to have."

Milah stopped and put a hand on her stomach. "I guess we haven't."

"A boy or a girl?"

"I … I guess I just want whatever comes and to hope they're healthy."

"I agree." He smiled and nodded.

She couldn't help but respond to his smile. "You're happy about being a dad?"

"I never thought I would be. I know I would have to be at some point. You know, continuing the De Luca line."

"I guess."

She remembered her father being so infuriated when her mother would miscarry. They didn't stop trying with her. Her mother made herself sick trying to please Antonio Russo.

"I've upset you."

"No, you haven't upset me. I was just thinking about my dad. He was … so angry that I came along. I was a healthy daughter, but he wanted a son."

"Milah, you are aware that he had more children,

right?"

She nodded. "Yeah, I know, and it's crazy that he didn't allow … any of them to take his name."

"It was the one part he stayed traditional about."

"Yeah, I guess." She shrugged. "Let's not talk about him. It will only upset us." She didn't want to end a baking night on an argument, and they would never agree on their opinions on each other's families.

"Do you miss him?" Damon asked.

"No." She didn't even have to think about the answer.

"No?"

"Do you miss him?" she asked.

"He was my sworn enemy, Milah. Not my father."

"Do you miss your father?"

"All the time."

"Oh." Milah nibbled on her lip. "I didn't have that kind of relationship with my father. He was never the kind of person who wanted a daughter." She forced a smile to her lips. "I'm sorry about your loss."

"Thank you."

Milah tested the cupcakes to see if they were cold enough to have the frosting. They weren't, but the cookies were ready to take out of the oven.

She slowly placed them on a cooling rack, being sure not to break them.

The scent of chocolate made her mouth water. This was what she'd been craving.

"What do you think your dad would think about our … situation?"

"He'd probably slap me silly."

This made Milah pause, and she quickly turned toward him. "He would?"

"Yeah, I knock a girl up, and she doesn't even

have a ring on her finger."

"Damon, I'm not going to marry you."

"You will, when you're ready and you see that we are good for each other."

"Sex doesn't work in a relationship. If it did, most men would marry their mistress."

"Some men do, and let's be fair, you're not really my mistress."

Milah frowned. "I have sex with you and we're not married."

"I'm not married. I'm not seeing you behind my wife's back. Also, we both know I didn't marry you to piss your father off. It was a power play."

"Wow, you're admitting that now."

"I've got nothing to lose. It doesn't mean that my end game wasn't to marry you, Milah. I will. One day."

"And you're totally sure of yourself?"

"I know what I want, and I know who I want it with."

"Oh, yeah, and what is that?"

"I want it all with you. Every single thing. I want to have this baby with you, grow old."

"Damon, stop it. I don't know what you're trying to do, but it's not going to work."

"Take away the De Luca and Russo name. What do we have?" he asked.

"We have nothing. There is nothing between us."

"That's where you're wrong. I know when there is no one to get in our way, we have each other. We have passion. If you actually gave us a chance, I think we'd succeed."

She nibbled on her lip, a little shocked. "Is that what you want? For us to succeed?"

"I lived in a home where my parents loved each other. There was no one else for either of them. I saw the way they both were with each other, and I want that. One day. I miss them both and I know they would be disappointed if I didn't give it a proper shot with the woman carrying my child. You're not a Russo to me, Milah. You're the mother of my child, and if you would give me a chance, a real one, opening your heart to me, I think we could make this work."

As far as honesty went, Damon shocked her.

Did he really feel this way? Should she trust him? Her child was growing inside her, getting bigger every single day.

She'd lived in a home where there was no love. No laughter. Her mother hating when her husband would get home. Milah didn't want to live like that.

Would it be so bad to give Damon a shot?

****

Damon chuckled as he watched Milah walking across the edge of the waves. When he got back home, he was going to give Raoul a fucking bonus. He's asked his friend what he would recommend to win over a woman determined not to want him.

A honeymoon without the wedding.

He could marry Milah in a heartbeat. He hadn't lied about that. There were men willing to do whatever he asked for the right price. What he wanted was to make Milah fall in love with him. To marry him on her own terms.

The flowers hadn't worked.

Neither had the jewelry.

Or the chocolates.

The late-night baking she enjoyed doing had seemed to work. He didn't understand how.

When he'd talked with Raoul, his friend had suggested going away where it was just the two of them. Minimum guards.

Seeing as he had several villas around the world, it wasn't a hardship to bring her to Italy, to his private villa that had a personal access to the beach. They were far enough away from anyone else, and he was free to just be with her.

There were no pressures of the city.

He had expected Milah to ask for Glory to come with them, but she hadn't put in the request.

Glory told him everything about Milah. All the finer details he didn't get to enjoy.

Milah's love of literature and pop music. How she enjoyed dancing when she thought no one was watching.

He wanted Milah to break down those walls and finally open up to him, but with each step forward they seemed to take, another step was taken backward.

Watching as the sun started to set, he saw Milah put her hand on her stomach. She seemed to be doing this more often of late.

Did she love their child? Was she protective of him or her?

Damon watched her, and he couldn't tear his gaze away.

She wore a beautiful pastel-blue summer dress with thin straps. When the sun shone on it at just the right angle, he saw her bare flesh beneath.

Her stomach was rounding nicely, but again, no real sign that there was anything in there. That would take time. He found himself getting excited about the future. At watching his baby grow within her stomach.

Throwing caution to the wind, he ran the small distance between them and rushed toward Milah.

She saw him running, released a scream, and started trying to get away from him, but he wasn't going to let her get away this time. He captured her in his arms, pulling her against him. Spinning her around, he lifted her, and Milah wrapped her legs around his waist. He lowered her slowly to her feet, cupping her face.

Milah tilted her head back to look at him, and as he stared at her lips, he just couldn't resist claiming them. Kissing her mouth, he traced his tongue across her lip, and when she opened, he took full advantage, plunging inside.

She wrapped her arms around his neck, and Damon tugged her to the sand, moving her to straddle his waist.

He didn't break the kiss once.

Milah's pussy rocked against his dick, and he wished they didn't have fucking clothes on, but there would be plenty of time to fuck her when they got back to his villa. For now, he just wanted to kiss her.

"Wow," she said, breaking from the kiss.

"I missed you."

She burst out laughing. "We haven't parted, Damon. You were watching me from the beach."

"And then I wanted to kiss you. Why did you run?"

"I don't know. I think I wanted you to catch me."

"Always." He pushed some of her hair behind her ear. He was quite happy to stay out here for the rest of their lives, but her stomach started to rumble.

"Embarrassing." She buried her head against his neck.

"Not at all. I have a question. In or out?"

"I think I'd like to eat in."

"Done."

He got to his feet and tucked Milah into his side, placing his hand on her hip as they walked back toward his gate. "Are you having fun?" he asked.

"The best kind." She rested her head against his

chest. "I don't know why you brought me here, but I do love it."

"My dad bought this place for my mom as a wedding present."

"He did?"

"Yeah. They had their vacation in Italy. I think in that very villa, but it was rented at the time. She loved it that much, and talked about how perfect it was, my dad wanted to recreate it for her, so he bought it. They spent their anniversaries here. Even after my mom passed, my dad would come here, just to be closer to her."

Milah didn't say anything, and Damon cursed himself for bringing up his parents.

Raoul had advised that he didn't bring up any … bad memories. Anything that could bring the De Luca and Russo feud into play.

"It is a beautiful home," Milah said. "I can see why she liked it."

"My mom would have liked you."

Milah stopped, and even though he could have forced her to keep on moving, he stopped right along with her.

"Don't, Damon."

"It's my life, Milah."

"I know, and I know what happened, so we don't have to keep repeating it."

"I'm not. I'm just sharing this with you, and our baby. That's all."

She nibbled on her lips, and he tugged her close, pressing a kiss to her cheek. "You're going to have to learn to trust me. I haven't said everything to be bad." He kissed her cheek again, and this time, they started to walk, heading back to the house.

Neither of them spoke as they arrived, and Milah excused herself to shower. She had sand in places that really shouldn't have it.

He chuckled, and as she went to the shower, he went into the kitchen, grabbing some food to fire up on the grill. Milah had already made a salad, and there were cheeses, fruits, and some sliced meats. He picked them all up, taking them outside.

The wine was there, but he hadn't opened a bottle as Milah couldn't drink, so he poured them both a glass of water.

By the time Milah arrived, he'd already fired up the grill and had their steaks in the oven.

"Something smells good," Milah said, moving toward him and surprising him as she wrapped her arms around his waist.

"Just doing the grilling."

"A man's job?"

"There's not much I can do to feed us, but grilling is something I can." He was about to tell her that his father taught him, but he decided to keep it to himself.

Milah had no fond parental memories, other than when her father wasn't around, but even then, her mother put training above everything else.

Turning over the steaks, he glanced over at Milah as she walked toward the table. Their lives had been totally different. He was surrounded by war but filled with love in his home. Milah had been surrounded by war everywhere. Her parents' hatred for one another.

"I see you grabbed everything out of the fridge," she said.

"I didn't know what you'd enjoy today." Her food preferences changed daily.

She grabbed a grape, putting it in her mouth with a smile. "I love it all today."

Damon finished with the steaks, putting them on their plates to rest. After setting a plate in front of Milah, he sat down opposite her. She picked up her water and took a sip.

"Are you enjoying it here?" he asked.

"Yes, very much so. I didn't think I would, but this place is so beautiful."

"To us and to the future," he said, lifting his glass.

Milah hesitated.

"What is it?" Raoul had also told him to find the strength to be calm, even when she infuriated him. In the beginning, when he first took her, he found everything about her to be infuriating. The past few weeks, he didn't find her to be like that. Not anymore. He enjoyed her company.

He never admitted this to Raoul or to his father, but there were things about Milah he found adorable, cute, and some he loved.

Like the pups back home. They were still growing, and every single day, Milah played mother to them. Or she did until he recommended they go away together. He had no doubt once they got home, she'd be back to babying the pups. It was something his father would have loved her for. Then there was the fact she loved to cook and bake. Even though it was costing him sleep back home, he loved to watch her in the kitchen. There he got to see her smile, which was another thing he loved.

She had the cutest dimples on her cheeks when she let go and smiled. He'd seen them a lot more in the past few days of being at the villa. What he hadn't gotten the pleasure of seeing was her dancing, and he hoped to see that soon enough.

Milah had the Russo name, but not the true nature of the beast. Her mother had stopped that awful grip of taking hold of her daughter, and Damon was so fucking happy with that.

"I … do you think we should toast to the future with us?"

"Milah, the last few days have told me that when we're not fighting or allowing this family feud to get in the way, you and I are good together. Haven't you enjoyed the past couple of days?"

She nodded.

"Then why can't we have a future? Nothing is holding us back. There is just you and me."

Milah stared at his glass, and he got to see those dimples once again. "You're right. To us and to the future."

He winked at her and took a sip.

"How about we go for a swim tonight?" Damon asked.

Milah nodded, popping a tomato in her mouth. She chewed for several seconds before swallowing. "I like that idea."

They ate their food, and Damon couldn't take his gaze away from Milah. They didn't talk, but it wasn't awkward.

This was their newfound freedom, he believed.

He noticed the way Milah kept sneaking glances his way, and he had to smile, he just couldn't help himself.

Milah was falling for him, and that was all part of the plan. It wouldn't be long before she was confessing her feelings and marrying him. Then he'd have his true revenge on the Russo family.

Even as he thought it, Damon couldn't help but look at Milah and that smile. She was so beautiful.

Chapter Fourteen

They'd been at the villa for a week when Damon had no choice but to return home. There was no way Milah was going to stay behind, so she followed him back to his country home.

He left for the city, and to avoid Glory, Milah explored his home.

She never tried to leave, so the guards were told to let her explore, and to do that, she got to find every single nook and cranny, including the large expanse of the attic.

The bedroom on the top floor had an access point. With no one around, she pulled the lever that lowered the steps, and she looked around to see if anyone would see her.

After climbing the steps, she glanced around the attic and couldn't make out anything. There was not enough light.

Descending the steps, she rummaged around the room and found a flashlight that had some working batteries. Once again, she made her way up into the attic, and for a second, she debated if she should do this. A lot of bad things happened in attics in horror movies.

Pushing aside her silly thoughts, she shone the flashlight around the room, and there was no big bad monster threatening her. She breathed a sigh of relief, but she heard a commotion coming toward the room.

Glory had become rather persistent of late, and she didn't wish to upset the young woman. Pulling the steps up, Milah sealed herself into the attic just as the door to the room opened.

"I'm sure she is fine," James said.

Glory released a growl of frustration. "Damon told me I have to keep an eye on her. He doesn't want anything to happen to the baby."

"Milah can take care. She is a good woman, Glory."

"I know. I know, but … I … think she knows that Damon, you know?"

"Asked you to be his spy?"

"I don't like doing it, okay? Milah is … she is so nice and sweet, but I think she knows. She is more closed off now than ever before. I just hope she knows that I'm her friend, regardless."

Milah refused to feel bad. She didn't just have herself to worry about anymore, but her child as well.

James and Glory talked for a short time and then left.

Milah didn't want to leave the safety of the attic. Turning the flashlight back on, she glanced around the space. There was nothing there. She took her time, shining the light on every single thing, and then stopped. Tucked away, right in front of her, behind a beam, was a box.

She reached for it, blowing off the dust that had settled over it. The lock was hanging free, and she removed it, opening the box to find a … book.

Shining the light on it, she saw it was a leather-bound book with no distinctive patterns. Milah picked it up, glanced over it, and then opened it up to the first page.

I was taken today.

Men came, threw a bag over my head, and there was darkness. I'd never been so afraid in my life. I didn't know where they were taking me, but then I saw him, a De Luca, not just anyone, but, Valentino De Luca. My father was going to marry me off, and now I'm trapped.

I've only met Valentino a couple of times before

at social events. Parties, and each time, he has ... intrigued me. Unlike some men who leer at me, telling me how beautiful I am, Valentino looks into my eyes. He doesn't stare at my body. He sees me.

No one else has ever seen me.

Milah slammed the book closed. This couldn't be. There was no way ... was this *the* Alicia Russo?

She'd heard whispered tales of the most beautiful Russo being stolen away by a De Luca, but that tale was dark. It was deadly.

What the fuck was this?

Turning to the front page, Milah looked over the words again.

She couldn't remember exactly what happened to Alicia Russo. She hadn't been the first daughter, but her beauty had been legendary.

Milah didn't know if she wanted to read more or ignore it.

Would it be so bad to read about her relative? She wasn't a grandmother but a great aunt to her.

Opening the book, she started to read once more.

I was a prisoner once again. I had tried to run away from my father, but my brother, Antonio had dragged me back. Like always, he was our father's puppet. The firstborn son. He already coveted the ring he so desperately wanted. Of course, he already had a son of the same name.

Milah paused and did a rough calculation. Antonio, Alicia's brother, would be her grandfather, which meant the son he had would be her father.

Wow, why didn't people name their kids something different?

"Don't you worry, little person. You're either going to be called Daniel or … Georgina, or something. You're not going to have the same name as anyone in my family, or your daddy's."

She hadn't thought of Damon being a father, but at that moment, she very much knew it.

This was going to be bad. Part of her didn't want to read this book. She had never met Alicia Russo before.

Valentino told me today that I was not going to belong to anyone but him. He would not allow my father to marry me off to anyone else. He owned me. No one else. There is no way a marriage could ever happen between us.

I'm a woman, but I'm not a fool.

De Lucas and Russos have feuded for generations. I don't even know why they did, and to be honest, I'm starting to think they don't know either.

So, he keeps me prisoner.

There are nights he comes to my room, and even though he doesn't touch me, he tells me to scream. He tells me to beg him. I don't understand why he is doing this, but each time he orders me, I do as I'm told.

I guess my father's teaching has been good for something.

Not once has he raised a hand to me. There is no hatred in his gaze. No anger. Sometimes, he will bang his fist against the door, throw precious items. He broke a lamp that was so beautiful, it surprised me. The room would always look a mess, and then he'd come to me, tell me to cry, and as I started to weep, he'd tear at my gown.

When his maids came, I looked a mess. It looked like … he raped me. I don't understand it.

Milah stopped reading and frowned. "What the

fuck?" Was Valentino mental? Why had he acted that way?

Blowing out a breath, she read on.

Valentino kept Alicia prisoner for days, if not weeks. The only solace Alicia had was to sneak her writings into this book. To tell of the time she spent.

The irony was not lost on Milah that even though kept as a De Luca prisoner, Alicia found a sense of freedom.

As the day wore on, Milah had no choice but to put the book away and make her way out of the attic. She hadn't put the catch on the stairs, so she was able to lower it and to climb down.

No one had found her.

Leaving the bedroom, she put her hand on the door and wondered if this was the very room where Alicia Russo was kept. There was so much about her family history she didn't know. Tomorrow, she'd find time to hide and to read more.

She needed to know what was going on between Valentino and Alicia.

Why would the mad De Luca pretend to rape Alicia? Why go to that extreme? She had heard Valentino was mad beyond understanding.

Milah rounded the corner and gasped as she came face to face with Damon. "Crap, fuck, Jesus."

"Wow, not what I was expecting."

"Do you have to go sneaking around everywhere?" she asked, putting a hand to her chest.

Her heart raced. She felt like she'd stumbled onto something important. Something forbidden that she shouldn't have been privy to, and yet, it also felt good to finally read something from an aunt she never got to know.

"This is my house," he said.

SAM CRESCENT

"Of course, it is. It is your right to go sneaking about wherever you want." She forced a smile. "Did business go well?"

"Better than expected. Would you like to go out with me tonight?" he asked.

She frowned. "Where?"

"I want to take you out to dinner."

"Why?"

"Can't a man and a woman enjoy each other's company without all the troubles that come with it?"

She pursed her lips and watched him. "I don't know. I guess it depends on what you're hoping to achieve."

"I'm not hoping to achieve anything. I just want the pleasure of your company, that is all. We've got a family to enjoy, Milah." He reached out and pressed his palm flat against her stomach, taking her completely by surprise. This was the first time he'd openly touched her like this.

Her mouth went a little dry.

Staring into his dark gaze, she had to wonder what he was thinking. What was going on in that head of his? Did she even want to know?

She sank her teeth into her bottom lip, already knowing the answer was yes. She did want to know what was going on inside his head. He was a mystery to her. One she hoped to take the time to uncover.

"Okay," she said.

"Glory's waiting for you to get changed. She will be helping you. You've got half an hour."

Milah didn't need that long to get changed. With Glory waiting for her, it kind of sucked the wind right out of her sails.

Glory.

The woman who was only pretending to be her

211

friend.

She kept a smile on her lips even as she followed Damon down the main stairs, heading to the bedroom they now shared.

Glory waited inside.

"Mr. De Luca has bought you a beautiful dress," Glory said.

"Yes, of course." She didn't know what else to say to her, so she followed the other woman into the bathroom. Glory stayed close by while she took a shower. She tried not to be affected by the woman's closeness, but it was kind of hard to ignore her.

She wanted to order her away, but that would have been cruel.

"Are you excited about tonight?" Glory asked.

"Yes."

"It sounds nice."

Milah agreed. She washed her body quickly and then rinsed her hair with some conditioner before stepping out. Glory was there with a towel, rubbing at her hair. "I can do that."

"I know, but I would like to help."

"No," Milah said. She was done playing this game. "I can take care of myself, Glory. I appreciate it." Clearly, she wasn't ready to call the other woman out on her games.

What happened to Alicia?

What happened to Valentino?

There were so many questions, and all she wanted to do was go and read that damn book.

"I tried looking for you today," Glory said. "The pups missed you."

"I went exploring the grounds once I took care of the pups," Milah said. "I don't like being cooped up for too long. I like to be outside."

Glory nodded. "You look beautiful."

"Thank you."

"I … thank you for being my friend," Glory said.

Milah glanced at her in the mirror, and she wanted to ask, to finally get it out in the open, but instead, she continued on as normal. A smile.

The lies were still forming between them. They were not friends.

"I'm nearly ready," Milah said. "Do you want to go tell Damon?"

The dress Glory had helped her into was on the tight side. Her stomach wasn't getting smaller, but much bigger. She felt a little swollen today.

Glory left the room, and as soon as she did, Milah collapsed on the edge of the bed.

"I know I was being a little mean there, but she's … she's not my friend. She works for Damon. Your daddy." She scrunched up her face. That was certainly a sentence she never hoped to string together. "I can't tell anyone this, but I think … I think I like him, and that is so fucking scary, and I'm going to try and not curse so much anymore. You've already got the Russo and De Luca genes, let's not add to it."

She rubbed her stomach, already feeling a great deal of love for the little baby growing inside her.

Regardless of how she felt about her baby's father, she knew without a doubt she loved her child.

****

Dinner.

Damon had spent way too much time working lately, and he didn't want Milah to feel rejected.

A nice, candlelit dinner. Soft music. The restaurant had other guests, and Milah looked so beautiful.

Glory had reported to him that Milah had gone

missing. They couldn't find her, but all the guards he spoke with told him that she'd been in the house the whole time. Was she trying to hide from Glory?

If so, why?

Why didn't she want to be with Glory? Did she know he used the maid to gain information?

"You look stunning tonight," he said.

"And you're full of compliments tonight. You look very handsome yourself."

He ran his hand down his jacket. "I tried."

The waiter came and poured them both some water. Milah thanked the waiter.

In his breast pocket, he felt the wedding band he had taken the time to pick out. Raoul had told him he'd been acting too hasty, but he'd wanted to get the ring and not miss an opportunity like this.

They were surrounded by people.

Milah was pregnant with his child. She was going to give birth as his wife.

"This is a nice place," Milah said.

"Milah, I know we got off on the wrong foot."

"Really? You could have fooled me," she said, laughing.

"I'm being serious."

"I'm joking, Damon. Come on, we can't be too serious." She smiled at him. "Our circumstances can't be changed but we're here now."

"True." He lifted his glass and took a long swig. "You're an amazing woman. Kind. Thoughtful. I didn't know enough about you when I made that deal with your father." He reached into his jacket pocket, and Milah's gaze went wide.

She reached over the table and put her hand on top of his. "Stop this."

"Milah!"

"I haven't asked for much, but I am begging you, not to … do this here."

He glanced around the room. Damon figured she could turn down a proposal when it was just the two of them, but in a roomful of diners, she'd struggle to do so.

"Milah."

"Damon, don't."

"I want to be a good man to you. A father to our child. I want to make up for everything that I've done, and the only way to do that is if you give me a chance."

Milah shook her head, and he saw the tears glinting in her eyes.

He was about to get on one knee and do a big speech, but Milah shocked him as she shoved her chair away from the table and stormed out of the restaurant.

Damon saw they'd gained some attention, but he sent a glare their way, forcing them to look away. No one paid him any attention as he rushed out of the restaurant. The shoes Milah wore were on the high side, so she didn't get very far.

His guards had always been warned to constantly keep an eye on her and to keep their distance.

"Milah!" He yelled her name.

"No, Damon. That's why you wanted me to go to a nice and fancy restaurant with you, isn't it?" she asked. "It has nothing to do with me or the baby, or to just spend some time together. It was an ulterior motive. Were those people actors?"

"Why don't you stop running away, and stand and talk to me?"

Milah spun around, and he saw tears running down her face. Ever since she'd gotten pregnant, she'd been more emotional, and he knew he was the one to blame.

"Talk to you?" She stepped up toward him. "How

can I talk to you when you clearly don't listen?" She stomped her foot on the ground and then growled. "I'm not doing this. We're not doing this."

"Milah, you're the fucking mother of my child."

"That is all I'm ever going to be. I told you once, and I will tell you again, I am not marrying you. You're not going to take away the one thing that even my father hadn't been able to take from me."

"Oh, yeah, and what is that?" he asked.

"Why should I tell you?"

He grabbed her arm as she tried to walk away.

"Get your hands off me." She tried to pull away. He didn't have a hard grip on her, but it was enough to stop her in her tracks.

"Tell me what you want," he said. "Name your fucking price. Tell me what it will take for me to get what I want."

"Is that all you care about? Getting what you want?" Milah asked. "You know what, I don't even know why I bothered to ask. Of course, that is all you care about, because that is all you know." She shook her head. "I'm not doing this here with you."

She spun on her heel, and Damon couldn't help but admire the curves of her ass. He wanted her.

Some men would find the constant fighting, the passion, too much to handle, but not him. No, he found this banter between them a turn-on. He looked forward to being with her. The women he'd been with in the past had all tripped all over themselves to be the woman he wanted, rather than be themselves. They wanted him to like them, to love them, but he'd found them so fucking boring.

Not Milah.

Never fucking Milah.

She never bored him.

"What is it with you women?" he asked, raising his voice. There was no one else around. It was just the two of them, as well as his men, keeping guard. "Why can't you just tell me straight exactly what you want? Why do you have to keep me guessing? I'm not a fucking genius. I can't read your fucking mind."

"Love!" Milah screamed the word, turning back to face him.

Her cheeks were red. Her hands clenched.

"That's the big secret. You can mock me if you want. Have a big old laugh about it because that's what the Russo woman wants."

Damon didn't know what to say.

"You've got nothing to come back at me? How I'm such a horrible person that no one will ever love me? How my name drives people away? Tell me, Damon, is that what you wanted to hear? I bet I look pathetic to you." She shook her head, and he saw a new trail of tears running down her face.

"Milah, stop."

"Just leave me alone, Damon."

"No, I can't do that."

"Why not?" she asked. "Because you love me?"

He gritted his teeth.

"Let's face it, Damon, I'd be dead right now if it wasn't for this baby."

"I never had any plans to kill you."

She laughed, but the sound was hollow. "Yeah, right. Of course, I'm going to believe that."

"You can believe what you want to. It's not going to change anything. I'm not going to tell you that I love you, Milah, because I don't. I care about you, and for now, that is going to be enough."

"And that's why I won't marry you." She put her hands on her stomach. She had moved toward the curb.

There were no cars coming or going.

He glanced back at his men to see they were still guarding, keeping a distance to allow them some semblance of privacy but not too far that they couldn't protect them if it was needed.

"Milah, do you think that is the only child we're going to have?" he asked.

"Yes."

He took a step toward her, but she stepped off the curb, and he had no choice but to stand perfectly still.

"I'm not like your dad," he said. "I'm not going to sleep with other women. Unlike yours, my parents loved each other. I was raised in a happy family. Full of love and support. I don't have half-siblings running around the globe. There is only me," Damon said. "And like it or not, it is only you and me, and that is not going to change. You're my woman, Milah."

"You can't stand me."

"Not true. It was your father I couldn't stand. You're your own person, and I see that. I see that you and me, we can make this work. It didn't start out as love, but it sure as hell doesn't mean it might not end like it."

He took a chance and stepped toward her. Milah didn't move.

"I never took you as a coward or someone who would take the easy way out," he said, moving a little closer. He didn't like this distance between them. He wanted her in his arms.

"Damon?"

"I'm not saying this is going to be easy. Fuck, is it going to be easy? You're a giant pain in the ass and that was before you even got pregnant." When he was close enough, he reached out and brushed some of her hair off her cheek, tucking it behind her ear. He grabbed the back of her neck and pulled her against him. She stumbled, but like so many times before, he was there to capture her.

He had no intention of letting her go.

Staring into her gorgeous blue eyes, Damon had a feeling he could look at them for a lifetime and that still wouldn't be enough.

"I can't promise that every single day will be easy. I doubt it will. This is you and me. We're going to set fire to this world, and we're going to get the chance to see it burn, and I know it is going to be one mighty fucking flame. What I do know is that there is no one else I want to do it with."

"You know, you're turning this into quite the proposal," she said.

"You'll remember this day for many to come." He stroked the back of her neck. "I'm not taking anything away from you, Milah. I'm trying to offer you my world. All you've got to do is be willing to take a chance with it." He pressed his face against her neck. "Because I'm willing to dive all in. No turning back. You and me."

She was still tight within his arms, and he didn't know if he'd won her over. This wasn't a speech he'd practiced. This had come straight from his heart, and he meant every single word.

"You're not going to hurt me?" she asked.

"Never."

"If you do want someone else, you'll tell me?"

"It's not going to happen. I will be a good husband to you, Milah. A good husband and a damn fine father."

Milah nodded. "Yes."

"Yes?"

"Yes, I'll marry you." She nibbled on her lip, and

he reached into his jacket pocket, taking the engagement ring out of the box. "That's massive."

"You can change it if you want. My dad gave this to my mother on their engagement. With how their marriage turned out, I think it might be a good luck charm."

Milah smiled.

The ring fit perfectly as if it had been made for her.

He hadn't done any adjustments, nor had he changed the ring for Milah.

Pulling her against him, he pressed a kiss to her lips, smiling at her. She finally had his ring. Now, he needed to get her down the aisle.

"Get down!" his man suddenly yelled.

Gunfire rained down, and Damon pulled Milah into his arms, pushing her to the ground.

"Russo whore!"

Damon looked up ahead as his men fired at the car that had been intent on killing Milah.

Getting to his feet, he pulled out his gun and fired, taking out one of the tires as he did so.

They would insult his woman.

How fucking dare they?

Rage made his hands shake. This was not the proposal he wanted to remember.

"Sir, there's blood."

He turned to see one of his men had gone to his knee beside Milah.

Blood coated the pavement against her chest on her right side.

"She got hit," his guard said.

"You two, chase that fucking car. I want the men responsible." He lifted Milah into his arms. "Call the doctor, tell him I'm about to make a house call."

"Milah, talk to me," he said.

"They were trying to kill me." Her voice sounded a little faint.

"Fuck, the baby. Talk to me, Milah. Don't fade away. I've got you. Please, come on. I'm here." He carried her across the street, going back to the restaurant where his car was already waiting.

He eased her into the backseat, following in behind her and holding her close.

Her eyes were closed, and panic hit him hard. "Milah, fucking talk to me, baby. Don't you go to sleep. There is no time to sleep. Not now. Not now."

She had to stay awake. Nothing could happen to her.

Not now.

Not ... fucking ever. He wouldn't allow it.

Milah couldn't die. There was no way he could live without her.

Chapter Fifteen

Dates and times mean nothing to me. I have no real indication of how much time has passed, unless I count this book, and I found this by accident. I'm well-fed and taken care of. Clothes are always provided for me, and until last night, I'd eaten dinner in my room.

Last night, Valentino came for me.

I expected the worst. Another night of forced screaming, but instead, he asked me if I'd join him for dinner.

He was so ... polite about it.

I'd never known a man to be so sweet.

He looked so scary. What man wouldn't with the few scars I saw peeking out from beneath the collar of his shirt. That's another thing I like about him, he's always looking rather dashing. He is a man in constant control.

When I'm with him around his home, I notice how his men respect him.

All of them do.

Not a single one gives me a sneer, even though I sense their judgment. I'm a Russo, so to them, I'm the enemy. Always the enemy.

There's nothing I can do to change that.

We walked down to dinner together, and I didn't feel like a prisoner. His maids served us, and he demanded they left us alone, and I wasn't frightened of him.

If I'd been at home, I would've been terrified of what was to come. My father wasn't a nice man. He was one hungry for power.

Did I miss home?

I hate to admit it, but seeing as I'm only writing in this book and not saying it aloud, no, I don't.

There's nothing to miss.

The endless threats of being forced into a marriage. The constant attacks. There is nothing I miss. Absolutely nothing. Why would I?

Valentino is a different kind of man. He's sweet, kind, and he makes my heart flutter. I can't believe I'm admitting that, but I am.

Even when he comes to the bedroom, and I have to scream, to me, it's just a game we're playing.

How I wish I knew what was going on inside that head of his.

Did he want me for himself?

Was this a power play?

So many questions, and I'm almost terrified to go hunting for the answers.

Would there be any point?

When my father takes me, there will be no hope for me. He's told me many times that men are only interested in virgins and with the rumors running rife around this very house, there is going to be no doubt whatsoever that I'm not a virgin.

Why does he do it?

Does he care?

****

We shared more meals together. I've lost count of the number of times he's come for me. Each night is the same. There is always a beautiful dress waiting for me. There's a sweet maid to help me change into. She works for Valentino.

Whatever I ask for is in my hands within hours.

A book.

A trinket.

There is nothing too much, and I don't know how it happens. I just know that I ... enjoy it.

I love being with Valentino De Luca, and the man

hasn't even kissed me yet. I'm starting to think he has no feelings for me at all.

Each night, we'll enjoy a nice, long meal together. I've never been one for a sweet tooth, but I will request dessert just to make my time with him last.

I find him so intoxicating.

What is wrong with me?

He stole me away. Took me from a life I knew, one that I hated more than anything in the world, and I'm ... happy.

Is it wrong for me to be happy?

My dad would have slapped me silly by now.

Valentino always asks me about my day. He wants to know if I had a good day. A bad one. What he could do to help improve my time with him.

How do I tell him that the only thing I want is a guarantee to never take me back? To never let my father get to me?

Even if he doesn't love me or care for me. I would settle for him having the mildest of feelings because I think I feel enough for him for the two of us. Is that so wrong?

I hate this.

I don't want to cry, but as I write this, I am.

Does he not know how I feel? How it feels to have his hands on me? After dinner, dessert, and a nightcap, he'd escort me back to my room, hand at the base of my spine. Some nights, he'd come into my room, where he'd give me demands. Nothing was ever inappropriate. If he needed me to change, he turned his back, or asked for me to change in the bathroom.

Does he want me?

Am I a fool for pushing this?

I... I ... I think I'm in love with Valentino De Luca, and I know in the end, those feelings would get me killed.

****

It happened!

Oh, my God. I cannot believe I get to write this, but Valentino De Luca, I have to write his name, to remind myself over and over again, that it happened. He finally kissed me. Not a sloppy drunken kiss, but something so much more.

His fingers danced in my hair. His gaze was on mine.

My entire body was frozen in anticipation, hungry for every look, every single touch. I've been wanting this kiss for some time, and I don't even know what led up to it. Maybe I do, a little.

Another dinner.

Another conversation that was going nowhere, and then I asked him why I was here. What did he hope to achieve? He told me. He told me that I was to be set free. I'm a rare and precious bird, and he saw me locked within the Russo cage, begging to get out. That he'd seen me so many times, broken. Each time he saw me, it was like another piece of my wings had been clipped, and he couldn't allow that to happen.

A bird.

Clipped wings.

He had no idea.

I told him he was a fool and that he was to send me back immediately. Things got a little ... heated.

I yelled at him. I screamed that he was a fool. That no one in their right mind would pretend to rape a girl to start some vicious rumors. That the lies he kept manipulating would hurt him and his people in the long run. Once my father found out the truth and that I was a virgin, and could be sold to whomever he chose, Valentino would be nothing more than a liar and a

225

laughingstock.

Oh, my.

I don't know what part of my rant set him off, but in the next second, his hand was in my hair, cradling my head, and his gaze was fierce. Like I had finally lit a fire inside him, and there had been no way to put it out.

He told me that no other man was ever going to know me. That I was his, and I needed to learn to accept it, and then, his lips were on mine.

I thought chocolate was supposed to send you to heaven, but I now know it's Valentino's kisses. Each and every single one of them.

My lips still feel tender.

His kiss was fire.

The heat, I never want to forget it.

I've never been kissed like that.

Under the mistletoe, I have. The drunken, sloppy kind of kisses where men forgot themselves, but never with full control.

Never like this.

This was a dream.

I loved every second of it, and what was more, I wanted to keep on kissing him.

I didn't want it to stop, but his guard had alerted him to some trouble, and there was no way for me to stop it.

How can I make him kiss me again? Would I look desperate if I ask him? Do I ... kiss him?

I don't know these rules. I've never cared to know, but for Valentino, I'm anxious to find out more. So much more.

****

Trouble is happening between De Luca and Russo.

This is not news to me.

SAM CRESCENT

Valentino called me into his office, forced me to sit down, and even poured me a whiskey. It was disgusting. I've only ever been allowed to drink wine or champagne. My father felt it was rather unseemly for a woman to be seen drinking anything that was designed for a man.

Men could keep the whiskey. It's gross.

With the war picking up speed, Valentino had told me everything. This was news to me.

I'm a woman. My father ignored me. Always did.

I was to be seen and not heard. To look pretty for my husband, but to keep my mouth shut.

Just thinking of all the rules my father imposed on me made me hate him even more.

Valentino looked me in the eye and asked me if I wanted to leave. If I wanted to go back home. The decision was mine.

He said I could have a day to think about it.

I didn't need a day, or an hour, or even ten minutes. I told him I didn't want to leave. He looked ... shocked.

This did make me smile.

Feeling bold, I got to my feet, and I don't know if it was because I've been living with Valentino for some time now, or just because I wanted to. But I approached him. He pushed his chair out a little as I stepped in front of him, and then, I sat on his lap, straddling him and wrapping my arms around his neck. I kissed him, hard.

Valentino's arms were wrapped around me.

The moment he grabbed my ass, I felt alive.

I wanted his touch.

With Valentino, I wanted everything with him.

I know it's a risk.

He's my enemy.

I'm a Russo.

227

He is a De Luca.

There is no chance between us. We will not work.

Our lives are constantly against it.

But when we're together, I can't help but feel differently..

I'm alive.

I'd give everything, even if it means to only be his mistress. I'm happy with him, and I hope he is happy with me. I won't go home. If Valentino will have me, I will stay with him.

****

Last night, I did it.

I ... went to Valentino De Luca's room.

I'd noticed my bedroom door was left unlocked the other night, and rather than ignore it, I decided to act on these feelings. Of course, Valentino could reject me. I'd accept it and go back to my father, without a word.

But our kisses were not losing their passion.

So, I recalled the path I'd been taken that first night, finding De Luca's bedroom with ease. The door had been open slightly. No guards interrupted me.

I wasn't stopped.

I wasn't sent back to my room.

I stepped into Valentino's room without fear.

He waited for me. In a robe.

He looked up and told me to close the door.

This was all my choice. My decision.

When I moved toward him, Valentino cupped my face and told me there was no going back.

I told him that I didn't want to leave. I told him that I wanted to stay with him.

Last night was amazing. He held me in his arms, made love to me, worshipped me. The pain was minimal.

I know I'm in love with Valentino De Luca, and I would do anything to be with him. Settle for a life as his

mistress. I'd be anything, just so long as I was with him.
****

Four months later

Milah closed the book and smiled.

Alicia Russo fell in love with Valentino De Luca. This was not the tale she had heard, but it was one that lightened her own heart.

Putting her hand on her swollen stomach, she gave it a pat.

"There is hope, my sweet girl. Always hope."

The past four months had been a little crazy. After she'd been shot, it hadn't been so bad. The doctor had referred to it as a through and through. Not exactly a nice way to think about her injury. It had hurt for several weeks after, but Damon had been so attentive.

On his last visit, the doctor had advised that she take better care of herself as he felt like Damon wouldn't survive it. He'd been so scared of losing her.

Damon hadn't said anything of his feelings to her.

Why would he? There was nothing to be said.

There were times that Damon was a little like Valentino. Apart from the nightly visits to create vicious rumors.

Damon had sent her to that open dungeon with the rats and the elements. The memory was enough to make her skin crawl. Since that moment, she had known only luxury.

Damon didn't love her.

She glanced down at the ring on her finger. He was currently organizing all the arrangements for their wedding. He wanted to marry her quickly.

She'd requested that her wound be healed before the wedding, and now that it was, he was going full speed ahead.

It didn't help that her dress had to be modified

every single week because the baby she carried was widening her waistline at an alarming rate.

"I still love you, sweet baby."

They didn't know the sex of the child.

The doctor had said to them on their last checkup that he could tell them, but Damon had insisted on waiting. She liked that.

Either a boy or a girl. She didn't care which, just so long as her child was healthy.

According to Alicia's writings, her father was only interested in his sons to carry on the family line. All the daughters were used as business deals. Pawns to be used and sold at his whim.

Kind of like her own father.

Valentino had saved Alicia from a life of pain and regret. He'd loved her.

Even though she hadn't read those words, she knew Alicia loved him. His actions spoke louder than the words that could be said.

Sliding the book back into its case, she placed it in the same position she did each time.

It had taken her a long time to read so far. Alicia's scribbles were hard to decipher, especially when she was happy or excited about something.

She particularly liked the writings of the day in the snow. It had fallen thick and fast. Valentino had forced her to dress up well for the weather, and he'd escorted her outside. It had been a wonder to read how he'd shaken off his stilted captor suit and enjoyed the afternoon with her. They had gotten into a snowball fight, and it was the first time Alicia had felt the evidence of his arousal.

Milah smiled, just thinking about it.

Their romance was like a crazy storm. She loved it.

Climbing down the ladder, she took her time, not wanting to fall and hurt herself. She only got the chance to sneak off when Damon was busy or away. She used this place as a chance to escape. With the stairs to the attic neatly folded away, she glanced around the room. She wondered if this was the room where Alicia had stayed. If so, it had been fully remodeled.

Her aunt sounded kickass.

Milah could relate to her so much. Her life with her father had been a horrible, confined one. There had been no peace, and certainly no freedom.

Even though Damon had kept her locked up in a bedroom for some time, there had still been more freedom.

Each meal time, they talked.

In the past four months since she'd been shot, it was like a barrier had broken down between them. He no longer saw her as a Russo, and she didn't see him as a De Luca.

They were going to be parents. Sharing a baby together.

Leaving the bedroom, she headed downstairs just as Glory was coming toward her.

"Mr. De Luca is waiting for you," Glory said.

Milah frowned and glanced at the time.

It was nearly six o'clock in the evening.

She had completely lost all sense of time and reality.

"I'm so sorry."

"I couldn't find you," Glory said.

"It's fine."

She walked downstairs, making her way toward the main dining room, not wanting to be late.

Damon was already at the table as she entered, and the scents filling the room made her aware that food had already been served.

Guilt gnawed at her as she rushed toward her seat.

He got up and helped her sit down.

She wasn't that far into her pregnancy that she couldn't sit or stand on her own. The time would come though. The giant ball in front of her was not deflating.

"Where have you been?" Damon asked.

"I'm sorry. I was exploring. Got tired and slept in one of the guest bedrooms. I didn't mean to be gone for so long." She offered him a smile.

He took her hand, pressing a kiss to her inner wrist. "I have something for you."

"Damon, you don't need to get me gifts."

"I know, but the moment I saw this, I couldn't resist, and you can't blame me until you see it."

Milah rolled her eyes, and then, she felt herself falling a little more in love with Damon De Luca as he held up a small baby romper. It was a plain white one.

"Oh, my," Milah said.

"I figured it was time we started to prepare."

Milah took the romper and pressed it to her face. "I love it."

"Good, because if you love that, then you will love this."

He pulled out of a small bag a pair of baby shoes, and Milah gasped at the cuteness of them.

"They're gorgeous."

"I know."

Milah got to her feet and threw her arms around his neck, pressing kisses on his cheek. "I love them."

Damon held her tighter. "Expect more of them."

"Our baby is going to be very spoiled, and I'm totally going to blame you."

"I'm the father. I can spend all my time spoiling

my son or daughter."

Milah kissed him again and went to her chair. "You really don't mind what we have?"

"Not at all."

"If our parents could see us now," Milah said and regretted it instantly.

"Some would be turning in their grave, others would be happy for us, I'm sure."

She nibbled on her lips as Damon served her some pasta. Her cravings had been driving her crazy. She had asked the new chef to make her a caramel sauce and chocolate pasta. Damon had looked at her like she'd gone mad, but it had been so good. However, now, the thought of eating that made her feel sick.

"What about …Valentino De Luca?" Milah asked.

Damon paused. It was only for a second, and if she hadn't been watching him, she would've missed it.

"How do you know that name?"

"Valentino was at the graveyard with your parents, and everyone knows the tale of the stolen Russo beauty."

Damon smiled, but it didn't quite reach his lips. "There are a lot of vicious rumors surrounding our relatives. Especially Valentino and Alicia. I have heard many variations myself. Tell me which ones you've heard."

"Just the two. One was that he raped her because he was mad and wanted her beauty for himself. Another is that they fell in love, but Alicia wanted to go home, and he wouldn't let her, so he killed her."

"I wasn't born when it happened," Damon said. "My grandfather was always a good man. I know my dad wasn't always happy with him. I don't know the truth and he was never forthcoming with what really happened."

"Oh," she said.

"Let's move on to more pleasant business."

He held out a notebook, and it was filled with different sets of flowers. Then there were napkins.

Milah looked at the selection, and she knew what Damon was trying to do. He was forcing her to make decisions on her wedding, even though she hadn't exactly been prepared to do so.

"Damon, please, I trust you."

"Milah, this is your wedding as well. I'm not going to make all the decisions. Also, you need to work on your vows."

"I thought this wedding was going to be a small event. There were no vows necessary."

Damon smiled. "When have you ever known a De Luca to do things by halves?"

"I guess you're right. It's all in or nothing, right?"

"Exactly how we roll."

Milah twirled her fork in the spaghetti, put a large serving into her mouth, and started to chew while also looking at the flowers, napkins, and there were even cake decorations.

She pointed at a cream-colored napkin that had their initials. She settled on white and red roses. The color of innocence and passion, which was how she felt their relationship was.

She finished her food as Damon pulled out a menu, and this time, she did groan. "Does it matter what they eat?" she asked.

"You're going to remember this day for years to come. I want it to be a special one. Full of all your favorite things. Trust me."

He took her hand once again and kissed her knuckles. She fell a little harder for him.

"Fine."

For the next thirty minutes, over a nice hot chocolate, they came to an agreement on the meal. He was going to handle the caterers.

"I can't believe we're getting married."

"It will finally put an end to the rumors surrounding us."

"What kind of rumors?" Milah asked.

"How I stole you away to keep you all to myself. How I'm like Valentino."

"They're accusing you of raping me?"

"And far worse."

"I'm sorry." She wrinkled her nose.

"I've had plenty said about me behind my back, sweet. Don't worry about it."

"Sweet?"

"Can I not call you precious names? You are soon going to be the mother of my child." He lifted her wrist and pressed a kiss to her pulse.

"What if he loved her?" Milah asked.

"What?"

"What if Valentino loved my aunt Alicia, and he took her to protect her because he knew deep down that there was a fate worse for her if she stayed."

"I don't know why you're so obsessed with this, but it doesn't matter. Alicia never survived what happened, and my grandfather, he'd later marry, have my father, and be known as one of the worst De Lucas to ever live."

She couldn't help but feel there was more to the man that she had hated just on nasty rumors alone.

What was the true ending of Alicia Russo and Valentino De Luca? And were she and Damon going to relive that same ending?

Chapter Sixteen

Damon stared at his fiancée as she rubbed some kind of cream into her hands. She wore a white negligee that, in the low light, showed off her body to perfection. It was indecent, and he loved it.

He bought it for her.

Ever since Milah had been shot in front of his eyes, and he'd feared her death, something had changed inside him. He couldn't put his finger on it, and he didn't quite understand it, but he had this overwhelming need to know that she was okay. That no harm was going to come to her. He had to know she was all right.

Raoul had told him he was falling for her, but he just laughed it off. He was not falling for a Russo.

But — he had to pause — was he?

Was there a chance that Milah had gotten beneath his skin, and now there was no turning back? He feared that he was indeed falling for her. Staring at her now, he saw the beauty, not just on the outside but also on the inside. The way she treated their new dog and the puppies. They were no longer confined to the room but had free rein around the house. Of course, it meant training them to go outdoors was a nightmare.

It had brought a new wave of laughter to the house. Even his most hardened of men had softened toward her.

Milah had this … air around her. She was destined to be loved.

He adored her.

Closing their bedroom door, Milah turned toward him with a smile.

Free of makeup, her cheeks red from the shower, and he saw the puckering of her nipples.

Her body was all his. He closed the distance

between them and cupped her face.

"You're early."

"I have a reason to be." He pressed a kiss to her lips, and she released a moan. "I have a bath to take, come with me."

He didn't give her a chance to turn him down. With his hand on hers, he pulled her across the room, going into his en-suite.

Damon let her go, and he watched her start a bath for him.

The negligee fell to the curve of her ass, but as she bent over, it rode up, and his little minx wasn't wearing any panties.

His cock went hard in an instant.

Removing his clothes was a task, and he had to be careful when it came to his dick, pushing the zipper of his pants down. Then he kicked them off until he was free from the confines.

Wrapping his fingers around his length, he watched her.

Pre-cum already leaked out of the tip, and he massaged it into his length. When she turned to look at him, he let his dick go, pretending he wasn't fooling around at all as he climbed in.

Milah got up to leave, but he captured her hand.

"Please, don't go."

"Damon?"

"I want to spend some time in your company. It feels like I haven't seen you. Is it so wrong to want to be with you?" he asked.

She smiled. "You must want to be with me to admit that out loud."

"See, you've got to try to not punish me. Besides, I need someone to scrub my back."

She rolled her eyes, but as he let her go, she

didn't make a run for it.

He leaned back in the bath and released a sigh of relief. "How have you been feeling?" he asked.

"Good. This little dude or dudette has been moving a lot lately."

"Do you want me to get the doctor?"

"Nah, I think movement is a good thing. They're very active."

"I'm starting to wonder if we should have gotten to know the sex. We're constantly trying not to go *he* or *she*."

Milah chuckled. "I don't mind not knowing. It's fun."

He loved that smile and those dimples.

He grabbed a sponge and offered her the soap. "Wash me."

"Yes, sir."

"Be careful. I could get used to that."

She laughed. "Could get used to it? I bet you already are."

"Only when it comes from your lips."

He lifted after she lathered up the sponge. She massaged it into his back, and she took her time washing him.

He loved her hands on him. Having all of her attention focused on him. Reaching out, he put his hand on her stomach, completely blown away by their baby growing.

Milah's tits had also grown, and she had gotten more beautiful in his eyes. Even with her weird eating habits. There was not a thing he'd change about her.

She was perfect. So fucking perfect.

She hummed to herself as she washed him.

When it came time to do his dick, he took the sponge from her and gave her the soap.

"Just your hands."

No matter how many times he fucked her, she still had the ability to blush, and he found that utterly endearing.

"You're beautiful," he said.

She chuckled. "What is with you and all these compliments? A girl could get used to them." It was meant to be a warning.

"Then I want you to get used to them. If I show any signs of being a dick, tell me."

She laughed and this one was real and throaty, and it made him want to fuck her even harder.

In fact, he was done with the bath.

Standing up, he climbed out and picked Milah up in his arms with ease.

"Damon, put me down. I'm way too heavy." She tried to swat at his ass, but he stopped her blows.

He carried her through to the bedroom, dropping her down onto the bed.

She giggled, wriggling beneath him. "You're crazy."

"I'm crazy for you," he said.

Milah gasped, and to stop any more questions, he slammed his lips down on hers. He wasn't sure why he had said those words in the first place. They had spilled out from nowhere.

It was the truth.

The past few months hadn't been part of his carefully orchestrated plan. It had been real.

It had been … between them, and it was so natural. Shedding the Russo name and their feud had been a breath of fresh air.

Kissing down her body, he quickly got to her tits and admired their full ripeness. They were so much bigger, and it wouldn't be long before they were full of milk for her to nurse their child.

He pressed them together and lathered each nipple before sucking it into his mouth. He paid close attention to each, licking and sucking, teasing her. She arched up, spreading her legs and making way for him, and he took it.

Damon reluctantly let go of her tits and started to trail his lips down, kissing her rounded stomach, then going down, toward her pussy. She was already slick with arousal.

Plunging two fingers inside her, he felt how wet she was, and Milah rewarded him with a throaty groan. That was the sound he relished.

She pressed onto his fingers, and he gave her what she wanted, fucking her with his digits. At the same time, he licked at her clit. He wanted her to come.

Sucking her clit into his mouth, he twisted his fingers inside her, finding that spot she loved that always set her aflame. He continued to tease her clit, and just like he knew she would, she came, screaming his name.

So perfect.

He pushed her through her orgasm, not letting it fade, and only when her begs and pleas were loud enough did he let her go, but he wasn't done with her.

Damon eased her onto her knees, and he pressed his cock to her entrance, then slid right to the hilt inside her.

Their moans mingled in the air.

He grabbed her hips and started to fuck her. Long, hard, deep thrusts. With her orgasm only just ending, he felt the tiny ripples of her surrounding him. He closed his eyes, loving every second of it. Each thrust drove them both higher, but tonight, he wanted to try something new.

With his cock still inside her, he nudged her up

the bed, following her. When she was near the pillows, he reached into his drawer and pulled out the nearly empty tube of lubrication.

Milah had been more than happy to explore with him, and he'd been preparing her tight little asshole for his cock.

He didn't know why, but he felt a primitive need to claim every single part of her. He wanted to own all that was Milah. He craved her body, and deep down, he wanted her complete and utter devotion.

Damon wanted Milah to be hungry for him. To not ever starve of her need for him.

It was selfish, but he didn't care. Just so long as he got what he wanted, he didn't give a fuck about anything else.

Running his hands all over her body, he kept his dick balls deep inside her.

He opened the tube of lubrication and made sure there was plenty on her asshole, getting her nice and slick.

Damon used his fingers to push some into her anus, and then, he eased out of her soaking pussy.

He didn't want to hurt her, so he made sure to use plenty more lubrication. Once he was covered, he eased the tip of his cock against her ass.

Milah tensed up, like she always did, but unlike that first time, she didn't jerk back. He'd told her to trust him, and she did. He pushed the tip of his cock against her tight opening, and she pressed out, and slowly, inch by inch, he sank inside her.

Damon was sure to take his time. Allowing her to become accustomed to the feel of him in her ass.

She was so tight. Just as he knew she would be. So tight.

When he was as deep as he could go, he paused

and gave her time to get used to him. While he did so, he ran his hands all over her body, taking his sweet time, rubbing her, touching her tits, and diving down between her thighs.

He stroked her pussy, slipping his fingers through her slit and stroking her clit. Her ass tightened around his cock, and he had no choice but to close his eyes as the pleasure was so fucking intense.

All he wanted to do was grab her hips and fucking pound that asshole. To go as deep as he could go.

Stroking her clit, he allowed Milah to set the pace. At first, she was super still, not moving, not even breathing, or so it seemed, and then it was like she came alive for him. She started to move on his cock, taking him all the way in, then pulling off.

He kept on teasing her clit, and he felt her orgasm starting to build. Rather than stop, he pushed her over the edge, and only when she was completely blown away by her orgasm did he grab her hips and fuck her, taking his sweet time, watching his cock as he claimed her ass.

It was impossible to make this last, their first time together like this.

Her ass was so fucking perfect. He couldn't control himself.

Slamming balls deep inside her after only a few thrusts, Damon threw his head back and groaned as he spilled his cum deep inside her asshole.

Mine.

All fucking mine.

No one is taking you away from me.

He collapsed over her but was sure not to give her too much of his weight. Conscious of her swollen stomach, Damon moved as they lay so he was spooning her. He hadn't pulled out of her ass, and he wrapped his arms around her, putting a hand on her stomach.

"That was intense," Milah said.

Kissing her neck, he breathed her in. "Did you enjoy it?"

"Yes."

"Good." He laid his hand flat on her stomach and nearly panicked as he felt an answering kick.

Milah chuckled. "Not the best time, but I think our baby is saying hello." She took his hand and placed it on her stomach again.

Sure enough, seconds later, a kick hit his palm. "Holy fucking shit. That is…"

"Incredible?" Milah asked.

"Yeah, does it hurt?"

"Not all the time. Sometimes. Our baby has a kick on them, and they like everyone to know they're here." She sighed.

Damon couldn't believe it. He felt his child kick. It was a wondrous feeling.

Milah sighed. "This is nice."

He kissed her neck. "And you better get used to it."

"I think I already am."

That was good, because he loved it, and he knew he loved Milah as well. He just hadn't said the words. He doubted he ever would.

****

Tears fell down Milah's cheeks as she closed the book.

Valentino and Alicia were together for a year. She sniffled. They had loved one another, and in those final days, Alicia had ended up pregnant with Valentino's baby. They were going to marry.

She opened the book again and stared at Valentino's scrawl.

MISTRESS TO A MONSTER

I had no idea my love had been writing about us this whole time. One single book for a year of memories. Alicia Russo was a precious gem. No one will ever see this, they will never know the truth, but here it is.

I, Valentino De Luca, failed my family. The very first time I met Alicia Russo, I knew she was the woman for me. Not just because of her beauty, and she was stunning, but her eyes. They were full of life. They wanted joy and laughter, and to actually live. The second time I saw her, that life was starting to ebb away. This is what our life does to people, or at least the Russo does.

They are monsters, and I saw what her father was doing. He was killing that fire that made her special.

I couldn't let it happen.

Alicia Russo deserved to fly. No, she deserved to soar.

So I did the unthinkable. I stole her. Kidnapped her. I never intended to harm her, but I needed people to think I was, and Alicia played along. She had no idea how I felt about her. How much I loved her.

She was my one true weakness, but being her captor was all that I allowed myself to be. Alicia was the woman to fulfill her own destiny. I was merely the man allowing her to be herself.

That first kiss, it would stay with me forever.

The night she came to me and told me she wanted to be with me, and only me, those memories I would cherish. This book is the truth of our love, and Russo, her father and her brother took her away from me. They killed her just so that I could not have her. Our baby was lost, and so was my woman.

They never claimed her body, and so I put her to rest where I will one day rest with her. My Alicia, I vow to kill every single one of the Russo men. I will slaughter them for taking you away from me. I love you more than anything else in the world, but to wipe out those men, I have to ... marry.

You are always in my heart.

If these pages are ever read, then to the reader, know this, a De Luca's love is not easily taken, and we're not easily pushed aside either. I will avenge you, my darling angel. They will never know true happiness again.

That was it.

Alicia had died because she'd fallen for Valentino De Luca. Her own father, Alicia's brother, had seen to it that she died.

A new wave of hatred ran through Milah. How dare they?

Valentino and Alicia could have been something special. Bringing De Lucas and Russos together. Finally ending this war, but instead, her own family had killed her.

She rested beside Valentino.

He hadn't allowed her body to go elsewhere.

Holding the book in her hands, she had to show this to Damon. To tell him that this feud must now end with the two of them.

Climbing down from the ladder, she didn't put it away, but left the room, heading down toward his office.

He'd told her that morning, that he'd be working with Raoul. She never asked him about his business. She would start to change that.

Going to the door, she paused when she heard raised voices. She was tempted to leave them to it, but when she heard her name, curiosity got the better of her.

Someone hadn't shut the door properly, and it was open enough for her to hear clearly without being seen.

"Don't you think you are taking it a little far with the wedding?" Raoul asked. She recognized his voice.

He was one of the few people who hadn't warmed up to her. Damon had warned her that Russo was responsible for a great deal of pain. She hoped one day, Raoul would see that not all Russos were bad.

"Enough of this," Damon said. "I am not going to keep on talking about this. It is done."

"What has happened to you?" Raoul asked.

"What has happened to me? You want me to stick to my plan, is that it? Don't you think I'm doing that? I'm not forcing Milah to marry me. The Russo line will end with her just as I always planned. Her child will be a De Luca. Our revenge will be complete. There is nothing of the Russo empire. It has fallen, and Milah was always going to be the last piece of the puzzle."

Sickness tightened in her stomach, and she felt a little dizzy. Getting pregnant was all part of Damon's grand plan, and she had fallen right into it.

Of course.

He'd always made sure there was no condom. Refused to wear them because he wanted her to get pregnant.

It was why he'd insisted on marrying her.

If she gave birth without being married, her child would be a Russo. He would have failed.

Damon was nothing like Valentino. He would never love her.

He was just a monster intent on destroying her. She had no doubt that once the baby was born, he was going to make her life miserable. He couldn't do that now. Not with her pregnant, he had to wait until she'd given birth safely.

That horrible son of a bitch.

Damon hadn't been falling for her or warming up

to her. All he'd been doing was preparing her for the final part of his plan. The complete annihilation of her family. Tears filled her eyes, and she slammed her palm against the door.

"How fucking dare you?" She yelled each word.

"Milah, what are—"

"So this was your big bad plan, huh? To marry me. To fucking destroy me and our child. No, sorry, my child, because you, you're not going to have anything to do with my baby."

"Milah, stop, this isn't—"

"Fuck you." She threw Alicia's journal at him, and then she tore off the engagement band. "You are never coming near me. You will have nothing to do with our child, and I swear, Damon, I will fucking kill you and put an end to all of the De Lucas and Russos together."

She spun on her heel and ran.

No guard stopped her as she fled the house, taking her as far and as fast as she could go, but being pregnant wasn't great. She was aware of her child.

"Milah, please. Milah, stop," Glory said, chasing after her.

Tears streamed down her face, and she was done with the farce. With putting on a show. She stopped, spun around, and glared at Glory. "And as for you, you can get out of my sight. I know you were never my friend. You always reported everything to him. To your master. Stay the hell away from me."

"Milah, please."

"No. Just stop. Stop with all the tears and the lies. Just leave me alone." Milah turned, and this time, she walked, fast. She didn't know where she was going.

All she wanted to do was to get away. To leave De Luca land. To put him behind her so she never had to look at his smug face again, but she couldn't do that.

Instead, she had no choice but to find solace elsewhere.

She knew exactly where she was heading. To the two people who could have put an end to this. Whose love was cut short by outside sources.

The cemetery was quite far from the house, and once she got there, she stopped just outside of the gate, looking at the gravestones. So much death. She swiped at her cheeks and stepped onto the grounds, seeing several names and finally coming to a stop where Valentino and Alicia lay.

Milah collapsed to the ground, several feet from the stones.

Were they finally together?

Staring at their names, she sobbed for them and for herself.

"I was falling for him." She covered her face with her hands and felt the huge loss and emptiness. "Revenge is so cold. It doesn't keep you warm, and it doesn't stop the hate. None of this is ever going to stop."

There were no answers.

"Everything I fell in love with was a lie. The long nights. The snuggles, the laughs. It was all false. He's not like that. He just had a bigger plan he was trying to concoct." She wiped the tears from her eyes and stared at the gravestones, knowing no good was ever going to come out of a De Luca and Russo union.

At the sound of a twig snapping, Milah spun her head toward the noise and saw one of Damon's soldiers approaching. He'd been there for several months, even before she arrived. She had no idea of his name.

"Leave me alone. You can tell your precious master that I'm not leaving the grounds." It would be dumb to.

She had a target on her back for just being a Russo. No matter where she turned, she was hated.

"I'm … I came to see you," he said.

Milah looked at him and frowned. "Why? I don't know you."

"I know you don't know me, but I … know you," he said. "Or at least I know of you. You see, my name is Ricky. My mother made sure that I was never to be named after him."

"Who?" She was confused by this man.

"My mother was a waitress at one of Antonio Russo's nightclubs. He's my…"

"Oh, I get it. You're one of my father's children," Milah said. She started to laugh. "Let me guess, you can't stand me either so you're going to kill me?" She put a hand protectively over her stomach.

"No, no, I'm not here to kill you. I'm older than you, in case you're wondering." Ricky still held a gun in his hand, it was the kind that she'd gotten used to seeing when the men were patrolling the grounds.

"If you're not here to kill me, then why are you here?"

"I … well, Antonio never accepted me. Even after a paternity test. He abused my mother, and so I vowed that I would never ask that man for anything. I found out about the De Luca and Russo feud and decided to work for his enemy. Then, I heard about you. I heard what he did, and I just knew that I had to meet you. I watched you from afar. I waited to see if you were like him or if you were different."

"And?" Milah asked.

"I, I would like to offer you a hug, little sister," Ricky said.

"Why?"

"Because we only have each other, and right now,

you're hurting more than anything."

"Ricky, you don't know me."

"But I'd like to."

"Damon will kill you."

"I've been loyal to him and him alone. I have sworn to protect him, and I will swear to protect you."

"Why now?"

"I don't want my baby sister crying. You've been happy until now."

"I was really fucking mad when I first got here."

"Yeah, but I didn't get the chance to know you. I've heard what people have said about you, and even though they hate to admit it, they know you're a good person, Milah. Russo or not."

"I hate that name."

"Me too," he said. "It gets kind of old hearing your mother scream it at night."

Milah glanced at Valentino and Alicia. There was no happiness here.

She got to her feet and walked over to Ricky. "You're my big brother?"

"One of them, I guess. Antonio wasn't known for being careful."

She wrapped her arms around him and hugged him. Ricky did remind her a little of her father, in his looks, but not in his temperament.

Chapter Seventeen

"Get your fucking hands off her!"

Damon glared at the man currently holding his woman. He'd already encountered Glory, but he'd figured Milah was aware of him using the maid to get close to her.

Milah wasn't stupid. He never thought she was, but she had only heard part of the conversation with Raoul. She hadn't heard the part where he confessed to how he felt about her. How he wanted to make it work with her.

Milah turned toward him, and he saw the anger in her eyes. "What part of *I don't want to see you again* don't you understand?"

"All of it." He looked at the soldier. "I will kill you."

The soldier merely glared at him, as if he had a right to do so.

Damon pulled his gun, ready to shoot the little prick, but Milah stepped in front of him. "No, you're not going to kill him."

"I'm not? I've got a soldier disobeying orders."

"He's my brother," Milah said. "I know all you want to do is wipe out every single last Russo, but he is my brother. Do not kill him."

Damon looked at the soldier, and sure enough, he detected the eyes, the distinctive brow.

"Don't," Milah said. "He has been working for you for months."

"I had a rat amongst my soldiers, feeding Russo information." He thought he had found the fucking vermin. He'd killed a soldier he'd detected on Russo payroll.

"I was the one who pointed him out," he said,

finally speaking up.

"Yeah, and now knowing you're his son, I have a hard time believing it. Step away from my woman." He wasn't going to risk killing Milah.

"No!"

"I didn't give Russo anything," Ricky said. "I had nothing to do with that old bastard. Not ever. He never claimed me as his. I heard him yelling at my mom once and he said she was a whore. That I could have been anyone's. That is not a man I want as a father."

"Why work for me?" Damon glared.

"You're his enemy and that made you my friend."

Ricky grabbed the gun, and Damon was ready, about to shoot when he lowered it to the ground.

Damon heard more of his soldiers approaching.

"I only wanted to see you tear down Russo. When you brought Milah here, I wanted to meet her, but I didn't know if she was like our father. She's not, and now, I just want to protect her. Family should take care of each other."

"Ricky, stop it," Milah said.

"Take him," Damon said.

"No!"

Milah threw herself toward him and started to beat at his chest. "Stop this. Just stop."

He grabbed her arms and shook her. "Do you think I'm going to trust the word of a man I don't know? This is your safety. Your life."

"No, all you care about is your child."

"Of course, I care about my child, but you're fucking blind if you think that is the only thing I care about." He nodded at his men, and Ricky was escorted away.

Milah sobbed, and he pulled her against his chest, but once again, she fought him like a wildcat. There was no giving in. No surrender from her. "Let me go."

He wrapped his arms around her, not allowing her to leave. He pressed his face against her neck, breathing her in. "Milah, please."

"No. You took him away."

"You know nothing about him. You don't know if he is lying to you. He is a stranger, Milah. Anyone could find out about the Russo and De Luca feud."

She slowly lost all of her fight.

"I'm going to find out who he is first."

"I hate you," she said.

Milah pulled away from him and started to walk away. He captured her arm and pulled her in close, but she spun around and slapped him hard across the face. "Don't ever touch me."

"Milah."

"I don't want to talk to you. I don't want to look at you. Just stay away from me."

He watched her go, and his hands clenched into fists.

Damon followed her as Milah rushed back toward the house. He didn't stop, seeing where she would go, and she stumbled back into the room where he'd put her when she was first given to him.

The door slammed shut.

He pulled out his cell phone and dialed Genius immediately, requesting all the information linked to the soldier named Ricky.

Damon hung up, and Raoul waited for him near the entrance of the basement. "Have you told her?" Raoul asked.

"I think it is best if you leave."

"Eavesdropping is never good for anyone, but avoiding your feelings is even worse."

"Raoul, leave, before I regret what I do."

His friend nodded and bowed, taking his leave.

Damon entered the basement. Ricky had been chained to a chair.

There were no cuts or bruises on him, and Damon was surprised. "You didn't put up a fight?"

"I have nothing to hide. I imagine you're running all my information through your guy, and you'll know everything soon enough."

"Yeah, what I'm not getting is why you're here. Why with me?"

"Because a son needs to have more of a reason to avenge his mother, to go against the man that never acknowledged him."

"Why get involved at all?" Damon asked. "If your mother was a one-night stand, and she had you, tough. Was she a leech?"

Ricky's jaw clenched, and Damon shook his head. "You don't have a fucking clue what you're talking about. My mother wasn't just a one-night stand."

"What was she then?"

He waited.

"She was his mistress."

"So, still a woman used for fucking."

Ricky tensed up, and Damon stared at him. "You're one to talk. Isn't that what you used Milah for?"

His hands clenched into fists, but he didn't strike. "Don't."

"You can call my mother out for being a whore, but Milah, she doesn't get hit by the same stick."

"If you value your life, shut your fucking mouth."

"I do value my life, and I value Milah's, as well as my unborn niece or nephew. Family means everything. Even as that piece-of-shit man tried to ruin my mother, she always believed that family was strong. She was the one who told me about Milah. That I had a sister. She asked me, on her deathbed, if I would take care of her. To be a good brother to her."

Damon burst out laughing. "You expect me to believe this?"

"I don't care if you believe it or not. We're not all bastards, but maybe your thirst for revenge on Russo has turned you into him, whether you like it or not."

Anger shot through his entire body. He wanted to put an end to the fucker's life, but someone must be looking down on him, because at that moment, Genius was calling him.

Damon just wanted to kill him and be done with it.

The man dared to touch Milah. No one but him touched Milah. She was his.

"What do you have?"

"A paternity test, and hell, yeah, this is Antonio Russo's child all right. He has been working for you for nearly five years." Genius whistled. "Damn good from what I see. He was a soldier as well. Trained in the art of killing. He has saved your ass so many times. It's why he's a main guard at your home. You can trust him."

"Thank you." Damon hung up. "Did Milah know about you before today?"

"No. Today was the first time I approached."

"Why did she believe you?"

Ricky shrugged. "I guess she is desperate for some family. Look, I know you want to kill me, and I didn't come forward and tell you who I was because I know what a Russo name means around here. I'm not my father. I just want to keep Milah safe, and you. You're a good man, De Luca, and I will accept whatever punishment you decide."

Damon glared at Ricky, hating the fact he sounded so fucking reasonable.

He left the basement, knowing he wasn't going to be able to kill the fucker although that was all he wanted to do.

Several of his guards were stationed outside of the basement. "Let him go."

"Sir?"

"Nothing is to happen to him. You have worked side by side for long enough. He is one of you." Damon left and made his way toward the main bedroom, where he found James and Glory.

The young woman was crying.

James had already asked if there was a chance he would be able to marry the young servant girl. Damon had never known it to happen, but with how fucked up everything was going of late, he didn't see a reason why not. He was going to grant Glory freedom. In fact, he already had, but Glory had asked if she could continue to stay and work for him. The only difference now was she left with James and came back every morning.

Why the fuck were people around him finding it easy, but he, he was facing a battle everywhere he turned?

There was only a lock on the outside of the door.

"She doesn't want anyone," Glory said. "She hates me."

"No, she doesn't," Damon said. "She hates me. Go. I'll take care of her."

James put a hand on his shoulder before pulling Glory into his side and leaving him alone. Opening the door, he saw Milah on the bed, curled up and sobbing.

"Leave!"

He closed the door, and Milah sat up.

Even with her face all puffy from tears, her lips swollen, and her hair all over the place, she looked so beautiful.

"What did you do?" Milah asked.

It was a fair enough question. He'd killed the kitchen staff who'd dared to disobey him. Ricky was the enemy.

"I found out who he is, and he is Antonio's bastard," he said.

"You killed him?"

"No. I did not."

"I don't believe you."

Damon took a deep breath. "There will be time for you to see him." He took a step toward her.

"Don't come near me."

"You didn't hear anything."

"Are you going to try and tell me that I misheard?"

"No. You heard part of the conversation."

"Getting me pregnant, marrying me, removing the Russo name, that wasn't part of your plan?"

"I didn't say that, Milah. It was part of my plan. An ever-changing one. At first, I wasn't going to marry you. I was going to breed you. Turn you into nothing more than my personal whore. Let your father see how the mighty fall. He gave you to me, and that was going to be one part of his punishment."

"I hate you."

"Your father made sure I had no choice but to change my plans. Like always, he had to take the lead, didn't he? He was never one step ahead of the game, but he sure liked to fuck up a lot."

"Your point?"

"I wasn't going to let him put you in danger, Milah."

"Why?"

"I started to care about you."

"Liar."

"I'm not lying."

"You expect me to believe you?" she asked.

"I don't expect you to believe anything. I'm telling you the truth, which I think you deserve. I'm telling you how it is. Do you think this is easy for me to admit?" he asked.

****

Milah scoffed. She couldn't believe he was making this about himself. Trust Damon to do it this way. "So you hate the way you suddenly care about me."

"It wasn't just now or the baby, okay? For fuck's sake. Do you think I like this?" he asked.

"Do you think I like hearing how you were only marrying me to make sure there are no Russos left? I'm a fucking Russo, Damon. You're never going to change that."

"You are not a Russo, Milah."

"Oh, please."

"To be one takes more than a last name. I've come to realize that now. You're nothing like your father or the men of your line. You're ... so much more."

Tears spilled down her cheeks, and she glared at him. There was no way she was going to let his words affect her. He was going to use her.

All that they'd been building together was a lie. A big fat, stinking lie, and she refused to be fooled by it.

"Russos are manipulative, cruel, and they don't give a fuck who they hurt in the process. All they care about is themselves, their own happiness. Your father was a prime example of that. He was Alicia's brother," Damon said.

"Did you know Valentino fell in love with her?" Milah asked.

"I didn't know. He was ... my grandfather was a hard man to understand. His hatred for the Russos was unlike anything I can describe."

"Read the book I threw at you. It tells you everything. It tells you how her father and brother, my dad, killed her. She was pregnant with Valentino's baby."

Damon gasped, and he shook his head. "I never knew."

"It's why he is buried beside her, Damon. Didn't you ever wonder why?"

"My grandfather always said that the Russos would pay for what they have done. The feud has been going on for so long, I don't even know what started it."

"But you intended to finish it?" she asked.

"Milah?"

"That's why you got me pregnant. It's why I'm here."

"You're here because I can't stay away from you. Do you think I give a fuck about every other woman out there? Do you think it drives me crazy to see other men touching women I've fucked?"

"I don't want to hear it."

"Only you, Milah," he said.

She glared at him.

"That night in the gardens, I don't know what you did to me, but it was like you put a spell on me, and since then, I haven't been able to get away from it. Yes, I thought of this despicable plan. All along, I was going to get you pregnant, but ... I didn't want to marry you. That was going to be the Russo punishment. Your father, his punishment was supposed to be seeing his daughter never married. Always at the mercy as a mistress to me. Never first place."

"Do you think my father would have given a flying fuck? He hated me, Damon."

"I wasn't going to go through with it!" Damon all

but screamed. "Do you have any idea what it's like to live with you? To be with you twenty-four hours a day and to try not to fall in love with you?"

Milah was about to yell at him, but then she realized what he'd said.

"Fall in love with me?"

Damon chuckled. "Yeah, I tried not to. I tried every single day not to give in. Not to feel this way, but nothing worked. Not a damn thing. I kept on ignoring it. Thinking it was just the guilt talking, but I didn't fucking care what I did to Russo. I was happy to make him hurt. To make him bleed, but you." He shook his head. "You got under my skin with those fucking kisses, and then you were a virgin. I have the sheets still."

"What?"

"I know, fucking sick, right? I have them because they are mine. No one else can take that away from me. I fucked the woman I fell in love with on that first night. For three fucking years I tried to forget you, but that one brief moment, and I had to have you. I thought it was because of my insane need to have my revenge, just like all the men in my family, but it wasn't. No, I see that now. I fucked up big time when it came to you. I should never have looked for you," Damon said.

"Do you really believe that?" Milah asked.

"I changed my plan so many times. Your father, he was a fucking piece of work. I thought he was going to demand marriage, and I would have done it to own you. I would do anything to have you. But when I said you'd be my whore, he didn't care. He gave you to me, and I was fucking glad. I heard that he intended to sell you to his highest bidder. I knew you were a virgin, Milah, even before we had sex. He was using that piece of information to sell you."

"What?"

"It's why I acted when I did. Everything is so fucking messed up. If he hadn't sent that fucking ring, and I realized why he sent that fucking ring. None of this would have happened. You would know by now that I fucking love you. There, I said it. I was trying to get you to fall in love with me, and I can say it was all part of my plan, but it wasn't. I wanted you, no, needed, you to fall in love with me because I fucking needed you!" He growled out the words. "Do you think I like this? How do you think I felt seeing you get shot?"

His eyes were wild, and he shook his head right before laughing. "It's insane, isn't it?" he asked.

Milah didn't know exactly what it was, maybe it was his voice, or the crazy look in his eyes, but she did actually believe him.

"You couldn't die. Holding you in my arms as you told me how much it hurt. I couldn't lose you. That's when I knew," he said. "No, I knew before then, but I realized I couldn't live without you. I'm not marrying you to give you my name, Milah. It started out that way as some fucked-up plan, but not anymore. I'm marrying you"—he sank to his knees on the floor in front of her—"because I can't live without you. I don't want to live in a world where you're not with me."

"You're lying."

"I know you think that. I could be lying, but I know what I feel in here, and Milah, I want you. Give us a chance." He crawled across the floor, and she gasped as he grabbed her hand. "Don't marry me. Have our baby without us getting married. See the next couple of months, the next few years, and I will prove to you that these are not lies. I will show you I'm the better man. I promise you."

"Then I get to leave?"

"No," he said, shaking his head. "I will give you

everything you want, but not that. I will do anything but let you go. I can't, Milah. Please, don't fucking go. Please, I am begging you."

He froze her to the spot.

Damon was on his knees, begging her, and what was more, he was crying as he did it.

This was not something Damon De Luca would do.

Could he be telling the truth? Was this possible?

She pressed her lips together as he continued to rain kisses on her hands.

Damon De Luca was a force to be reckoned with. He was not a man brought easily to his knees.

She thought back over the past several months, seeing his face flash, the smiles, the teasing. At times, it had been like a completely different man.

This would be the time to bring a De Luca to his knees. She could take everything from him.

He loved her.

A true Russo would do this.

She opened her mouth and then closed it.

Alicia was a Russo. She had fallen in love with Valentino De Luca, and she never got the chance to see her baby born or to marry the man she loved. She had died long before her time. Killed by the hands of her family.

Valentino had lived the remainder of his life to torture the men responsible for taking his love away.

This cycle had to end.

She was never a malicious person. Her hatred of her father was very fucking real.

She wasn't going to allow him or his greedy life to impose on her any longer. The Russo and De Luca feud would end here.

All it took was one person to finally put an end to

it.

She pulled her hands away from De Luca's, and he fought her, but she climbed off the bed. Then she shoved him against it and turned to straddle him as he sat on the floor. She cupped his face, tilting his head back to look him in the eye. His gaze was so cold it took her breath away.

"I love you, Damon De Luca. We're going to get married. So I'm going to need that ring back, and we're going to raise beautiful children. This rift between the Russos and De Lucas ends today. You and me, we will finish this. This feud will end in love. Do you understand me?"

He grabbed the back of her neck, pulling her close and drawing her lips down to his. She wrapped her arms around him. With her stomach in the way, it was hard to get as close to him as she wanted, but she didn't care.

His touch, his love, that was all she needed. She didn't need anything else.

She didn't know how much time had passed before he pulled away, but when he did, he already had the engagement ring out, and he slid it on her finger.

"I'm so sorry."

"Don't be. I don't want the Russo ring. None of our children do, but I think you should give it to Ricky."

Damon nodded.

"You're not going to argue?" She frowned. "Did you kill him?"

"No. Ricky is not dead. It turns out he has been one hell of a guard around this place," Damon said. He stroked her hair back behind her ear. "You're so beautiful. You know that?"

She cupped his face and kissed him. "I love you."

"And I love you. Don't leave me."

"Don't ever give me a reason to leave."

"I won't."

He held her tightly, and Milah finally felt like she belonged. Damon hadn't just put on a show, she knew that. Some people would think she was a fool, and she could imagine her father and grandfather spinning in their graves because she hadn't dealt a killing blow to him.

She loved him. There was no need to destroy him. The thirst for vengeance had caused enough death, and she was going to end it once and for all.

"Valentino really loved her?" Damon asked, pulling away.

Milah nodded. "It's all in the diary. I found it in the top floor's attic."

"I've never been up there. Valentino made the room out of bounds for a long time. My mother had it redecorated not long after he passed. She said the room had once been a shrine to something."

"It must have been Alicia," Milah said.

He nodded.

"Read the diary, Damon. For me."

"I will do anything for you, Milah. All you ever have to do is ask."

Epilogue

Five years later

Some people would have called her a fool for believing Damon. Milah watched from the table on the porch as the man himself chased after their five-year-old son, Daniel, and their two-year-old daughter, Alicia.

The moment she held her little girl, she had known what to call her. Damon had said he wanted to lock her away so no men would ever touch her.

Damon De Luca had proven his words to her, time and time again. They had gotten married a month after their confession to one another about their feelings. Milah had been nervous about leaving her Russo name behind, but the moment she looked at Damon, she had known she was doing the right thing.

Not once did he turn his back on her. Their honeymoon had been one of the most amazing times of her life. She'd been heavily pregnant with Daniel, so it hadn't been particularly exertive, but Damon had shown her how to make love everywhere.

She smiled at the memories and looked toward the chuckle to see Ricky coming toward her. Milah had gotten to know her brother. Damon had taken the effort to reach out to more of Antonio Russo's children, but that had caused a few problems. Some of the women had convinced other men that they were their children, and so to let them know they are Russos would have caused a whole heap of trouble.

Milah didn't mind.

Ricky was her big brother, and over the past five years, they had built up a sound friendship.

Damon had also given Ricky the ring, but her brother hadn't wanted it, so, one day, all three of them had gone out on a yacht, and she'd flung it into the ocean. The curse of the Russo would never be seen or heard from.

"How are you feeling?" Ricky asked.

Milah put a finger against her lips. "I haven't told him."

Ricky whistled.

The only reason he knew that she was pregnant was that he'd been there during several days of her morning sickness. She hadn't gotten a test and she didn't want to tell Damon unless she knew for sure.

"Not told me what?" Damon asked, approaching with Daniel wrapped around his leg refusing to let go, and Alicia in his arms, looking tired.

"That is my cue to leave," Ricky said, and she glared at him.

Ricky was a good uncle, and he even got along with Damon as well.

She smiled as Daniel pounced on his uncle's leg, and Alicia simply settled as if she was going to sleep. Her babies were so precious.

Damon cupped her face, kissing her passionately before taking a seat. "What do you have to tell me?" he asked.

Milah nibbled on her lip. "I wanted to get a test done first, but I think I might be … pregnant."

She stared at Damon, waiting for a reaction. They had said they were going to wait until Alicia was a little older before having more kids, but they hadn't given themselves time, and now, she was pregnant.

He stared into her eyes, and the smile on his lips brought one to her own. "Have I told you lately how much I love you?"

"You tell me every single day." She smiled at him. "And I love you for telling me all the time."

"Good, because I love that you trusted me, Milah.